# TRICKED

A NOVEL BY

TYRONE WALLACE

Life Changing Books in conjunction with Power Play Media
Published by Life Changing Books
P.O. Box 423 Brandywine, MD 20613

This novel is a work of fiction. Any references to real people, events, establishments, or locales are intended only to give the fiction a sense of reality and authenticity. Other names, characters, and incidents occurring in the work are either the product of the author's imagination or are used fictitiously, as are those fictionalized events and incidents that involve real persons. Any character that happens to share the name of a person who is an acquaintance of the author, past or present, is purely coincidental and is in no way intended to be an actual account involving that person.

Library of Congress Cataloging-in-Publication Data;

www.lifechangingbooks.net
13 Digit: 978-1934230473
10 Digit: 1-934230472

# ACKNOWLEDGEMENTS

First, I would like to thank myself. I thank myself for never giving up on what I know I can accomplish. And thanks to my higher power for instilling in me what it takes to keep pushing on regardless of what obstacles are in front of me.

To my Mom, Carolyn Wallace, you are the woman that I hope my future wife could be like. You ooze all that I want my wife to be. To my siblings, Ben, Renee, Russell and Alisha, I love you all.

To my 9-5 working family as a pathology tech, I thank you all for showing me another side of life that I never was exposed to before. And lastly, thanks to life itself for allowing me to live and experience what it has to offer in order for me to grow.

Until my next masterpiece,

***Tyrone Wallace***

# ONE

She loved everything about him. His swagger, smile, DC slang, and lastly, the way he slammed dick to her since she was in the seventh grade. Tyra sat comfortably in the passenger seat of her man's brand new silver, 2014 Mercedes Benz S550, as it rode smoothly along Florida Avenue. Her eyes were fixated on him, as his head bobbed back and forth to the grimy lyrics of the rapper, Wale. Tyra reached out and pushed the volume button downward on the steerling wheel, bringing tranquility inside the car.

"Cash," she said, with a smile on her smooth, cocoa brown face, "I wanna talk."

Cash gazed at her grinning. "Now?"

She looked at him as if he were crazy. "What'cha think? I just said I wanna talk didn't I? "

"If it's about what we talked about yesterday or the day before that I ain't tryna talk about it. Now, turn Wale back on." The grin on his face had disappeared.

"Cash, don't do this."

"Tyra, do what?"

"You know what I'm talkin' 'bout. What's goin' on?"

"Girl, ain't nothin' goin' on." He attempted to turn the volume back up, but Tyra smacked his hand away.

"Cash," she shouted!

"Damn! Okay, talk."

"Why you been havin' that gun tucked on your waist for the last month now and how come when we get back home, you gotta go in the house first and check it out? It's like you lettin' me know it's safe to come inside."

*Damn, I can't get nothin past this girl and she definitely won't let up 'til I tell her somethin',* Cash thought to himself.

"Cash, answer my question?"

"No!"

"What'cha mean, no? We've been together five years and you decide now to get on some secret squirrel shit!"

"A'ight girl, what'cha damn mouth." Cash shot a wicked glance over at Tyra, whose arms were folded across her chest. "I'm doin' some foul shit to this nigga."

"What nigga and what'cha do to him? I need to know."

"Later for the details, but I'ma tell you this, I owe the nigga sixty g's, and have been owin' him for five months now."

Tyra shot him a cold stare. "Who you owe, Pat?"

"Nah, this nigga Dre hooked me up with somebody that I never met before."

"Dead Dre?"

"Yeah."

Tyra put it all together in seconds. Since Dre had been killed three months ago, Cash had decided he wouldn't pay the dude since Dre made the transaction without Cash being present.

"Cash, why didn't you just keep coppin' from Pat? He was givin' you a good deal."

"Yeah, but the nigga Dre had a sweeter deal."

"Cash, how sweet was the deal if you got somebody after you?"

"I don't wanna talk about it no more. I ain't payin' the nigga and that's that. He don't know me anyway."

"Well, why you paranoid then?"

"Cause the word on the street is he found out who I am, but I don't believe that cause I wasn't wit' Dre when he copped from that nigga."

"What you and Dre get from him?"

"We went half on three kilos for only 40 g's and was fronted three kilos wit' the promise to bring back 60 g's. Now, that's enough about that."

"Wont'cha just pay him out the money you have in the safe at home. You got over a hundred g's in there or more."

"I said that's enough about that shit!" Cash finished his firm comment just as he pulled up to their house on Rhode Island Avenue.

"You mad?" Cash asked breaking the silence.

"Yeah, I'm mad," Tyra spat, her arms still folded across her chest. "I can't believe you doin' this when you have money. You willin' to jeopardize your life as well as mine over money." She turned her head away from Cash and looked up at the porch of their rowhouse.

"Tyra, I'm not jeopardizing my life or yours. I promise you that, and you know I keep my promises."

"Oh really?" Tyra swung her head in Cash's direction.

"Come on now, slim, you know a nigga keep his promises."

"Example," Tyra said.

"Example? What'cha mean example? You playin' right?" Cash asked.

"I'm waitin'." Tyra folded her arms.

"Okay. I promised you that I was gon' move you outta that dirty ass apartment you and your mom lived in, and I did. "

Tyra smiled.

"I gave you ten g's to furnish our crib, just like I told'cha I would as soon as we moved into our new spot. Now, how many niggas at sixteen woulda done that?" Cash grinned proudly.

"Not many cause they didn't have money like you did at that age," Tyra said.

"I also promised you that we'd be movin' into our house before you turned nineteen, and look, we've been here for seven months and you ain't even nineteen yet."

Tyra dropped her arms and pulled Cash's face towards hers. "Cash, I love you so much," she said, just before their lips collided and their tongues began a familiar dance.

Cash was first to break from their intimacy. "Oh yeah," he said, sounding out of breath. "I also promised you that I'd give you 25 g's after you graduated, which I did and by the way girl, what'cha doin' wit' that bread other than buyin' Chanel and Gucci handbags. Plus, all that other girly shit?"

"I still have twenty g's left," Tyra said proudly. "I might buy me a car soon, I'don't know."

"Have you put some of the money in the bank like I told'cha to?"

"Not yet. I'ma do that this week."

"So, you got'cha twenty hidin' in the crib?"

"Yep." She smiled.

Cash ran his lips into Tyra's, giving her a peck. "Let me go check this crib out," he said.

"Okay." Tyra gave him a peck on his lips and let her hand intentionally slide down his body stopping at the zipper of his jeans. She took his dick out and stroked it and before he could say a word, she dropped her face down and sucked his jimmy causing Cash to moan in delight. Tyra ended her attack on his manhood right before he was about to climax, lifted her head and stated boldly, "I want some of this tonight."

Catching his breath, Cash answered, "No problem. You got that." as he made his way out of the car and disappeared into the house.

As usual, she would wait for Cash's signal that everything was clear which normally took about four or five minutes, so she gathered her Louis Vuitton speedy bag and bottle of Rose Moet. *Any minute now*, she thought, looking up at the house.

After four minutes had gone by, Tyra started to hum one of Beyonce's songs, still waiting for the signal to come inside the house. When four minutes turned into five, she wondered what was taking her man so long. Her eyes shot up toward the top of the house when she saw the light to her and Cash's bedroom flick on. It stayed on for twenty seconds or so before going dark again.

"What is he doin'?" she mumbled to herself. "I'm goin' in." She grabbed her things, got out of the car and headed up the steps.

Reaching the porch, she noticed Cash had left the front door ajar. She stepped inside and shut the door behind her.

"Cash!" she yelled, while standing in front of the mahogany wooden door. Her eyes quickly adjusted to the darkness as she looked in the direction of the staircase that led up to their bedroom. Suddenly, she heard a creaking sound.

"Cash!" she yelled again. "Ca...," she commenced to yell for a third time, but she didn't get his name out completely because of the rapid footsteps she heard coming from above.

*What is he doin' up there*, Tyra thought, as she headed towards the kitchen and placed her bottle in the refrigerator. Tyra grabbed her purse and proceeded upstairs to the second floor. When she reached the top of the stairs, her heart sped up quickly. Something wasn't right, none of the lights were on. *I know he's not tryin to play a damn trick on me,* she thought as her eyes pierced through the blackness and landed on the closed door of her bedroom.

"Ca…Ca…Cash!" Her feet began to shuffle in baby-like steps toward her bedroom door, where she placed her right ear up against it. When she didn't hear anything, Tyra sucked her teeth then let out a deep sigh. She knew what was going on and smiled.

Cash had gone into the house, took a quick shower, then ran into their room and hopped into bed. He knew she wanted some dick and probably was waiting in bed naked under the sheets. This didn't surprise her. Cash had played tricks on her before, only this time, she didn't find it very funny because he had left her outside in the dark and hadn't returned to get her. *Good thing I had sense enough to come in,* she thought to herself.

She turned the doorknob and stepped into the dark bedroom. Tyra thought about turning on the lights, but she decided not to. She wanted Cash just as much as he wanted her, so the quicker she could get undressed and hop into bed, the sooner they could be fuckin' like two rabbits.

"Cash!" Tyra snapped, as she made her way over to the dresser kicking her five-inch, Jimmy Choo, stilettos off. Although the room was still dark, she could make out the hump in the bed where Cash was laying.

"Cash!" she snapped again, after receiving no response from him. "Oh, I know you ain't come in and fall asleep on me when you knew I wanted some." Tyra stepped over to the bed and poked Cash, whose entire body was under the sheets. He didn't budge.

"Cash!" She rapidly snatched the sheets from his body.

Frustrated, Tyra turned toward the nightstand and switched on a lamp, bringing light to the room. She was shocked to see that Cash was fully dressed, lying on his back. His eyes were closed with his arms at his sides. "Boy, if you don't wake up and give me some dick."

She lightly jabbed him in his stomach, “I’ma hurt’cha.” Cash didn’t budge.

Tyra gazed down at him again. Something about him looked different. Her eyes traveled down his body then back up, and that’s when she saw it. Blood. Dark red blood oozing from the back of his neck and around his shoulders.

She screamed at the top of her lungs, throwing her hands up to her mouth. Tears instantly began to roll down her face. Her legs fell from beneath her, causing her ass and the hardwood floor to become one. Realizing in her hysterical state she had to go get help, Tyra sprung to her feet and ran to the bedroom door. She swung the door open, and a silhouette of a man was the last thing she saw after a hard blow landed on her face.

Minutes later, she woke up with a burning sensation in her lungs. Tyra couldn’t breathe and smoke hovered all around her. She could barely see but she knew she was laid out on the floor. Then it hit her, she was in her bedroom. As Tyra sat up, she coughed from the tightening in her lungs. There was intense heat clawing at her back. She swung her head around and saw the bed her and Cash shared on fire.

“Cash!” she shouted, leaping to her feet. Tyra threw her hand up to her mouth, taking small steps, in an attempt to reach the burning bed where Cash laid. The heat from the fire stopped her in her tracks and the smoke made its way up her nose, causing her to gag. Then, as if she was Magic Man David Blaine, her feet were lifted off the floor, as her body distanced itself from the burning bed. She was literally being carried backwards, out of the blazing room by a pair of strong arms wrapped around her torso.

“Tyra, Tyra, girl, get up off this couch and go get in your bed,” Cherry, Tyra’s best friend, said. She was staring down on her discombobulated, but awoke crony.

Tyra sat up on the sofa and rubbed her eyes.

“What time is it?” she asked, groggily. The light in the living room was blinding her.

"It's two o'clock in the morning." Cherry sat her purse down on the coffee table. She rested her hands on her curvaceous hips, while her eyes wandered over Tyra, who wore a white t-shirt that stopped below her knee caps, and a knock-off Louis Vuitton scarf over her head.

"You have fun at the club?" Tyra asked. She made eye contact with Cherry, giving her the once over. Cherry wore a tight black skirt, BCBG straggy high-heeled sandals, and a white peplum shirt that covered her double-D cup breast.

"Yeah, and I wish you could've come wit' me for a change."

Tyra knew what Cherry was insinuating, so she quickly changed the subject. "You know I just had that dream again, right?"

Cherry hissed, "Look Tyra, you dreamin' 'bout what happened that night ain't nothin' new. You've been havin' that dream for a year and a half now. I don't mean to be a bitch or nothin', but you need to get over what happened and move on wit'cha life. I know that Cash meant the world to you but ain't nothin gon' bring him back. You been cooped up in this apartment for the past year and half. It's 'bout time you get out and do somethin'. What's the sense in you bein' beautiful if you don't have the opposite sex goin' out his way to be wit' you."

Cherry was right, Tyra was extremely beautiful, as in hour-glass figure beautiful. She stood 5 foot, 6 inches without shoes. Tyra weighed 140, with most of her weight coming from her ass. Her skin was a rich cocoa brown, and flawless by nature. She was a deep is-land/tropical look like Chili from the group TLC. Her hair was jet black and wavy, stopping at the middle of her back when let down. Tyra was bowlegged, which heightened her walk. She had light brown eyes, dark full eyebrows and lashes, with luscious gorged lips, almost the size of singer Erykah Badu.

Tyra stood up from the sofa and folded her arms staring at Cherry.

"I just need more time, Cherry," Tyra said.

Cherry gave Tyra a stern look. "Girl, please. So, a year and a half ain't enough time for you to pick up your life and move for-ward?"

"It's enough time, but I ain't ready. I'll see you in the

mornin'." Tyra stepped pass Cherry and walked to her bedroom. She climbed in her bed and put the covers over her head, crying silently in the dark.

Since Cash's death, Tyra's life had been nothing short of non-productive. She felt there was nothing to really live for. On numerous occasions, she told herself that she wished her old neighbor, Mr. Dobson, had never carried her out of the house to safety. She would've rather burned up in that fire with Cash than to be on earth living without him. Tyra just couldn't get over the fact that she'd lost everything she loved in just that one night; Cash, her 20g's, the house, clothes, and the money in Cash's safe, that she didn't actually own. Tyra was sure whoever had killed him had taken everything, including his S550.

Cash was her world. They had been together since he was fourteen and she was thirteen. She had even went against her mother's wishes and moved in with him at the age of fifteen. Although she was told by her mother, that if she moved out she'd never be allowed to move back in, Tyra moved in with Cash anyway. That caused them to grow apart, so far apart that when Tyra became homeless after the incident, her mother refused to give her shelter.

She told Tyra when she came knocking, that hell would freeze over before she would allow her back into her home. Then she slammed the door in Tyra's face and shouted, "Go to hell where your no good ass father is!"

That statement hurt Tyra to the core. Her father had died from an overdose of heroin when she was twelve, so she knew what her mother was implying. Her words only meant one thing, and that was she didn't mind if her only child was dead.

After that day, Tyra had no where else to turn, so she ended up on the doorstep of her junior high school friend, Cherry, who accepted her with open arms. Since that day, Cherry had singlehandily been taking care of her without throwing it up in her face. Though, at times, she wanted to yell out to Tyra, *get a job, bitch*!, she never did. Cherry knew Tyra was hurting and she didn't want to add salt to her wound by telling her to do something she wasn't up to.

Cherry was happy when Tyra decided to start doing hair in their apartment about a month ago. That was a plus, because Tyra brought things for the apartment that she never had before. Only thing is Tyra would give her the money to buy the things, she wouldn't step foot out of the apartment for squat, as if she was scared to go outside.

Still silently crying in the dark, Tyra thought about her dream and how, after all the time that had gone by, she still had a vivid picture of what happened that February 20th night. Every time she had that dream, it seemed so real, every detail of it was the exact way that night had occurred. Tyra often wondered after she'd wake up from the dream, who was it that did it? Who had gone through all the effort to lay him down in their bed, as if everything was okay? Who had set the place on fire? Had Cash fought back? And lastly, why didn't they kill her?

Tyra assumed Cash was killed because of the money he owed to the dude he told her about that night. She still didn't know who the dude was or anything else about him for that matter. What she did know was that if she ever found out who did that to Cash, she'd have them and their entire crew killed even if she had to do it herself.

She wiped the tears from her eyes and took a deep breath. "Cash, I loved you so much," she muttered to herself. "But I have to move on. Cherry is right, ain't nothin' I can do to bring you back. I promise you that you'll be the only man I'll ever love and I won't mess wit' anotha' drug dealer. Matter fact, I hate all drug dealers. You were killed because of drugs, so for that reason I hate 'em."

Tyra folded up into a fetal position and quickly fell asleep. But instead of dreaming about that night, her dreams were about starting a new life.

# TWO

The headboard of the bed banged up against the wall with every thrust Big G took. The pair of small pretty hands on the bottom of his stomach wasn't enough to stop his flow. In fact, it was only egging him on.

"G…why…you…gotta…go…uh…uh…uhhh…I'm 'bout to cum…" "Push all that dick in me…" She didn't get the rest of her words out. G drove his dick deep into her pleasure nest until he felt his head touch the back of her wall.

Her body jerked wildly under him, indicating that she was having an orgasm. Her pretty, high yellow face that resembled actress, Jada Pinkett, was now that of a creature straight out of a horror movie. She took hold of G's muscular arms, squeezing them tightly as her climax was coming to a halt.

"My turn now." G grinned down into the woman's face that he'd met only an hour ago at a club. He pushed his dick into her with brute force, then quickly slid out of her and stood upright on his knees. He pulled the condom off his dick and continued to stroke his shaft until his semen blasted onto the stomach and chest of the woman.

A few minutes later, G exited the bathroom after cleaning himself off. He was still naked from head to toe and his dick was swinging to and fro' with every step he took. He stopped his stride when he reached the bed. The women he had just fucked was on it, with her back up against the headboard. Her petite body just as naked as his.

"Your dick still have hang time even on the soft, huh?" Her eyes shot all over G's six foot three body.

G stood at the side of the bed, looking down on the woman

who told him her name was Tammy. His eyes traveled from her gorgeous face, down to her pretty French pedicured toes.

"Didn't I tell you to get dressed?" he said.

"Yeah, but I though you might…" She tossed the pillow from her lap, revealing a small patch of pubic hair above her vagina. It was in a triangle shape. "Want some more of this before we leave." She grinned.

A smile eased across G's handsome, cinnamon brown face that resembled rapper Cam'ron's. *Bitches will do just about anything for money,* he thought.

That was the real reason why she had no problem jetting to the hotel with him. *Money*, and G had plenty of it. Everybody that came in contact with him knew it, and Tammy was no exception.

She spotted G in the club rocking a black, Gucci sweatsuit, at least a 5 carat ice piece around his neck, black Gucci sneakers, and standing near the club's bar in a cocky stance that shouted, *I'm that nigga.*

After she approached him, and they shared small talk for about ten minutes or so, G led her out the club and to the parking lot, where his shiny, black Escalade sat on 25-inch Giovanna rims. She wanted to state her commitment to him right then and there, but she played it cool and hopped into the passenger seat as she was told, without as much as a goodbye to her friends. Nobody was gonna fuck up her chances of rolling with a nigga that was doing the damn thing. She was going to put her pussy game, ass game, and whatever else game down, so she could be in G's stable of women she knew he had.

G took a step back. "Come sit at the edge of the bed," he said, pointing to where he wanted her to sit.

When she did as she was told, he stepped in between her legs with his dick in her face. He was so close to her that he could feel her breath, blowing a slight breeze on his manhood.

"You got this big thing all in my face, like you want me to do somethin' wit' it," Tammy eyed G's dick.

"I do, but for now, I want'cha to look up at me so I can ask you some questions."

Tammy lifted her head.

"Keep it real. Why did you come to this hotel room wit' me?"

G asked.

Tammy looked at G strangely. "Why you ask me that?"

"Just answer me."

"Because you look like you got paper, plus you tall and fine as hell." Tammy grinned faintly. *Damn, I hope that was the right answer.*

"So, what'cha want me to do? Hit'cha off wit' some money for this episode, or I get'cha number and you get mine, and we hook up whenever the time is right?"

Tammy thought on G's words. She did want some money, but which was better for her, money now and never see G again? Or money later and see G often?

"We can just exchange numbers and hook up from time to time," Tammy said. "I know you paid and all, but I like you too. Plus…" She dropped her head down and eyed G's joystick again. "You workin' wit' somethin' every bitch need in her life." Tammy lifted her head back up and smiled a sexy smile at G. "I wanna taste you." She grabbed his dick with her left hand. With her right, she ran it up and down his well defined abs. "So, can I taste you or what?"

"Who gon' stop you? I damn sure ain't." He folded his arms across his chest and watched as she took him into her mouth. His dick began its maturation in seconds, and in minutes he had a powerful orgasm that shook his soul.

"Did you like how I sucked your dick and swallowed your nut?" Tammy posed to G. They sat in the truck in front of a house where Tammy told G she lived off of Columbia Road.

"I ain't gon' lie, you did'cha thing," G said, while glancing at the time on his Navigation screen.

Tammy saw that he was looking at the time, and said, "I know it's one in the mornin', so I'ma let'cha go. Don't take too long to holla at me." She opened the Escalade's passenger door and stepped out.

"Don't worry, I'll get at'cha," G stated, as Tammy shut the door. He didn't wait for her to reach her porch before pulling off.

Riding along Columbia Road, G retrieved his iPhone from his

pocket and tapped Roc's name on the screen. He placed the phone up to his right ear, checked his rearview mirror for any sign of the law, because they'd been cracking down on driving while talking on your cell phone.

"Is she the one?" the male voice on the other end of the phone asked G, without so much as a hello.

"Nah, she ain't the one," G answered. "She answered my questions just like all the other bitches did. She's the third one this week lookin' for a nigga wit' dough that they can be wit' from time to time, and who would break bread wit' 'em. That's all good and shit, but that's not what we need right now. We need a bitch that don't have no respect for a nigga, is all about the paper and not impressed wit' what a nigga got. She'll work if she have' ta to get her own shit. Oh yeah, and she gotta be a dime."

"So, the broad you went to the room wit' tonite didn't qualify for what we need at all?"

"Nah, but I plan to keep her lil' fine ass 'round though." G grinned broadly, while his mind played back the scene in the hotel room.

"So, what's next? We gotta get somebody," Roc said.

"We gotta keep tryin' 'til we get the right girl for what we tryna do."

"Okay, it's your call," Roc said.

G rolled his driver's side window down, just as he was stopping at a stoplight. He stuck his left arm out the window and waved for the driver that was behind him to pull alongside his truck.

G saw the black 745LI BMW with 22-inch chrome Sabatini rims pull up beside him. He reached in his lap for the pink thong panties that Tammy had given him before they exited the hotel's building. He hung the thongs out the window.

"G, you a nut, slim," Roc said, looking at the thongs his boss waved freely out the window. "I'll see you tomorrow."

G watched as the stoplight turned green and the 745 sped out, as if it was in a race. He let the thongs drop in the street.

He had to play his mirrors hard now since Roc wasn't trailing him. No telling what thirsty, broke niggas were up to. He had learned his lesson a long time ago when he was robbed by an unknown crew of broke young'uns, whose life ended only two days after their caper. G had learned many lessons since starting in the game some fourteen years ago. He was twenty-eight now. That's why tonight, and all the other nights since he'd been looking for the right woman to do the jobs he wanted done, he had Roc trailing him from the club and to the hotel that he had already reserved. He knew women had game too, and it wouldn't be nothin' for them to have some niggas follow them to the hotel and pretend like they were robbing them both, when in reality he'd be the only one being robbed. He was hip to the games growing up in the streets could teach you. But still, with all that he knew, he persisted adamantly on picking women up from clubs, in search of finding the right one. *Back to the drawing board*, G thought to himself as he headed towards his next destination.

# THREE

"Damn, Tyra girl, you laced the shit outta my hair," Sam, Tyra's customer said, while looking into a handheld mirror.

"I'm glad'cha like it," Tyra replied, standing behind the chair her customer sat in.

"Girl, when you gon' stop doin' hair in your crib and start workin' in a salon? You need to be workin' at *Class Act Salon* or *Bubbles*, up town. Bitches all over need'ta know who you are fa'real."

"Sam, this ain't the first time I did'cha hair."

"It's your third time hittin' me off, but this time you out did'cha self."Sam placed the mirror on the fake marble square table next to her. "I'm goin' in the bathroom and look at it in the big mirror." She sprung from her seat, and in three steps, she was out of the tiny kitchen Tyra called her salon. The sound of the phone ringing again caught her off guard. She looked at it with an evil eye. She knew who was calling, the same person that had called thirty minutes ago.

"Hello," she said.

"She in yet?" the deep, raspy male voice asked.

"Nope."

"Where the fuck she at? It's almost ten o'clock."

"I don't know and I told'cha that a half hour ago."

"But she got off at seven, right?"

"Smoke, don't ask me what'cha already know."

"Shit!"

"I'll let her know you called."

"Just tell her I'll call her tomorrow and tell her I said that's fucked up she wasn't there to catch my call like she said she'd be."

"A'ight, I'll tell her." Tyra shook her head and made hissing sounds with her mouth, when she hung the phone up. She gathered up her hair supplies off the table.

She secretly didn't like Smoke, not because of anything he did to her personally, but because he was and probably still is a drug dealer, although he's behind bars. Although she knew it was wrong that she didn't like Cherry's man, she couldn't help it. Tyra just felt that her friend could do better for herself than Smoke.

"Tyra, I'ma give you somethin' extra for bangin' my shit out," Sam said, as she entered the kitchen. "Here." She handed Tyra ten twenty dollar bills.

"You must be gettin' it at that club. You givin' me an extra fifty dollars."

Sam gazed at Tyra, with a sly grin on her face. "I ain't on no bitches or nothin', but you'd make a livin' if you was dancin'. You got that tropical look and a nice frame. Shit, you like that."

"Thanks for the compliment, but I can't see myself naked in front of a room full of niggas."

"Girl, that shit ain't nothin' once you get used to it. All you think about after a while is the money. Besides, you can make a lot more dough if you do a lil' more than dance. If you know what I mean."

"Yeah, I know what'cha mean."

"Well, let me jet," Sam said, walking out the kitchen and into the living room.

"Make sure you sleep wit' somethin' on your head so your hair can last longer," Tyra stated, opening the front door for Sam.

"I will. See you later, and tell Cherry I said call me."

"Okay."

After cleaning up the mess she made, Tyra took a quick shower, got dressed and made her way to the living room sofa.

Instead of turning the T.V. on, Tyra just stared at the screen. Her mind replayed what Sam had said to her about stripping. Even though she told herself she'd never strip, she still thought about it.

She pondered on the money. She knew that some strippers made a killing dancing. Not to be conceited or anything, but she told herself she knew if she danced, she'd receive top dollar. Shit, she thought to herself, *if Sam, who is skinny, gap toothed, and a five in the face, whose only apparent asset are her large breasts, could rake in dough, she knew the body she was blessed with, she'd get rich quick if she chose to show a lil' skin.*

Tyra broke her stare and looked around the living room. It wasn't much. The most expensive item in it was the 25-inch T.V. She and Cherry were living on a tight budget. Well, at least Cherry was, because it wasn't until two months ago that Tyra had any money at all.

They had made an agreement just a few weeks ago that Cherry would pay the rent and buy gas for her '09 Nissan Sentra. Tyra would pay for the phone and cable bill, and other necessities like toilet paper, soap, and towels. They both agreed to buy their own food and clothes, although Cherry had paid for Tyra's clothes before Tyra started making money from doing hair.

Tyra thought back to how the living room that she and her mother shared looked. She could remember vividly how empty it was. If she took a deep breath, she could still smell the stench that filled the entire apartment. Her mother didn't clean, so she didn't either. It wasn't that she didn't want to. Tyra just never knew how it was supposed to be done. It wasn't until she had turned ten years old that she realized the way they were living was trifling. Tyra found that out when she invited one of her school friends over to play with her.

Her friend told her flat out as soon as they stepped foot into Tyra's apartment, "Yuck! What's that smell? Damn, your house dirty as shit!" Then her friend stormed out the door.

That incident woke Tyra up, and from that moment on, she was investigating why her home was the way it was. She found out that both her parents were dancing with lady heroin. By the time Tyra was bold enough to voice her opinion about the conditions of the apartment, two years had past and her father was dead, leaving her mother in a state that wasn't approachable.

Tyra dealt with her housing status for three more years, before she moved out. Although by the time she moved out her mother had kicked her heroin habit, the apartment was still dirty and smelly because she was so used to not cleaning for years that she became accustomed to her habitat.

No longer wanting to think about her past, Tyra reached for

the remote control and flicked on the T.V. guide channel to see what time it was. She contemplated whether or not to get dressed and take a walk outside. She'd been taking walks for a month now, trying to get back into the swing of things but, she still hadn't been out to a club, a movie, or even to get groceries. She felt she wasn't quite ready for that yet.

Just as Tyra made up her mind to take a walk, Cherry came through the door looking very upset.

"How was your day?" Tyra asked.

Cherry didn't respond, she stormed passed Tyra without even acknowledging her presence, walking into her bedroom and slamming the door.

"Damn, I wonder what the fuck is wrong wit' her," Tyra mumbled with a puzzled look on her face.

Tyra sat back on the sofa and surfed through channels settling on a re-run of *The Real Housewives of Atlanta*. Her eyes were on the comic, but her mind was on Cherry. Curiosity made her rise from the sofa and head to the back, where she placed her ear against Cherry's bedroom door. She could hear Cherry talking to and answering her own questions in a muffled voice. Tyra thought to herself, *what the fuck is that about?*

"Cherry!" Tyra called out.

"What?" Cherry shouted.

"Girl, you okay in there?"

"I'm okay."

"Can I come in?"

"Yeah, come on in."

Tyra stepped into the room and found Cherry sprawled out across her bed on her back, still in her Walmart work uniform. She had her arms folded over her face, as if she was hiding it.

"Girl, tell me what's wrong?"

"I'm okay."

"Get'cha ass up and talk to me!" Tyra barked.

Cherry sprung up and scooted to the edge of her bed. She looked at Tyra with an exasperated expression on her red face. "I got fired today, okay! And for no reason at all."

Tyra didn't respond. She looked at her friend and saw that she had been crying. She had never seen Cherry like this, so she didn't know what to say to her.

"Me and two other people got fired. They gave us our last checks and said they had to let us go. That's bullshit!"

"They didn't say nothin' 'bout why they fired y'all?"

"No, our boss just called us into his office and told us our services were no longer needed. Ain't that some shit, and I've been workin' there for three years."

"That's fucked up," Tyra said, as she watched Cherry take off her work shoes.

"You damn right that's fucked up," Cherry said, taking off her uniform. "And I always worked my ass off too."

Tyra stared at Cherry, who stood in nothing but her underwear and bra. She watched her walk to her closet and place her uniform on a hanger, as if it was going to be used again.

"I can't believe this shit, man," Cherry stated. "After all I gave their asses, I oughta' just go down there and burn the store and the sorry ass management down to the ground."

Although Tyra heard what Cherry said, she didn't respond. She knew her girl was just hurt by the events of the day and that Cherry would never do no mental ass shit like that. Instead, her eyes were on Cherry's body. It wasn't her first time seeing her friend naked, but it was her first time really paying Cherry's body any real attention. Cherry was definitely big boned, light skinned, almost white. Her body was attractive though. She stood an even five foot four, and weighed one hundred sixty pounds. She wasn't fat and sloppy, just healthy looking. She had thick, strong, shapely calves and thighs. A little pudgy in the stomach area, but not much, nothing clothes couldn't hide. Her tits were big, and her face, on a scale of one to ten, was a seven. Cherry's biggest asset, Tyra thought, was her ass. It was phat, not like hers, but like a big girl's.

"Smoke been callin' here," Tyra said reluctantly, not really wanting to give Cherry the message.

"Fuck him!" Cherry shouted, at the top of her lungs. "He left me out here to go through all this bullshit. If he was out here, I wouldn't even have'ta have a job."

"So, you'd just depend on him, huh?"

Cherry looked at Tyra with a cold stare. "Tyra, don't go there. I know where you goin'."

Tyra decided to drop it. "So, you gon' look for another job?"

"Not right away, but you know I have to. I gotta pay this rent cause I don't want us to get kicked out."

Tyra begin to stress over Cherry's last words. She dreaded being kicked out in the streets. She already had nothing and the thought of being homeless too didn't sit well with her.

"Sam came by today. I did her hair. She gave me two hundred. We can use it towards the rent and yeah, Sam said for you to call her."

"Is that all the money you workin' wit'?"

"No, I have three hundred all together. You want it?"

Cherry gazed at Tyra and saw her willingness to help out. "Nah, you hold onto your dough. I'll come up wit' somethin'."

"You ain't gon' go back to strippin', are you?"

"Nah, my strippin' days are over."

Moments later, Tyra was in her bedroom lying across the bed thinking about some of the things she and Cherry discussed. When Cherry said if Smoke was out of jail, she wouldn't have to work, Tyra became angry. She resented that fact that Cherry made that remark because, years ago she thought just like that. Back then, Tyra believed that all she had to do was look pretty, fuck him good, cook for him and spend his money. Her whole life had evolved around Cash and now that he was gone, she had nothing. So now she vowed to never let her life be centered around another man. She wouldn't respect a man just because he had things. Her respect would be gained only if he wanted her to work in order to possess the same things that he had.

"Don't worry, girl, everythin' gon' be a'ight."Cherry said, sticking her head into Tyra's room.

Tyra could tell from the tone of Cherry's voice that she'd calmed down. Tyra sat up when she heard Cherry's voice, but when she looked at her bedroom door, Cherry wasn't there.

Tyra smiled, but behind her smile, she was frowning because she wanted to be in a position financially to help Cherry. She didn't know anybody that would've done what Cherry did, and still was doing for her. The only way she would even have the chance to do that, was to let her guard down a little more and be a part of society.

# FOUR

He sat quietly in the last row of pews, observing the crowded funeral home as he watched young men with black t-shirts on, displaying the face of the deceased, stand in line for their turn to view the body. The mournful cries of men, women and children were all around him but he wasn't fazed by it. He'd come there for one reason and one reason only, to get his man.

He saw the man he was waiting on stand up from his seat in the front row, view the body and turn to exit. He knew there were only two places he could be headed, the restroom, or outside to the parking lot. When the man strutted down the aisle and passed him, he stood up to follow.

Moments later, he was a few feet behind the man in the parking lot. He reached inside his suit jacket, retrieving his black Taurus 9mm with the silencer attached from his holster.

He scanned the lot for witnesses. *Just my luck, everyone is inside,* he thought to himself. The man, who had retrieved his cell phone and was now preoccupied by conversation, never once looked back to see what was about to go down.

He slowed his stride when the man reached a silver Acura. He watched his prey stick his key into the driver's door and step into the car. In about four giant steps, he was at the driver's side window. Pffft! Pffft! Pffft! Three bullets shattered the windshield, entering the man's chest and head.

Sliding into his black Chevy Corvette coupe, he rode smoothly through the funeral home parking lot. Four blocks away from the crime scene, the man behind the wheel was dialing a number on his cell phone.

"Hello?"

"It's done."

"You were right."

"I know. Too bad I had to put his peoples in a box, so that nigga Paul would show his face."

"Yeah, too bad."

"You find her yet?"

"Nah, not yet. But I hope to real soon."

"Okay. I'm out."

"That should be in your mail box."

"Yeah, okay."

Thirty minutes later, the Corvette drove into a gated apartment complex in Greenbelt, Maryland. As he entered his building, he stopped at a column of mailboxes and stuck a key into Box Number B7. He smiled when he saw the white envelope and read the front of it. Def walked across the black plush carpet that draped most of his apartment and strutted into his bedroom. He placed the envelope and his cell phone onto the dresser, and looked into the mirror.

The man that stared back at him looked to be Malaysian, caramel colored skin. He had strong narrow facial features, with a curly half-inch afro. He had a deep set of mesmerizing, dark brown eyes, and stood five ten.

He took off his clothes, revealing his gun holster's strap still over his shoulders, weapon in tact. He snatched the envelope up and opened it. Pulling out the check, he looked at the number $25,000 and the name the check was made out to: Johnny Walker. One of three alias that he used.

A couple minutes later, he was dressed in workout gear performing his regular five days a week, hour and a half workout consisting of the treadmill, pull ups and shadow boxing. That routine, he believed, kept him younger physically than his thirty years of age.

After his workout and shower, he settled in his living room to relax. He pressed power on the remote and the 55-inch television came to life.

"We have breaking news," the anchorwoman said, beginning the twelve o'clock news. "There has been a shooting in the parking lot of Allen's Funeral Home." The camera escaped the anchorwoman and zoomed in on the funeral home and the parking lot. "You can see the officers surrounding the silver…what I believe is an Acura with the white sheet covering the driver's door of the vehicle. The victim is still inside the vehicle at this time. My sources tell me that the victim, believed to be of male gender was attending the wake of a young man that was murdered just days ago. Now, this isn't confirmed as of yet, but my sources say that no one interviewed thus far saw or heard anything unusual. What we can tell you is that no one has been apprehended in connection with the shooting. More details will be provided as they become available."

Def turned the volume down on the television and dialed a number on his cell phone. In three rings, someone picked up. "Hello, check cashing."

"This Def, Roy."

"Hey, what's up partna?"

"You. I'ma come through today. I got the twenty-five."

"No problem. Come in a half hour or so."

"I'll be there."

Def hung up then headed to his bedroom. He seized the envelope with the check in it from the dresser, but stopped to stare into the mirror. He grinned because it was funny how his faced looked so young and innocent, when in reality, he was a stone cold killer, and had been for many years. He liked it that way because he didn't look to pose a threat but was as vicious as an untamed bull.

# FIVE

"Girl, how you get those tickets?" Cherry said to Sam, who sat next to her on the sofa in her apartment.

"I didn't get my usual three hundred from my trick. I got a hundred and the tickets."

"So, basically your skinny ass tricked for them," Cherry uttered, shaking her head while grinning.

"And you know it." Sam stuck out her tongue, revealing her tongue ring.

"Girl, you ain't gon' never change."

"Shit, why should I? I'm livin' good." Sam looked Cherry in the eye. "How 'bout you? How you livin'?"

Cherry's eyes dropped to the floor. "You really wanna know?"

"Yeah."

"Well, me and Tyra was barely able to pay rent this month. We got a lil' food in the frig, and both of us need clothes. I ain't find no job yet."

"Girl, I don't know what the fuck you waitin' on. You better get'cha ass back in the club and get'cha some dough or find you a nigga wit' some bread."

"I don't wanna do the dancin' thing no more and I don't wanna cheat on Smoke either."

Sam hissed. "Bitch, please! That nigga locked the fuck up, he can't do shit for you right now. He ain't leave you out here wit' money, so do you and get'cha some money. Shit, Smoke been in for three years now, and by the way, I know you ain't tellin' me you ain't had no dick in three years."

Cherry looked at Sam and smiled. "Nah, I ain't sayin' that. I had some dick, but not no relationship dick."

"Oh, I thought so." Sam gazed down the hall towards Cherry and Tyra's bedrooms. "What's takin' Tyra so long to get dressed? I don't wanna miss none of Jay-Z's performance."

"Girl, you know this gon' be Tyra's first time goin' out in almost two years, right?"

"Yeah, I know. I hope she still have some style wit' her. I don't want no bum lookin' bitch around me," Sam said, rolling her neck.

"I don't think she lost that. You gotta remember, Tyra was fly before that nigga died. She just stuck in a rut right now. After tonite though, I think she gon' be a'ight." Cherry smiled.

Sam shook her head up and down. "Yeah…yeah, she gotta still have it goin' on."

"I'm ready y'all." Tyra had entered the living room.

Cherry and Sam stood up from the sofa to look Tyra over. They both had long faces. Tyra looked good, rockin a pair of ripped skin tight jeans with a black faux-leather shirt, and studded peep-toe pumps.

"How do I look?" Tyra spun around in a circle.

The two women who had met four and half years ago at the strip club where they both worked said in unison, "You look good, girl!"

"Now, let's roll up outta here," Sam said, leading the way to the front door. "We rollin' in my car."

Before they could get out the door, the phone rang. They all stopped in their tracks.

"I'll get it." Tyra ran to answer the phone. "Hello."

"You have a pre-paid call from Smoke." Tyra let the rest of the recording play, then pressed five on the phone as she was told in order to accept the call.

"Yeah, Smoke, what'cha want?" she said into the phone.

"Put Cherry on the phone."

Tyra thought for a second then grinned. "We on our way out the door to go see Jay-Z at the Verizon Center."

"What? How y'all get tickets to that show?"

"Does it matter?"

"Yeah, it matter. I thought y'all money was tight? And I

thought you was still stayin' in the house all the time."

"Our money is tight and as for me stayin' in the house…" Tyra took a deep breath, "Those days are over."

"Oh yeah, so you over that nigga's death, huh?"

"I wouldn't say that but I'm gon' move on wit' my life."

"Good for you. Now let me speak to Cherry before y'all bounce."

"They already went out the door." Tyra lied.

"Who is they?" Smoke snapped.

"Cherry and Sam."

"Sam? Y'all hangin' out wit' that freak bitch?"

"I gotta go. What'cha want me to tell her?"

"What Cherry have on?" Smoke ignored Tyra's question.

"I'm just gon' say she got somethin' that'll make niggas holla at her." Tyra smiled broadly.

"Tyra, come on girl!" Cherry yelled.

"I thought'cha said they already went out the door? You a lyin'…"

Tyra cut him off. "Gotta go." She hung up the phone.

"Who was that?" Cherry asked Tyra as they were on their way out the door.

"That was Smoke," Tyra said.

"Don't tell me what he said, I don't wanna know. I'm in a good mood and don't want him spoilin' my night with his bullshit. Now, let's roll up outta here."

The Verizon Center was packed like sardines. Tyra wasn't used to the noise so, she held her hands up to her ears, dancing in place. Sweat made its way down the sides of Tyra's face. She saw women and men doing dances that she'd only seen in videos. She looked to her right and saw Cherry and Sam emulating the dances she witnessed other people doing. She smiled, because watching the dance moves verified that she'd been out of the loop. Tyra continued to watch. *Damn, my ass been off the scene way too long. I wonder what else I've been missin'? I hope it ain't nothin' significant,* she thought.

"Cherry! Cherry!" Tyra tapped her home girl. "I gotta go use the bathroom and get me somethin' to drink. Come wit' me."

"Girl," Cherry said near Tyra's ear, "I ain't heard nothin' you said but come wit' me. You go 'head cause I ain't tryna miss none of the show. Besides, I'll be pissed if I'm not here and my song, *Niggas In Paris* comes on." Tyra watched Cherry go back into her dancing mode.

It took her almost ten minutes to maneuver her way through the crowd, and make her way to the ladies room. When she got there, she waited in line. As she stood, her eyes roamed over the women around her. They all had on their best outfits, even one overly fat girl. Tyra looked down at herself and was happy with what she wore. At least she wasn't out of the loop on how to coordinate her gear, even if she wasn't sporting high price brand names.

From the restroom, Tyra made her way to one of the many concession stands facing yet another line.

"May I take your order?" a smiling, young looking black man asked when Tyra approached the stand.

"Can I get a bottle of water?" Tyra uttered with a slight smile as she dug into her pocket for her money.

"That will be five dollars," the man said.

"*Damn, has it been that long since I've been out?*" Tyra was in motion to hand the man her money, when someone behind her grabbed her wrist, and said, "I'll pay for that."

The tall man that stood behind her handed the man behind the concession stand's counter a ten dollar bill.

Tyra snatched her hand from the man's grip. "Don't put that in the cash register." She gazed at her intruder with a scowl on her face. "I don't know him and I can pay for my own stuff."

The intruder smiled at the man behind the counter, who smiled back.

"Here you go, my man." He gave back the man's money and took the five dollars that Tyra handed him.

"Let me holla at'cha for a minute," the tall man said, as he walked behind Tyra with his eyes glued on her ass.

Tyra was so pissed by the encounter that she never looked back.

He jumped in front of Tyra and put his hands out in front of her. "Hold up a minute, shorty," he said.

Tyra stopped walking. Her pretty face displayed an evil look. "What'cha want? I'm tryna get back and enjoy the show."

"Why you ain't let me pay for your water?"

"That's what'cha stopped me to ask?"

"No."

"Then what's up?" She looked him up and down. He wore a pair of expensive Pradas, blue jeans and a white t-shirt with a picture of his face on it. On his wrist was a costly Rolex watch with a diamond bezel, and a long platinum chain hung down his neck with a letter G diamond medallion. *That shirt is super corny, but the watch and chain have at least 7 carats. Drug dealer*, she thought to herself.

"I'm tryna get'cha number," he said.

"For what?"

"To call you."

Tyra took a sip of her water. "What's your name?" she questioned.

The man grinned broadly, then said, "G," grabbing the medallion on his chain. "But some people call me Big G."

Tyra sighed and rolled her eyes. "Look, G, just gimme your number and I'll call you."

"No problem." G reached into his pocket and pulled out a piece of paper with his name and number already on it.

Looking at the paper, Tyra said, "You were prepared for this, huh?"

"Yeah," G replied. "It comes with the territory."

"Well, I'll call you the first chance I get."

"You do that." G responded.

Tyra started to walk away when G stopped her. "Hold on." He reached into his pocket, pulling out a bankroll. Peeling off three hundred dollar bills, he tried to pass them to Tyra, but she refused to accept the money.

"What's that for?" she asked G.

"For your name and a reward for lookin' so good."

"I don't want your money," Tyra said verbally, but in her mind she said, *Damn, I need that money.*

G tried to place the money in her hand, but Tyra moved it away, saying, "I don't want no money that I didn't have to work for."

G smiled, nodding his head, as if he were acknowledging something. "Okay, what if I told'cha I had a job for you?"

Tyra stared at him suspiciously. "I would ask what the job was."

"All I want you to do is call me. That's the job."

Tyra thought on it. *That was weak but I need the money.*

"All I gotta do is call you, right?"

"Yep." G handed her the benjamins. "I didn't get'cha name," he said.

"I didn't give it," Tyra snapped, stepping off.

Before she got lost in the crowd, she looked back to where she'd left G standing and saw him talking to a short, fat, black dude with a baldhead. The man was dressed fresh but not as fly as G. It appeared that they were smiling, staring in her direction, but she doubted if they could see her through the crowd of people because she could barely see them.

Thirty minutes after the show ended, Tyra and Cherry sat in Sam's blue VW Beetle, while Sam stood outside talking to a brother with dreads. Tyra let Cherry in on what happened to her.

"You gon' call him, right?" Cherry asked.

"Yeah, but I don't know how soon."

"You better, if he gave you three hundred just to call him. Shit, we need the money. I ain't find no job yet and you ain't doin' a lot of hair. So, get at that nigga, girl. Goin' by what'cha told me, he caked up."

Tyra shook her head in agreement to what Cherry said, but she still wasn't feelin' the whole situation. It wasn't that she was afraid to make the call. It was just she vowed not to mess with another drug dealer, and G, she knew fit a drug dealer description.

# SIX

Cherry entered her apartment and shut the door behind her slowly. Reaching the living room sofa, she looked down to find it empty. She knew that meant Tyra was in her room, probably asleep. As she headed back to the door, Cherry was careful not to make much noise.

"C'mon," Cherry said, grabbing the man's hand and pulling him into the apartment.

They went straight to Cherry's bedroom, shut the door and turned on the light.

For the first time since they'd met two hours ago at one of DC's hottest clubs named Ibiza, they were able to get a good look at one another. Cherry liked what she saw. The dude, whose name she'd already forgotten, stood about five foot eleven, with a bulky build. He was what sisters called a chocolate brother.

"Damn, that dark lightin' in the club was robbin' a nigga from seein' your real thickness" he said, looking Cherry over, and smiling from ear to ear. Cherry gave up a fake smile. She really wasn't diggin' him as much as he seemed to be diggin' her. She had one mission on her mind.

"Okay, let's get off this how I look stuff…,," Cherry paused, hoping he would say his name, which she'd forgotten.

"Lee," he said.

"Yeah, Lee. Let's do what we came to do."

"You ain't gotta say no more. I respect yo' hustle." He reached into his pocket and pulled out a hefty knot of money. He thumbed through the dead presidents, until his counting came up on three hundred and fifty dollars. He handed Cherry the money.

"Thanks." Cherry stepped over to her dresser and placed the money down. But when she gazed at the picture of Smoke, a feeling of guilt came over her. Cherry was getting ready to do something she hadn't done in years, trick.

Four and a half years ago, when she was still strippin' and there was no Smoke trickin' was a normalcy. She did it for two reasons, money and fun. It paid well and she liked to see how niggas would come up off the ducketts just to get between her thick, but what some skinny bitches would call fat, legs. Cherry continued to strip until age eighteen when Smoke came into her life. When she told him she was a stripper, he asked her to stop. Smoke took care of her financially, as well as sexually but then after only a year into their relationship, he got locked up. The Feds took the house they lived in and Smoke's Benz. The only thing Cherry had left out of their relationship materially was the Nissan Sentra that he'd brought her that was in her name. Cherry's daze was broken when Lee approached her from behind. Until that moment, she had forgotten that he was even in the room, her eyes still fixated on the photo.

"You a'ight?" Lee asked. He'd already taken off his clothes and stood in nothing but his boxers and socks.

"Yeah…yeah, I'm a'ight," Cherry said, flipping the picture down on the dresser. She turned and faced Lee, and the only thought that came to her mind after seeing him in his boxers and socks was, *It's all about the money. I'm broke, damn it.*

"You got condoms, right?" Lee questioned.

"Yeah, I have some," Cherry replied.

He reached behind her to unzip the strapless body con dress she wore. She wiggled the dress down over her ass and down her thighs.

"I don't know if you felt it while we were dancin' or what…,," Lee dropped his boxers to his ankles, "But I'm tottin'. I need a magnum condom, baby."

Cherry looked down at the long thing that hung between his legs and wanted to pull her dress back up. She'd never seen a dick that big in her life and to make matters worse, it looked to be on the soft side.

Cherry shook her head. "Please tell me you're already hard."

Lee grinned macho-like. “Nah, he ain’t hard yet, but when he get there, you’ll know.”

Several minutes later, Lee’s statement became a reality. His huge dick stood out from his body, at least eleven inches.

“I told’cha you’d know when it’s hard,” he uttered to Cherry, who was rising from her knees after giving him fellatio.

Cherry stood in front of him, stroking his dick while gazing down at it. “I don’t know if I’ma let’cha put that thing in me. I might have to give you head ‘til you bus’off. I’ll have to give you some of your money back.” She looked at Lee, waiting for a response.

“You ain’t gotta do that. All you gotta do is let a nigga put a lil’ bit in you.” He grinned.

The four walls that concealed Cherry’s bedroom couldn’t contain the yowls, even if they were made of steel. She yelled with every thrust Lee took.

“Oh shit!” Lee huffed, “I’m cummin’.” He exploded into the condom and subsequently within a matter of minutes, Cherry was walking him out of her apartment door.

Cherry let the shower water rinse the soap from her body as she gently caressed her sore vagina, wincing from the pain.

Wrapping her towel around her, she proceeded to open the bathroom door and was caught by surprise.

“You have fun?” Tyra spat standing so close to Cherry’s face that she could damn near hear her heartbeat.

“Shit!” Cherry screamed, stumbling backwards with a frightened look on her face. . “Girl, you scared the crap outta me.”

“Oh yeah,” Tyra replied, with an unpleasant look on her face.

“Yeah.” Cherry picked the towel up from the floor and wrapped it back around her. “What’cha doin’ up?”

“How long?” Tyra posed the question to Cherry.

“How long what?” Cherry responded.

“How long you been bringin’ niggas in here after comin’ from the club?”

Taken back by Tyra’s question, Cherry said, “What?”

“You heard me,” Tyra snapped.

Cherry twisted up her face. “I heard’cha, but I’m wonderin’ what made’cha ask me that.”

"Cherry, come on, the entire buildin' probably heard all that noise you were makin'."

Embarrassed, Cherry threw her hand up to her mouth. "Girl," she began in a muffle, "You could hear me? I didn't know I was that loud."

"Well you were. I thought somebody was killin' you."

"Girl," Cherry dropped her hand from her mouth, "That nigga had a big ass dick. That shit felt like it was gon' rip my insides up."

"Who was he?"

Caught off guard, Cherry didn't want to tell Tyra the truth.

"Uh," said said. "I um."

"Don't tell me you don't know him." Tyra folded her arms across her chest and slid her neck back.

"Nah, I know him. He…,,"

"What's his name?" Tyra pressed.

Cherry cursed herself inwardly for once again forgetting the man's name who had just ran up in her, no less than thirty minutes ago.

Tyra shook her head in a *shame on you* way. "You don't even know the name of the niggas that put his dick in you."

"Nah, I know his name. You just caught me off guard wit'cha question."

"Cherry, give it up and come clean."

Relinquishing, Cherry spat, "Okay. I met him in the club. We danced a lil' and I told him we could fuck for some money…,," Cherry paused to capture the reaction she knew would come from Tyra and sure enough, Tyra's face got long and her jaw hung. Since she had already let the cat out the bag, Cherry decided to continue. "He said money wasn't a thing, so we rolled out from the club and came here. I fucked him…nah, he fucked me then he left."

"So, when you start trickin'?"

A little offended by Tyra's question, Cherry uttered, "What'cha mean when I start trickin'?"

"Money for pussy is called trickin', right?" Tyra said smartly.

Sensing where their conversation was headed, Cherry said, "Tyra, let's talk about this tomorrow."

"Nah, you bringin' niggas up in here you don't even know.

You playin' a dangerous game."

Cherry had thought about whether or not it would be safe for her to take him to her crib and after thinking it over, she decided it was worth the risk. For the most part everything went smooth, except for the fact that he had a monster in his pants, which she hadn't expected.

"You know what Tyra, it was a dangerous thing for me to do, but didn't nothin' happen. He came here, paid me, fucked me and left. That's it."

"Yeah a'ight. So, let me ask you again since you didn't answer me a while ago. When did'cha start trickin'?"

Cherry rolled her eyes and sucked her teeth. "Look Tyra, we fuckin' broke. We can barely pay rent. Nah, scratch that, we can't even pay rent, not this month comin'. We need clothes for the winter and lil' shit around the house so, what else do you suggest I do?"

"You still didn't answer my question," Tyra said, unmoved by Cherry's words.

"I started trickin' tonite, damn it!"Cherry shouted. "I don't know what part of what I just said you didn't understand, but we fuckin' broke and by the way, if you would get off that bullshit that you're on and call that nigga that you met at the Verizon Center, maybe I wouldn't have to sell my ass. Won't you sacrifice somethin' for a change for the both of us? You know that nigga got bank. Any nigga who gives a bitch three hundred just to call him is caked the fuck up. Now, can I get by?"

Tyra stepped to the side and Cherry walked out of the bathroom, into her bedroom. Boooom! She slammed her door shut. Cherry unwrapped the towel from around her and allowed it to tumble to the floor. She climbed into bed and was on the verge of crying.

She wanted to cry because she didn't feel in control. Her status had changed from being head of the household to tricking to survive. As a matter of fact, she was damn near on the verge of flipping out from her current circumstances. Cherry was strong but even she had her breaking points. She felt helpless and didn't know what to do about it.

Cherry had been taking care of herself since age seventeen when her grandmother died. Her grandmother had raised her after her parents ran off and left her at an early age. With the one person in her corner gone, Cherry stripped, sold her pussy and still graduated from high school on time. Now, here she was forced to go back to her old ways, which she had vowed not to do.

As Cherry closed her eyes, she said to herself out loud, "I hope Tyra get in touch wit' that nigga. I know he's paid. If she don't I'm not gon' have no problem wit' sellin' my ass for some paper but I won't be takin' care of her, not this time. If she don't make enough by doing hair, and she's not willin' to open her legs to get paid, well I'm sorry to say but she gotta step." After those words, Cherry dozed off to sleep.

# SEVEN

G stepped inside the famous Saint's Paradise Cafeteria to the smell of southern cooked food. He smiled when he spotted the person he was there to meet.

"You made it on time, I see?"

" Of course," G replied, sitting down at the table across from the petite, red-boned woman who wore a navy blue business suit. "I can't stay long though, I gotta go meet Roc."

"How's he doing?"

"He good." G slid the woman's plate of food towards him and started eating.

"G, why didn't you just go up to the counter and order your own food?" she asked.

"Why should I? There's food right here." He polished off the bake cheese ziti.

The lady shook her head.

"Okay, Jill, tell a nigga how his bank look?"

"There's not much to tell you. Tess, the white girl, finally paid up and Lou, the china man, paid up too."

G smiled. "I thought I was gonna have'ta put a price on their heads about my money."

"G, like I told you a long time ago, the people I deal with aren't corner drug dealers, so they might be a little late on payments from time to time. They run businesses, they can't make fifty, sixty thousand in one day."

"Nah, they can just ask to borrow that much. Well, what else?"

"That's it. Oh, by the way." Jill looked at G, in a pleading manner. "They both asked me if it were possible next time, if you could charge twenty-five percent on what they borrow instead of fifty percent."

G gave Jill a cold stare.

"Okay, I see you aren't going to say anything. The look on your face says it all."

"I'ma say it anyway. I could charge them one hundred percent on my shit. They better be glad it's just fifty percent."

Jill stared at the man she had known since they met five years ago at Howard University's homecoming football game. That year, she was finishing her last semester, majoring in business administration. They had met that day, and two days later, she and G were in a five star hotel room in downtown DC fucking like it was the last day on earth.

She had fallen in love with G that day, and wanted to express that to him but for some strange reason, she didn't and it was a good thing she hadn't. After only three weeks into their fling, G showed her exactly what he was about, coming to pick her up with another woman in the truck. He conveyed to her the woman's name and that she'd be tagging along with them to a club and then to a hotel for a threesome. She didn't even have a chance to ask him a question about who the woman was.

Needless to say, she didn't tag along with them, and it took her two weeks after that day to accept G's phone calls. From that point on, they maintained a business relationship only.

"G, you're in the loan sharking business, right?" she asked.

"Yeah, ever since I was fourteen."

"You loan people money and collect your money back, plus fifty percent interest, right?"

G shrugged his shoulders. "And what'cha tryna say?"

"You ever heard of a tax break?"

"Yeah."

"I think you should give interest breaks for some of your people."

G slouched low into his seat. "And that interest break will be just for the people in your circle that I do business wit' through you, huh?"

Jill nodded and smiled.

"You're so fine, you know that right?" G said.

"I know." Jill ran her tongue over her teeth.

"I ain't givin' no breaks, slim. If I give your corporate clique a break, I gotta give my street niggas a break." G shook his head no. "That ain't happenin'."

"Okay, I tried." Jill threw her slender pedicured hands up in the air, indicating defeat.

"Yeah, you tried." G stood up from the table.

" Did you leave your car alarm off and your door unlocked, " Jill inquired.

"Yeah."

"It should be in your overpriced ass car." Jill rolled her eyes at G.

G grinned. "You took your money out, right?"

"Don't I always," Jill snapped.

"See ya later," G said, as he walked away.

G slid into his candy apple red Bentley Continental GT that sat on 20-inch chrome Lorenzo rims. The smell of the new car's tan leather seats rushed up into his nostrils, reminding him of how sweet life was for him.

He looked over in his passenger seat at the Nordstrom shopping bag that Jill had someone she obviously trusted place there. He grabbed the bag and looked into it. He lifted up the cheap sweater he knew was hiding the one hundred and forty thousand dollars and bingo! There lay the money, wrapped in rubber bands, the hustler way. He had schooled her a while ago that he always wanted his money this way. He didn't have to count his money because Jill had been loyal since he met her.

While cruising along New Hampshire Avenue listening to rapper Drake's latest CD, G felt his cell phone vibrating in his pocket. He retrieved it and scanned the number of the caller. He smiled and said, "What's up, girl?" as he turned the music down.

"You," a soft voice replied. "Where you at?"

"I'm around."

"I miss you already."

"Oh yeah. What'cha miss?"

"You and that dick."

G grinned. "I just bounced from your spot this mornin'. You miss a nigga already."

"Shhiiitt! The way you fucked me last night and again this mornin' Shhh! You got that type of dick that'll hook a bitch like a drug."

"Your shit ain't nothin' to play wit' either, you got some good pussy. You surprised the shit outta me. Your lil' ass can take some dick."

"If I wasn't never practicin' wit those anal beads that I have, I would'na been able to take all that dick you got."

They both laughed.

"Look, Tammy, I'ma get at'cha later. I'm gotta take care of somethin' right now."

"Okay. You think I can see you tonite?"

"Maybe. What kind of surprise do you have for me?"

"I'll give you a hint. You get two scoops of ice cream. One strawberry, one chocolate."

"If you sayin' what I think you sayin', I'll be over later."

"See you then."

"Bye." G said, but before he could put his phone down it rung. "Yeah."

"Where you at, slim?" Roc said.

"I'm on my way," G replied. "You got everythin'?"

"Yeah."

"A'ight. I'll see you in 'bout ten minutes."

Twelve minutes after getting off the phone with Roc, G was parking behind Roc's ride, in front of the barbershop his uncle owned off of North Capital Street.

He grabbed the Nordstrom bag and stuffed it under the driver's seat. He stepped out of the car, activated the alarm and headed into the barbershop.

"Look who steppin' up in the house," an older man said from the back of the shop. "The owner of this shop comes around when he feels like it."

"C'mon on, Uncle Pete," G said, as he made his way from chair to chair, giving each barber a pound. "This ain't my shop, this your shop. You runnin' things around here."

"I wish that were true, young buck," Pete said, when G reached him. They hugged. "You still gettin' a cut of the money I make up in here," he said, in G's ear.

"Don't forget I put all the dough up to purchase this joint. I should be gettin' a cut."

"Yeah, you have a point." They broke their embrace. "So, when is my last payment again?" Pete gazed at G from under his glasses.

"In two years. You got two more payments."

Pete nodded his receding hairline while smiling. "I can live wit' that young'un." Pete noticed the look his customer was giving him, so he quickly jumped back on his job. "Your parents would've liked what'cha did for me."

"I know," G responded. "Roc in here, right?"

"Yeah. He in the back, in my office."

As G walked towards the office, he thought about his parents. They had died so young. A car accident on one New Year's Eve had taken their lives. G had just turned eighteen, and his sister, Olivia, seventeen. His father, Gary, worked as a janitor at Children's Hospital, and his mother, Daisy worked at DC Office of Aging as a cook. Although they didn't have what society called high paying jobs, they took damn good care of their children, always finding a way to buy them things they didn't really need and it was greed that led G, at the age of twelve, to the streets. He began stealing clothes from out of stores. But his reign didn't last long because he got busted and since he had stolen so much from the store, he had to do time in a juvenile center. He was given two years with an R, meaning Restriction, at Oak Hill Juvenile Facility.

G stepped into the office to find Roc sitting behind Uncle Pete's desk with his feet kicked up. He was asleep, his baldhead hanging off the back of the black leather chair.

Booommm!! "Wake your ass up, nigga!" G slammed his hands down onto the table.

Roc quickly woke up."Damn, G man," Roc said. He straightened his Armani t-shirt out and regained his composure.

"Nigga, it's four o'clock in the afternoon and you sleepin' and shit." G walked around the table and sat in the chair.

"Shit, last night that bitch wore me the fuck out," Roc piped, with a shake of his head.

"That's cause your fat ass ain't in no shape, nigga," G barked.

The statement G made was true. Roc wasn't in shape. He'd let his once ripped up physique turn into fat. He no longer deserved to claim the name Roc, which represented his use to be body. He stood five feet six, and weighed 225 pounds. If he weren't a nigga that had a little money, he would've been fat. His appearance, although he was overweight, was a reflection of his money.

"What's up? Where the bread at?" G quizzed.

"Right there under the table."

G retrieved the black backpack and looked inside.

"Two hundred g's in there. You know I already took mine out," Roc explained.

Again, G didn't have to count his money. Roc had been loyal to him since he started his loan sharking business, when they both were locked down as juveniles at Oak Hill, the place where they met over fourteen years ago. In the joint, G used to do what they called one for two or two for three's.

At first, G worked alone on his hustle of toothpaste, cookies, chips, candy bars, frontin' niggas for products who in turn, paid him back his original plus an extra. When his hustle got plentiful, he needed help, and since there were only two people he had befriended to the point of trust, he put Roc down with his hustle, he was the boss, and Roc was the worker. That relationship trickled out onto the streets when they both were released at age fourteen. Once G hit the streets, he started lending out money. No more jailhouse items, and as time went on, he was deeply rooted into the loan shark game.

G zipped the pack back up, and said, "Anything new on those niggas?"

"Nah." Roc stood in front of the table, staring down at G. "We know where they at, it's just too many niggas round 'em."

G gritted his teeth and shook his head. "Man, these nig…" The vibrating feeling in his pocket let him know his phone was ringing. He pulled the phone from his pocket, read the number and answered it. "Yeah."

G's facial expression changed within seconds. He spoke into

the phone for five minutes before ending his call.

"You won't believe who that was, slim."

"Who?" Roc asked.

"The Verizon Center," G said, grinning.

"The Verizon Center?" Roc had a perplexed expression on his face.

G stood up from the chair, with the backpack in hand. "I gotta be at Hechinger Mall in the Safeway's parkin' lot in two hours. I'll call you later on tonite."

"Be safe nigga, and tote the fire on you," Roc said, as G exited the office.

# EIGHT

With nothing on but her purple thongs and bra, Tyra rambled through her bedroom closet for something to wear. She pulled out a pair of black leggins, a long sleeve cheap looking, sweater and her wedge heel Puma sneakers. She ran out of her bedroom and into Cherry's in search of a coat. With no luck, she realized Cherry must've had the only coat in the house on her back when she left out the apartment earlier in search of another job.

"Damn!" Tyra cursed out loud. "I know it's cold outside and I don't even own a winter coat. I've been in this damn house so long that I'm bout to go and meet this guy and I'ma freeze to death. He'll probably think I'm crazy as hell showing up with nothin' but this sweater on my ass." Tyra thought to herself, *the minute I get my hands on some money, I'm goin on a shoppin' spree for me and Cherry.* At that moment, Tyra reflected back on how she had lost everything in the fire. "I love you Cash," was the last thing she said as she headed out the door.

Twenty minutes later, Tyra was standing outside in front of the Safeway grocery store at Hechinger Mall. Her arms were folded across her chest, and her legs clenched together. She wondered whether standing out in the November chill was such a good idea. Maybe the person she was waiting on had stood her up.

Her eyes roamed over the grocery store's parking lot. When she didn't pinpoint the vehicle that had been described to her, she turned to leave.

Beep! Beep!

Tyra stopped in her tracks. She glanced in the direction where the sound of the horn came from. There, cruising slowly up toward her was a pretty, candy apple red, Bently Continental GT. She'd only seen one before in the latest rap videos. The Bentley stopped in front of her, rims shining from the sun that beamed down on them. The driver's side window came down.

"I hope you weren't standing out here too long," G said. "I had to stop for some gas."

Tyra didn't respond, she walked around the front of the car and hopped into the passenger seat. The new car smell and the heat that she needed so badly immediately put her at ease.

"Your car must be around here somewhere. You don't have no jacket or nothin' on," G said.

"Nah, I don't have a car. I don't have a jacket on cause I only live a few blocks away," Tyra revealed. She nonchalantly ran her eyes over G. She saw the diamond studs in each of his earlobes.

"You want me to park and we talk? Or ride and we talk?" G offered up as options.

"You can park," Tyra stated.

G found a parking space in the lot. "You know you a beautiful girl, right?"

"Am I?" Tyra asked, sarcastically.

"Don't act like you don't know that. I know niggas tell you that all the time," G stated.

"Nah, they don't."

"Well, I'm tellin' you." G looked at Tyra. "You got that tropical look. Are you Brazilian or somethin'?" He looked at her long wavy hair that was pulled back into a ponytail.

"So, I guess you wonderin' what I wanna do wit'cha, huh?" Tyra nodded her head up and down.

"Okay. Let's get down to business. As you know, my name is G." He extended his hand for an official greeting. "What's yours?"

"Is my name really important?"

"Yeah," G snapped. "When we talked at the Verizon Center, you didn't give me your name. When I talked to you earlier, you didn't' give me your name. Damn! What's wrong wit' givin' a nigga your name?"

"Tyra, my name is Tyra."

"Okay, now we gettin' somewhere. You work, Tyra?"

"If you call doin' hair in my crib workin', then yeah, I work."

G nodded his head. "So, you an entrepreneur, huh?"

Tyra twisted up her lips, she wanted to say a broke one, but she held her tongue and instead said, "You can call me that."

"You make good money?"

Tyra wanted to yell, *Hell no*, and tell him how broke she was, but she didn't, instead she said, "Not really."

"Would'cha like to make good money and purchase your own salon?"

Tyra stared at G, who stared right back at her.

"Doin' what? Cause I don't sell ass, and I don't sell fuckin' drugs either." She rolled her eyes at him.

"So, that's what'cha think I am, a pimp or a drug dealer?"

"You tell me."

"I'm not neither one, I'ma businessman. I…,," His cell phone rang, cutting him off. He dug it from out of his pocket and answered it. "What's up, sis?"

Tyra looked out the passenger window, while G talked on the phone. She saw a group of young boys pointing at the car as if they were playing the game of, *that's my car.* She laughed to herself, just as G was ending his phone call.

"You willin' to take a ride wit' me?" G asked Tyra. He slid his phone back into his pocket.

" I don't know. First, I gotta know who you were talkin' to on your phone."

"That was my sister."

"How I know that? You could've gotten somebody to call you at this particular time cause you knew you'd be here wit' me. That way, it'd look like you had to go. You ask me what'cha just asked me and I say yeah, and you take me somewhere and kill me."

G smiled broadly, he liked what he had just heard. Her words let him know that she was sharp, and that's what he needed.

"You want me to call her back and let you talk to her?"

"Yeah," Tyra said, plainly. As G was going into his pocket, Tyra stopped him. "I believe you, now, where we ridin' to?"

" Bethesda, Maryland. To a store me and my sister own together."

"You and your sister tight?" Tyra turned and asked G.

"Hell yeah, like peas and carrots. When my parents died, it was just me and her. We had each other's back then and still do to this day."

Tyra surveyed G with a smile on her face. "So, you're not a drug dealer?"

He shook his head. "Nah, never had been."

"Good, cause I hate drug dealers and don't ask me why."

"Well, I'm not a pimp or a drug dealer. I'm in the loansharkin' business and the owner of two stores. I own a clothin' and a porno store. So, you gon' take that ride wit' me?"

"Yeah, you seem a'ight."

Half an hour later, the Bentley was parked in the lot of a mini mall. The entire ride to the mall, G and Tyra didn't talk much. They listened to music like Kanye West and Lil' Wayne.

"C'mon in the store wit' me. I'ma head straight to the back and you can wait out in front. But while you waitin' for me, go 'head and pick up anythin' you like and place it on the counter. I don't care how much it comes up to."

Tyra looked at G with a puzzled expression. "Won't you lose money?"

"Nah, I'll put it back, so pick up anythin' you like."

When they stepped into the store, G did just as he had told Tyra he would. Now, alone, she looked throughout the store. Meek Mill's latest hit pumped from out of speakers that were hung around in corners of the ceiling. As people browsed through clothes, she looked around the store and noticed it was a unisex clothing store with nothing but the hottest brands of Hip Hop gear.

After Tyra picked out a few things for herself, as well as Cherry, she took them up to the counter, where a dark skinned woman stood behind a cash register.

"This all?" the woman said with a smile.

"Yeah." Tyra looked around. She didn't know if the woman had seen her enter the store with G or not.

"Honey, you lookin' for G?" the woman asked.

Tyra shook her head.

"I already know you supposed to get rung up without passin'

me a dime. It's okay." She placed Tyra's things into two bags. "I didn't see you walk in here wit' a coat on, so I think you should place this jacket up here also." She handed Tyra a black, insulated Helley Hanson jacket.

As Tyra was trying the jacket on, G was approaching her with a tall brown skinned woman in tow.

"Tyra, this is my sister, Olivia," G said.

Tyra looked the woman over. She summed up G's sister's appearance in three words, *looks like money*. Olivia had to stand at least five feet eleven inches, with pricey knee-length Christian Louboutin boots on her feet. Her body was slender. She rocked a short, cut hairstyle, like Halle Berry used to. Her cinnamon brown face and smile were beautiful. Olivia wore just a little make-up, and when she stuck out her hand towards Tyra for a shake, Tyra saw that she had French manicured nails.

"Hi Tyra? My brother told me you're a friend of his. Any friend of his is a friend of mine."

"Thank you," Tyra said, after they freed hands.

"I must say this before I go," Olivia began. "You're a beautiful young sista. You have some beautiful hair. If my hair could grow that long, I wouldn't be rocking it like this. Now...,," she kissed G on his cheek, "I got to go finish this paperwork before I close up."

Tyra and G walked out the store.

"You go 'head to the car, the door is open. I gotta go check on the white boy that I have managing my porn shop. Oh, unless you wanna go in there wit' me." G smiled wickedly at Tyra.

"Both of your stores are in this mini mall?"

"Yeah. So, you didn't answer my question. Do you wanna go in wit' me?"

"Nah, I'll pass. You go 'head, I'll be in the car."

Tyra sat in the passenger seat smiling as if she had won a prize. She couldn't believe her luck. *Why her*, she thought. Why she had to come up on a nigga that was balling out of control? He didn't even know her and he was treating her as if they knew each other for years. *What did he want*, she began to think. No man gave things or did things for women without wanting to be paid back in some way. She thought as soon as he stepped into the car she was gonna ask him.

G slid into the driver's seat when Tyra said, "What'cha want for givin' me all this stuff? I told'cha I don't sell no ass and I told'cha that I didn't want nothin' that I didn't have to work for."

G pulled off. "I'ma lay everythin' out to you," he began. "Like I told'cha earlier, I'ma loansharker. While my store business is legit, my loansharkin' thing ain't, so what I need you for is bait. I loaned some money out to a couple of niggas that had the balls not to pay me back. They hard for me to get to, since I'ma nigga and the muscle I have on em' is a nigga too. My man trailin' em' can't get to em' 'cause they always rollin' deep. That's where you come in. I need you to get them alone. Now, I'ma keep it real. Not all of 'em are in DC, some of them pussy ass niggas skipped town. You followin' me, right?"

Tyra shook her head.

"Now, this job pays real good. You…,,"

"Are they drug dealers?" Tyra asked, cutting him off.

"Yeah. They niggas that needed more loot to cop bigger shit."

"I'll do it," Tyra said, with a little bitterness in her voice. She didn't have to think hard on this and there was no need for G to explain any further.

"You sure?"

"Yeah, I'm sure. When do I start?"

G peered over at Tyra. "You wanna know how much it pays?"

"How much?"

"Between ten and fifteen a nigga."

Tyra eyes sprung open, she knew he was talking thousands.

G reached into his pocket and pulled out a knot of money. He placed it into Tyra's lap. "That's five g's. That's for you to buy yourself more clothes. " G reached to open the glove compartment. A cell phone fell into her lap. "That's yours. You don't have'ta worry about payin' the bill. The number is logged in the memory. You'll meet my man that's gon' be by your side on this. He's the one that'll do all the dirty work. He good, don't worry. There are only two niggas in my life that I trust and get down wit' and he one of em."

"He a killer?"

G shook his head. "Pretty much."

"Let me ask you somethin'?" Tyra said.

"Go 'head."

"When you saw me at the Verizon Center did you approach me in the way that you did to holla at me on a relationship/sex thing or for this job?"

"For this job. Although, to be real wit'cha, you bad in a way that I wanna fuck wit'cha. But I need you for this job. I tested you at the show when I tried to pay for your bottle of water. When you didn't allow me to pay for it, I knew you were the type of broad that likes to do for yourself and when you told me you didn't want no money you didn't have to work for, I knew you wasn't one of those broads that wanna live off a nigga. You'll grind for your own shit. You want me to drop you off back at the Safeway?" G smiled.

"Please do," Tyra uttered, "I don't want'cha to know where I live just yet."

When G pulled into Safeway's parking lot, he said, "And another thing, you haven't complimented me on the ice you see me wearin' or my car. I like that. You ain't impressed wit' what a nigga have."

Tyra gathered her things. "Why should I? That's your shit, not mine. Now, when you gon' call me so we can get this started?"

"When I call you, all three of us gon' meet up together."

"Okay."

"Stay pretty," G stated as he watched her step out of his car.

When Tyra entered her apartment, Cherry was sitting on the living room sofa. She didn't even bother to look up to see who it was coming through the door. She was staring at the television. Tyra stepped up to the coffee table and sat the two shopping bags on it. That got Cherry's attention. She gazed at the bags then at Tyra, who was smiling down at her.

"What's in those bags, girl? Where you get that bangin' ass jacket?" Cherry looked Tyra up and down.

Tyra handed Cherry the bag of things she had gotten her. Cherry immediately dug her hand into the bag and pulled out a pair of leather jogging pants.

"These mine?" she asked Tyra.

Tyra shook her head. "Yeah, everythin' in that bag is yours."

Cherry froze with the jeans held up to her waist. She gave Tyra a crazy look. "The po-po ain't gon' kick in the door any moment, are they? You ain't go rob nothin' did'cha?"

"Nope. I called that nigga and you were right, he is caked the fuck up."

They both screamed at the top of their lungs.

"Girl, I told'cha. I knew that nigga had some serious paper." Cherry paused. "Now, what'cha do for him? I know that nigga ain't spend all that money on you for free."

Tyra had to think fast, she definitely didn't want Cherry to know what she was about to get into. "Girl, I'm not gon' lie." Tyra threw a shameful look on her face. "I sucked his dick until he came in my mouth."

Cherry dropped the pants she was holding to the floor and covered her mouth with her hands. "I know you didn't," she muffled, "Not your miss-holier-than-thou-ass."

"And I was a lil' rusty, too. You know, since I ain't sucked a dick in like two years." They both laughed.

Tyra dug into her bag for the money G had given her. She sat the money on the table and watched Cherry's eyes bulge. "Twenty-five hundred for you, and twenty-five hundred for me. You my girl."

"He hit'cha off wit' money too so, you wasn't that damn rusty," Cherry said.

Tyra giggled, but behind her giggle, she thought, *I'm 'bout to start a new life. Some people may think it's wrong what I'm 'bout to do, but not me. I'll be gettin' rid of people that hurt other people anyway. If it wasn't for drug dealers, this world wouldn't be as fucked up as it is now. So, I'll do my part and help get rid of some of 'em.*

# NINE

He stepped out of his car into the chilled night air in front of a red brick house, on a fairly quiet street in Rockville, Maryland and headed towards the door. In his right hand, he gripped the strap to a black duffel bag.

Stepping onto the porch of the house, he smiled. The front door was opened. He proceeded in and walked up the stairs that led to the second level of the house.

The sound of Rick Ross connected with his ears the moment he reached the top of the steps. As he walked closer to the door he became very excited.

He turned the doorknob and stepped into the dimly lit bedroom. His eyes widened at the two naked bodies.

Smiling as if it were his birthday, he quickly removed his clothes and switched his duffel bag with an identical one from the bedroom's dresser.

Focusing back on the bed, the two women lying on their backs watched him closely. Looking at one of them meant you were looking at them both. They were identical twins.

When he had first met the twins three and a half years ago, he couldn't distinguish between them. But once they started having a ménage-a-trois, he could easily tell which one was who.

"Daddy, what'cha waitin' for," they said in unison. Their voices barely hovered over the music that was still playing.

Daddy grinned broadly. "Nothin'." He climbed his naked body up on the bed in between them. "Everythin' straight wit' the coke, right?" he asked.

"Is everythin' straight wit' the denaros?" Cita quizzed.

“Yeah, it’s two hundred and twenty-five g’s in there, plus a g for what we ‘bout to do.”

“A’ight poppi. Get this line of coke up off my stomach so we can get this shit started. I want some of that big dick,” Rita spat.

Daddy loved when they talked to him like that. Ever since he had met them at a private party, they talked aggressive like men. That turned him on. Although prior to meeting the twins, Daddy wasn’t interested in sellin’ drugs, that changed when they told him, they’d both fuck him when he copped from them and he could get his kilos at a reasonable price. He agreed, while still holding down his other hustle. But, it was one thing he never thought he’d indulge in and that was sniffing coke.

The twins had him doing coke for a whole year now, and he liked it, especially when they were about to get busy. Although lately, he found himself sniffing powder in between his monthly visits, he allowed himself to accept his lack of discipline.

After taking in a few lines, Daddy laid out on his back in anticipation for the twins who were taking in a few lines across the room. Crawling up on the bed, the twins stationed themselves in between his legs.

They hadn’t even touched his dick yet and it stiffened up. “What’chall waitin’ for?”

“Shut up!” Rita shouted boldly, as she grabbed hold of his dick from the base and squeezed it, causing it to swell up more than it already was. Then, as if that was her cue, Cita lifted her head up and clamped her mouth on it.

Daddy moaned loudly. He watched his dick disappear in and out of her mouth. Then she suddenly stopped, took her mouth off him, slid a condom over his dick, and mounted him. Rita crawled up toward him and stood above his face. She grabbed onto the headboard for support and squatted down. He didn’t protest. His tongue began flickering fiercely at her clitoris, causing her to lament in the same manner as her twin.

An hour later, Daddy was dressed and on his way out the twin’s house with a duffle bag filled with fifteen kilos of coke. He made it out to his car then dialed a number on his cell phone.

“Hello.”

"Yeah, this me, slim. I got that. You ready?"

"Yeah."

"I hope so cause you know I like to get rid of this shit as soon as possible and yeah, I don't know how much longer I'ma be hittin' you off. I've been at this shit for three and a half years and I ain't feelin' it no more. This hustle ain't me, my other hustle got my heart."

He hung up with his caller and thought about what he had just said. He had been pondering on quitting his drug hustle, but if he did, it would mean no more twins. They were the reason he hadn't quit yet. He knew however, that someday disaster would come knocking at his door if he didn't. *As much as I'll miss them, it's time*, he said to himself as he sped away.

# TEN

The silver, Porsche 911 that sat on dipped chrome factory rims, zipped into Safeway's parking lot in Hechinger Mall. The man behind the wheel was running late for a meeting.

He slowed his ride down when he spotted the car he was looking for. He quickly pulled up next to it and parked. He grabbed the Sony DVD recorder from his passenger seat and stepped out the car.

"Sorry I'm a lil' late," he said, as he slid into the backseat of the Bentley.

"Don't worry 'bout that, slim," G said, looking into the backseat at Def. He smiled because his hit man had finally arrived.

Def's eyes bounced over in the passenger seat at the woman that sat next to his friend and employer. She sat looking straight ahead, not even acknowledging him.

"Tyra, this the man you gon' be workin' wit'," G stated.

Tyra turned around in her seat and looked at Def. She couldn't help but notice his curly hair. It was definitely a turn on. They both stared at each other until G interrupted their trance.

"Def, this the lovely Tyra, and Tyra this my man, Def."

Def sat in his seat at a loss for words. When G had called him a week ago and conveyed that he'd found a beautiful broad to help carry out their hits, he never thought she would be a dime.

"Hi," Tyra uttered. She extended her hand out for a shake.

G gawked at Def because he knew Def was going to leave Tyra hanging. G had learned over fourteen years ago when they first met at Oak Hill, that Def didn't believe in shaking hands with a person he'd just met. However, G thought that Def would at least shake Tyra's. G shook his head as he looked over at Tyra, who'd withdrawn her hand. He knew she was pissed. He stared at Def, who looked at him as if to say, 'You shoulda' told her'. *Damn.* G thought, *I knew this nigga was cold to niggas, but I ain't know all these years he was cold to bitches, too. I wonder how he treat his moms...,,oh damn, I forgot, he was locked up from age thirteen to twenty-one because of his mom. That nigga did juvenile life for killin' his alcoholic stepfather who killed his moms. I'm glad I kept in touch wit' this nigga after I got out. I'd rather him be on my team then on another nigga's.*

"This ain't the dude who takes care of people for you, is it?" Tyra asked. She looked at G, but rolled her eyes at Def.

"Why you ask that?" G asked perplexed.

Tyra gave Def a hard stare. "Cause he don't look like he no killer. He look like a young'un that just started comin' out the house."

G and Def smiled at one another. They both knew Tyra's statement was motivated because she'd just gotten dissed and needed to retaliate.

Def flipped out the camcorder's small screen, then pushed the play button. He handed the camcorder to G. "The nigga wit' the dreads is the one Roc put me onto. As you can see he 'round a lot of niggas." Def cut his eyes over on Tyra who he caught staring at him.

"Where he at, in this shot?" G posed the question to Def because he wasn't familiar with the dread or the area in the photo. This had been a loan Roc made. He would give Roc a certain amount of money a week to loan out. Roc would collect when the money was due, original pay back plus interest.

He didn't know half the dudes Roc dealt with. They each had their own clientele. It was just that Roc had more niggas that didn't pay up and had to get dealt with than him. But overall, he was the one that called all the shots, not Roc. When someone didn't pay up, that Roc loaned money to, Roc would come to him and tell him and he would say whether Def should take them out and in the case of the dread, the decision was already made.

"He in front of the pool hall off of Branch Avenue. He play that spot every Monday and Tuesday," Def revealed.

G passed the camcorder to Tyra. She looked at the screen. "Is he Jamaican?"

G turned to Def, who shrugged his shoulders. "We don't

know," he said.

Tyra looked up from the screen. Her eyes went from Def to G. "What'cha mean y'all don't know? Didn't you loan him money that he didn't pay back?"

"I didn't hit him off personally," G exclaimed. "My man Roc did."

Tyra looked at Def. "Didn't I hear you say Roc put you on to the dread?"

Def shook his head no.

"Well, shouldn't you know whether he's Jamaican or not? You didn't ask Roc?"

Def shook his head no again.

"Well you should've."

"Why?" Def asked, making his question the first word he'd spoken to Tyra since he stepped foot into the Bentley.

"Cause if he Jamaican, I have to approach him in a different manner."

"And which manner is that?"

"Let me worry about that," Tyra spat smartly.

Def and G eyed each other. Tyra handed the camcorder to Def then placed her attention on G.

"I have questions. How much time do you give to your customers to pay you? And if they dead how you gon' get paid?"

"Three months, the longest six. Reason being is if you wait too long to get at them 'bout your money, they might get too big for you to get at them and for your last question, I don't get paid, but my dough long so I don't sweat the fact that I had to kill a nigga 'bout my money."

"So, in three months, if they don't have it, you approach them 'bout it and if they don't have it then, you give them another three months. After that, if they don't have it you get them taken out."

"Pretty much."

"What if when you're about to take them out they have the money?"

"If they don't have it on 'em right there on the spot, they dead."

Tyra looked at Def, who smiled wickedly.

"Can you play pool?" G asked Tyra.

"No, but I can side bet."

"You drive?" Def asked.

"Do I have a car? No. Do I have a license to drive? Yeah."

Def fixed his eyes on G. "We gon' need to be in separate cars to do this hit."

"What's today?" G said, more to himself. "Today is Friday, by Monday mornin', I'll have a car for you," he told Tyra.

"No. You don't have to do that. I can get my girlfriend's car. She ain't workin' right now."

After informing Tyra all they needed to do in order to pull the hit off, Def stepped out the Bentley and into his Porsche. He drove the small rocket on wheels quickly out of the Safeway's parking lot, and five minutes later, he was dialing a number on his phone.

"Hello."

"Yeah, this me, Roy," Def said.

"Hey, what's up partna?"

"You man. How'd the check come through for you?"

"Great man. Everything's straight now. You finished."

Def beamed, and he had a right to. The twenty-five thousand dollar check he'd given Roy a few weeks ago was the last of the eight twenty-five thousand dollar checks he had to give him. Usually Def would receive cash from G for his hits, but he asked G to pay him in eight twenty-five thousand dollar checks so he could pay Roy, the man he had purchased his house in Maryland from a year ago.

Roy was a businessman that owned a string of check cashing joints throughout the city, and a few nice houses in DC and Maryland. Def had met Roy through G, who in turn, met Roy through Jill. G wanted to buy a house a couple years ago and Roy was who Jill had hooked him up with.

"Okay Roy, if I need to holla at'cha in the future, I'll let'cha know."

"A'ight partna. Take care."

Def closed his phone and slid it into his pocket. He beamed even brighter now and again, he had a right to. He had an apartment, which he only used to store his weaponry and park his Corvette that he drove only to lay on his target and to execute them. His house was where he called home, kept all his money, and parked his hundred and twenty-five thousand dollar Porsche.

Def turned onto Highway 295. He drove like a bat out of hell, zipping through cars doing ninety. In no time he was exiting off the highway and parking in a small parking lot that was reserved for the residence in the baby brick building.

He stepped out of his car, triggered the car's alarm and walked into the gloomy, smelly building that he could never seem to get used to after so many years.

Approaching the front door of the apartment, he read the sticker above the peephole. *Don't Fuck With Me!* He chuckled. As many times as he read the sticker, the phrase still tickled him.

He knocked on the door twice. A minute later, the door opened slightly. On cue, he stepped into the dimly lit apartment that smelled of cooked cabbage.

"Hey there young soldier."

"What's up, Old Man Bootney," Def replied, locking the door back up.

"You came a lil' early today, huh? It's around six o'clock, ain't it?"

"Yeah, it's 'bout that time," Def said, as he watched the old man walk slowly with his brown cane over to the living room sofa.

"I thought you was coming around nine o'clock?" The old man slowly reclined his rail thin six-foot body down onto the sofa, letting out a grunt when he was fully seated. "Hey, before you sit down, go and get me a drink from out the frig," he said to Def.

Def stepped through the beads that hung over the threshold before entering the kitchen. He opened the refrigerator and grabbed the bottle of *Wild Irish Rose* and headed back into the living room. After handing the old man the bottle of legal poison, he sat down next to him. Def's eyes roamed around the living room which consisted of little or nothing, just the sofa and framed pictures all over the walls.

There was one picture that Def's eyes always seemed to get stuck on. That was a picture of the old man when he was young, with a smiling little boy resting on the back of his neck and a beautiful woman by their side. He knew the history of that picture. That was a picture of the old man's wife and kid who had died in a house fire while he was away fighting for Uncle Sam.

"Old Man," Def began, staring at the side of his face. He watched as he guzzled his drink down. Looking at the old man drink the way he did, Def could see why his brown, gray bearded face had a droopy look to it and why his bubbled eyes stayed red and wrinkles ruled his skin. "Why they call you Bootney again?" he asked.

Old Man Bootney dropped the bottle from his lips. "You want the short or long version?"

Def smiled. "Give me the short version."

"Cause back in the day, me and your pops used to kick ass all over Southeast. They named me Bootney cause when I kicked ass, I used to put my foot in peoples asses from my boots to my knee." He chuckled at his words.

Def's father, who had been missing in action since Def was nine years old, was good friends with Old Man Bootney since childhood. But not even he knew where the man, who went by the name of Zek, was after twenty-one long years.

It was once said that Zek had been murdered and buried by a gang leader after he had beat the leader in a one-on-one fistfight. It was also said that Def's stepfather, the man Def had killed, was responsible for killing Zek and tossing his body in the Anacostia River, just so he could be with Lola, Def's mother.

"So, since we on names. Why they call you Def again?" Old Man Bootney asked.

Def grinned. He knew the old man was playing tit for tat. "I got that name from the cop that locked me up after I killed my stepfather. He said I looked like death when they pulled up in front of my building. When he took me to the precinct, he just kept callin' me death and from there on that name followed me. But I spell my name D.E.F., not D.E.A.T.H."

Old Man Bootney nodded his head and took a swig of his wine. "Two days ago when you dropped by, you said it was a gal you were supposed to meet. What happened?"

Def shook his head and frowned. "I met her."

"And," Booney said.

"She…,," Def looked at Bootney, who was staring back at him. "She bad man, but the bitch is too witty and any bitch that's witty is trouble."

"Why you say that?"

"Cause a man is intimidated by a broad that's too sharp. A man needs to feel superior over a woman at all times. If he don't they'll surely clash. Plus, what her job calls for her to do, she gotta tone that shit down."

"So, I take it that you seen her in action, huh?" Old Man Bootney smiled, revealing a pair of off white teeth.

"Yeah, and the bitch was snappin' the whole time."

"You had to do somethin' to her for her to act like that. Women are very vindictive."

Def thought about the handshake she tried to give him, which he didn't accept. "Maybe you right old man. But I don't know, I got a bad vibe from her. For some reason, I sense that she got beef wit' niggas."

"You could be right. After all, she ain't in on doin' what she'd agreed to do just for the money. No, no, no…,," Old Man Bootney shook his George Jefferson receding hairline head. "For a woman, especially if she's as beautiful as you say she is, to get involved in what she's 'bout to get herself into, she has to have somethin' missin' in her life that's makin' her available for somethin' like this and like I said, it ain't just for the money."

Def shook his head. "I hope my opinion of her is wrong cause I don't want us to get off on the wrong foot. Right now she's needed. I can't get to these niggas without her. If I could, believe me, I would've never told my man we needed a bitch. You know I like to work alone."

"I know," Old Man Bootney agreed. He had complete knowledge of Def's lifestyle. Def had revealed it to him years ago. Def allowed his head to tilt back and rest on the back of the sofa. He smiled and grunted. "Man, I don't think I've ever seen a broad that beautiful before. I didn't get to see her body fully, but I know she thick. My man wouldn't have chosen her if she didn't have no ass. He know niggas checkin' for bitches asses and if they have the face to match it, that's even better."

"Sounds like she has your nose opened, boy," Old Man Bootney grinned.

"To be honest, she do, but I ain't gon' let her know that."

"Yeah. Why we talkin' 'bout women. "It's 'bout that time, ain't it?" Old Man Bootney smiled at Def. "You ain't sent one of them over in like a month. I'm rejuvenated now."

Def laughed. "Old man you sure cause I came over after your last run wit' one of 'em and you could barely move."

"I'm ready, boy. Not get one of them gals over here."

"Okay." Def stood up from the sofa. "Which one? Kelly or Diana?"

"Kelly, the big boned one." Old man Bootney had a huge smile on his face. "She suck a helluva dick."

Def walked to the front door. "A'ight, I'll call her up and tell her to get over here ASAP. Now come on and lock this door behind me. I'll see you in a couple of days."

As he walked out to his car, he thought about the two women he paid a monthly fee to sex the old man. They were young whores, but they were clean. They treated the old man good and that was important to Def because he thought of him as a father.

Riding along 295, Def thought about Tyra. He wondered why she agreed to be a part of their operation. He knew it had to be about more than just money. He dared not to ask her because he knew she wouldn't tell him the truth. So, he pondered. *If she last in this operation without gettin' herself killed, her motive for comin' on the team will reveal itself in due time.*

# ELEVEN

Tyra couldn't stop thinking about him. Especially, his pretty boy, caramel colored face and curly hair. She wondered what his body looked like out of his clothes. From what she saw, he was slim, maybe cut up. When they had locked eyes inside of G's Bentley, she almost wet her panties, something that had never happened to her before. So, she knew something between them would transpire, but what she had no idea.

Although she was attractive to him physically, mentally she knew he would prove to be a challenge. She recognized that when she tried to give him a handshake and he left her hanging. Tyra wanted to reach into that backseat and smack the shit outta him but, instead she verbally assaulted him by insinuating that he didn't look like a killer. Even though she was still pissed about him trying to diss her, she still laid in her bed at almost two o'clock in the morning thinking about him. But, Tyra knew her attraction to him couldn't be revealed because she couldn't allow herself to be emotionally involved with a man in the line of work that Def was in. She had seen it all before, drug dealer or hired killer, they would soon be eradicated either by a jail cell or worse, death.

Tyra dozed off to sleep and awoke almost ten hours later to the sounds of her cell ringing

"Hello," she murmured.

"What's up, slim?"

"Who this?" Tyra asked.

"Damn, how many niggas you gave your number to already?"

"Oh, this G," Tyra stated as she sat up on the side of her bed.

"Yeah, this me. You ready for today?"

"Yeah."

"Tyra, let me get'cha full name and date of birth."

Tyra frowned into the phone. "Why you want all that?"

"I gotta check you out before you do your thing."

"Check me out how?"

"You know, make sure you ain't hot."

"Hot! What'cha mean hot?"

"Just give me your name and date of birth and I'll call you back."

Tyra hissed. "Tyra Young. I was…,,"

"You don't have a middle name?"

"No."

"Okay, go 'head."

"Tyra Young and I was born on February 5th 1995."

"Damn slim, I thought you were older than nineteen."

"Well, I'm not. Is that a problem?"

"Nah, no problem at all. Look, I'll call you back later. Oh yeah, can you still get'cha people's car?"

"Yeah, but you know what? I was thinkin' maybe I shouldn't use her car. What if things go right today and I leave the hall wit' the dread and people see my car trailin' his ride.

"Don't worry. I'ma talk to Def about what'cha just said and get back wit'cha in a minute."

Tyra looked at the small clock on her dresser that read: 12:06 pm. "What time you gon' call me back?"

"Round three o'clock."

"Okay."

Tyra placed her cell phone on the nightstand and headed to the shower. By three o'clock, she had already gotten dressed and ate a nice lunch when her cell phone rang.

She let her phone ring two times before she answered it. "What he say?" she asked.

"What who say?" Def answered.

Tyra's heart fluttered. She knew it wasn't G on the line, but Def. "Oh, I though you was G."

"Nah, this me. He told me to let'cha know he had his friend that work at the precint check you out and you good. A nigga gotta make sure you ain't workin undercover so, that's what he meant by checkin' you out. Now, about that car thing, don't worry, I'ma pick you up in my ride. Where you live?"

"I don't want you to know where I live, so I'll meet'cha at Hechinger Mall."

"Yeah, okay. But I don't like to be seen at the same place too many times, so I'll meet'cha in the lot of Modell's, not the Safeway, at five-thirty." Click.

The sound of Def abruptly hanging up on Tyra appalled her. She took the phone from her ear and looked at it with a scowl on her face. "I know he didn't just hang up on me like that." She nodded her head, with a grin and said, "Okay, it's on."

At exactly five-thirty, Tyra was stepping into Def's black Corvette as she stood in front of Safeway. As she slid into the car, she immediately felt Def staring at her.

"What's up? Why the look?" she inquired, looking Def over.

He had on black from head to toe.

"I ain't late, am I?" Tyra knew why he was looking at her with a stone expression on his face. He'd specifically told her that he didn't like to be seen at the same place too many times, and she knew that, but did otherwise out of spite.

Tyra watched his eyes travel over her outfit that consisted of the black Helley Hansen jacket she got from G's clothing store, a grey tunic, jeans, ankle length boots, and her long hair pulled back into a high bun.

Def turned his head from her and pulled off. They rode in silence until Tyra finally decided to ask him about the new plan to get the dread since she wasn't in her own car.

"Def, so what's the plan now that I ain't in my own whip?" Tyra questioned.

Def turned and looked at her, but didn't speak. Tyra grinned.

"So what, you got on all black and that hard look on your face to indicate that you're in killer mode, huh?"

Def didn't respond, he just kept his eyes on the road. Five minutes later, he turned onto the street with rows of semi-run downed houses. He parked behind an old blue Pontiac Bonneville SE. He didn't kill the Corvette's engine, he just let it run.

"The new plan is this. Since you don't have a ride to pull up in front of the pool hall, you gon' pull up on foot. That's it. That's the only thing new about this plan." Def was staring at Tyra, who stared back. "You gon' step inside the spot and act like you lookin' for the nigga named Mike-Mike that I told'cha play the hall only on Tuesdays. But, of course, he ain't gon' be there because today is Monday. If your game tight and you manage to get the nigga away from all those niggas he be wit', we straight. You jus' gotta get the nigga in his car alone with no niggas taggin' behind y'all."

Tyra shook her head. "I can do that. Now, let's ride near the hall. I wanna get this over wit'."

"We a few blocks from the hall. Jus' walk straight down this street and turn right. You'll see the hall from there and yeah, reach in the glove compartment."

Tyra retrieved a small plastic bag from the glove compartment and pulled out a spiral curled, black wig.

"That's if you wanna disguise yourself a lil'."

Tyra swirled the wig in her hands. "You picked a good wig, it's bangin'." She placed the wig on her head and stepped out the car but before shutting the door, she asked, "If I get him to drive us somewhere like to a hotel, please make sure you follow us. Okay? "

Def wanted to smile, but he didn't. "I got'cha, don't worry."

It took Tyra between seven or eight minutes to reach the pool hall's entrance. When she did, she stood a couple of feet in front of the red painted door. She looked up at the big blue and white sign that read: *Rack 'Em Up*. Tyra looked around at all the cars that were parked out on the street in front of the hustler's hangout spot. Her eyes spotted nothing but expensive whips from Audi's to Range Rover's.

*Damn*, Tyra thought to herself, *now I'm gettin' nervous*. She could now hear the music that hummed from the other side. She reached to pull on the door handle, but it was locked. She noticed and rang the buzzer. A few seconds elapsed before the big red door opened slightly revealing a six foot five inch burly, dark skinned man. He stared Tyra down and smiled, displaying a set of crooked, but white teeth. "Hey there sweet thing," he said.

Tyra uttered a weak, "Hi." She folded her arms underneath her chest, to indicate it was cold.

"Oh, my bad. Come on in. I know it's cold out there."

The pool hall was lit with pockets of clouds from smoke hovering in the air that coincided with the smell of marijuana. The sound of rapper *Jadakiss*, pumped from speakers that weren't visible. The music was loud, but not loud enough, that people couldn't chat with each other. Rows of pool tables filled the room and each one was occupied by men. Tyra noticed immediately that she was the only woman there, and she became increasingly nervous. As she walked towards the small bar, her legs became weaker. She was glad when she finally reached the bar and slid onto one of the six stools.

Tyra spun around on her stool and scanned the hall since there was no one behind the bar to service her. None of the men seemed to notice her. They all appeared to be focusing on the games they were watching. She spotted the dread she'd seen on the camcorder playing a game of pool at a table in the far end of the room. A group of men stood around the table with serious looks on their faces.

"Hey young lady."

Tyra almost toppled from her stool out of fear from the woman's voice. Composing herself, she turned around and faced the woman behind the bar. "Oh, hi. Hi you doin'?" Tyra stared at the middle-aged, heavy-set woman.

"Honey, it's Monday night. No women supposed to be in here. Big Totty know better than that." She peered over at the front door of the hall at the man that had let Tyra in. He saw her staring at him and smiled, with a shrug of his wide shoulders.

"He's tryna set'cha up honey." The woman placed her eyes back on Tyra.

Tyra looked behind her then back at the woman. "Why you say that?" she inquired.

"These guys gon' be on you like sharks on meat once they recognize you in here. You see, Monday's and Tuesday's are for men only. I've seen women come in here before and all these men in here be tryna rap to them. So, whatever reason you came in here, you better spit it out and I'll see if I can help you before you get bombarded wit' propositions for some ass." She smiled at Tyra. "All of em' in here got money, so you know that's the first thing they gon' come at'cha wit'."

Tyra half smiled at the woman. "I'm lookin' for Mike-Mike." Def had told her to ask for him, not only because he knew he played the pool hall, but because that way when the dread ended up dead, the word would be that Mike-Mike had something to do with it.

"Hold on, honey." The woman raised her hand and waved for Big Totty to walk over, but out the corner of her eye, she saw a man from the far end of the room, walking towards the bar. "Honey, here comes one of them now. We'll just ask him if Mike-Mike is in here."

Tyra turned and saw the man coming toward the bar. She was in luck, it was the dread.

"Hey, what's up, Ms. Moore?" the dread said when he reached the bar.

Tyra observed him from head to toe. She immediately noticed he had no accent, so he wasn't Jamaican. He just wore his hair in long, flowing dreads. *A fashion statement*, she thought, *not a religious one*. She ran her eyes over his outfit. His light brown complexion looked good up against his money green, Polo hooded sweatsuit and Timberland boots. He stood about five feet ten inches, with a husky build.

"Hey, Dread." Ms. Moore nodded her head in Tyra's direction. "This young lady is lookin' for a fella named Mike-Mike. You know if he's in here?" *So, Dread really is this nigga's name*, Tyra said to herself.

Dread gazed at Tyra, while shaking his head. "Yeah, I know him, but he ain't in here."

Tyra slid off the stool. "Okay, tell him Ann came lookin' for him." She turned to walk off, but Dread grabbed her by the arm. She turned to face him.

"Hold on, slim," he uttered, his eyes running over Tyra's body. "You don't fuck wit' that nigga Mike-Mike like that, do you?"

Tyra looked down at his hand that was still gripping her arm. "Can you let go of my arm?"

He dropped her arm.

"So, do you?"

"Do I what?" Tyra asked.

"Fuck wit' that nigga Mike-Mike like that?"

"What if I said no?"

Dread smiled. "If you said no, you can leave this hall wit' me."

Tyra frowned and spun around on her boots. Not to walk off, but to give him a good look at the phat ass that was stuffed in her pants. He reached for Tyra's arm again, believing she was about to step off from what he had said to her.

"Okay, just me and you then."

Dread looked at Ms. Moore, who then walked off. "What'cha mean?" he said to Tyra.

"Just what I said. Mike-Mike be payin' for this ass." Tyra turned around and let him get another good look.

Dread squinted up his face. "Damn! You fatter than a ma-fucka. How you even get that ass in those pants is beyond me." He stared hard at Tyra's face. "And you pretty too." He shook his head and grabbed at his crotch. "How much?"

Tyra rolled her eyes at him. "If you askin' me how much I charge, then you can't afford me."

"Nah." Dread pulled a bankroll from his pocket. "I'm just askin'. I can afford anythin' I want includin' you."

Seconds later, Tyra stood at the front as Dread walked to the back of the hall. He stood, pointing in her direction while talking with one of his flunkies. *Oh God, here he comes so git'cha yourself together girl,* Tyra mumbled under her breath.

"You ready to bounce?" he asked looking at Tyra.

"Yeah, let's roll."

Minutes later, Tyra sat in the passenger seat of Dread's dark blue BMW X5. She was super nervous now. She made sure not to touch anything inside the car. Def's words played back through her mind. *You don't want your finger prints connected to no dead man. Even if you never been in the system before, I believe they keep prints for future reference. So, if you get knocked for somethin', they can connect your prints wit' old prints and put'cha at the scene of the crime*, Def had said to her.

A million questions ran through her mind. Why was she so nervous when the man that sat next to her was a drug dealer? Was Def following the X5? Where was Dread going to be killed?

Because Def had told her he'd strike when he felt the time was right, would she have to go in the hotel room and fuck Dread because Def didn't do his thing before they got to the room? Tyra remembered telling him that she didn't want to fuck Dread and he responded, "*Tell G that, maybe he can find someone else to do the job if you can't.*"

"You want some of this?" Dread asked Tyra, breaking into her thoughts. He held a lit blunt in his hand that Tyra didn't even see him roll or light up. "This purple haze," he added.

Though Tyra had smoked weed in the past, she hadn't done so in about two years. She wanted to accept the weed from him just to calm her nervousness, but she chose not to. "I'm okay, I don't smoke like that."

Dread pulled hard on the blunt, held the smoke in for a few seconds, then blew it out, clouding up the mini SUV. "Girl, you don't know what'cha missin'," he said. "This shit is potent."

As they approached the parking lot of the hotel, Tyra looked out the window scoping out the lot. She was hoping to spot the Corvette Def was in, but she didn't.

"Let me finish off the rest of this blunt," Dread uttered. She wanted to take the blunt from him and smoke the rest of it up, but just when she had made up her mind to do so, the SUV's back, left side door swung open and Def was in the back with the door already shut again. His left hand was on Dread's left shoulder, while his right hand held his Taurus 9mm with a silencer on it, against the back of Dread's head.

"One question," Def began. "Do you have the money Roc loaned you? All I want is a yes or no and yeah, put'cha fuckin' hands up so I can see them."

Dread complied by placing his hands above his head. He let the blunt in his mouth drop into his lap. At once, it started burning through his velour sweatpants, where it landed near his crotch.

"You bitch!" Dread piped, his eyes cut over to Tyra. He didn't move his head. "You set me up."

Tyra didn't respond, she was too busy wondering whether or not Def was going to shoot Dread in her presence.

"Yeah man, I got Roc's money," Dread said.

"Where?" Def asked.

"At my crib. I'll…,," Def stopped him.

"Slim, look in your rearview mirror."

Dread did and he was staring into the cold eyes of Def. Pffft! Def put one in the back of Dread's head, causing his body to slump forward onto the steering wheel. The bullet went through his head and out the front windshield.

Since the silencer had muffled the noise from the gun, what had just happened didn't register to Tyra right away. It wasn't until she looked at the blood that had splattered onto the front windshield that she realized Def had blown Dread's brain out. Tyra began crying hysterically. She rubbed her face and looked at her hands. Dread's blood was on them. "Shit!" she yelled.

"Tyra. Tyra!" Def shouted. "Tone the fuck down!"

She continued to sob, despite Def's demand. She still shook her hands as tears fell down her face.

"Tyra!" Def snapped. He grabbed her left wrist and Tyra's hands stopped shaking. Her sobs became a mild weep. She stared at Def with tears still running down her face.

"Listen to me," Def began, he was looking Tyra in her watery eyes. "Don't touch nothin'. I'ma get out and come open the passenger door for you. Okay?" Def didn't wait for her reply, he stepped out of the vehicle and made his way around to the passenger door. "Come on," he said, after opening the door.

Inside Def's Corvette, Tyra sat motionless. She'd gained her composure, but she was still shaken by what had taken place.

"You okay?" Def asked her, while driving along Alabama Avenue.

"Did'cha have to do that while I was in the car?" Tyra asked. She was staring at Def with a scowl on her face. She snatched the wig off her head and placed it into the glove compartment.

"I did that to break you in," Def said, seriously. "You needed to see that this ain't no play shit. Niggas gon' be killed." "By the way…,," Def turned his head towards Tyra. He grinded his teeth together, causing his jaw muscles on both sides of his face to flare out. "Do I still look like a young'un that just started comin' out the house and, do I look like a killer now?" Def got no reply from Tyra.

A few minutes later, Def was turning off Benning Road and

into the parking lot of Modell's.

"Take me to the front of my building. I live on Maryland Avenue," Tyra said, finally revealing where she resided.

Def pulled up in front of her building. "G told me to give you this." Def reached into his coat pocket and pulled out two bundles of cash that were wrapped in rubber bands. "It's five g's in each knot. He said for you to call him."

Tyra took the money and stepped out of the car, but before shutting the door, she leaned down into the car and said, "By the way, the answer to your question is, yeah, you still look like a young'un that just started comin' out the house and you don't look like a killer...,, you are one." She shut the passenger door and walked into her building.

When Tyra stepped into her apartment, she was glad Cherry wasn't home. She definitely didn't want Cherry to see the specks of blood on her face. She quickly undressed and took a shower. She removed the money from her jacket and sat on her bed. Tyra took the rubber bands from the two bundles and tossed the money into the air. After cleaning up the mess and putting the money away, she found herself lying on her bed thinking about Def. What he had done earlier had frightened her initially, but as she pondered on it, she was turned on and couldn't wait for it to happen again.

# TWELVE

G stepped inside the store in Good Hope Marketplace. He walked towards the meat department and pushed the service buzzer. A light skinned man with freckles on his face appeared.

"What's up big Al?" G said, as he made his way around the counter.

"What's up big G?" Al said, shaking G's hand.

"You slim, I came to get that." G stared into the big man's face that looked scared.

Al's eyes dropped to the floor. "Man, I ain't got it."

G folded his arms across his chest, something he did often when he felt supreme in the presence of someone. "Slim, you goin' on six months. I…"

Al brought his eyes up from the floor and looked at G with a big smile on his face. "I'm just kiddin', I got'cha money in the back. C'mon."

G followed Al through a pair of swinging doors, but while doing so he thought, *this nigga wanna play games, but I'm serious 'bout my money. He doesn't know, but if he didn't have my dough, his fat ass was goin' six feet under.*

G stepped out of the store with 50 g's stuffed in his pockets and hopped into his Hummer.

"He didn't have your money," Roc said sitting in the passenger seat.

"Yeah, he had my shit!"

"Good," Roc spat. "Cause we already have too many niggas to lay down as it is."

G looked at Roc, who displayed a three-inch straw sticking out of his mouth.

"Nigga, when the fuck you start chewin' on straws?" G asked. "For the last two weeks, you've been chewin' on those shits."

"I don't know, slim. I just picked this shit up out of nowhere."

Roc turned towards his business partner. "G, what's up? Let me in on how that shit wit' the broad and Def went down."

G smiled. "Oh, I ain't tell you?"

"Nah."

"Man, they slumped your man on the first try. Tyra got the nigga alone and Def put in that work."

Roc grinned. "So the broad came through, huh?"

"Yeah, she did good. She doesn't know this, but Def told me she had a lil' breakdown from watchin' him punish that nigga."

"He killed slim in front of her?" Roc questioned.

"Yeah, he said he had to break her in. But he said she got over the shit quick."

"Slim, that nigga Def a cold ma'fucka," Roc said, shaking his head.

"Yeah, he is, and that's why he's on our team."

"So, when I'ma get to see the broad, Tyra?" Roc asked.

"You already seen her at the Verizon Center."

"Nah, I ain't get to see but a glimpse of her. She was surrounded by a crowd of people when you pointed her out to me."

"Oh yeah, you right. Well, I don't know, she only on board to do her job and that's it. We don't need to be socializin' wit' her on a regular."

"So, since she as bad as you say she is, you ain't tryna hit that?"

"Believe me," G said, letting out a sigh, "I'd love to tap that ass, but she on board like I said to do her job."

"What about Def? You think he tryna hit that?"

"I don't know, but I doubt it. He said she's a bitch, and she told me the other day she didn't like him. But despite how they feel about each other, I think they gon' work good together."

G turned off of Alabama Avenue and onto Gainesville Street. He parked in front of a brick building.

"Let me go get that," Roc said, stepping out of the truck.

As G watched Roc walk into the building, a text message came through on his cell phone. A naked Tammy appeared on the small screen as he pushed the play button on the video.

"Hey baby," she said. "Where you been? I haven't seen you in a few days."

G smiled widely, while staring at her perky breast.

"I know you miss this." The camera moved from Tammy's breast, down to her flat stomach and onto her shaved pussy. Then it showed her plump ass. "Call me." Tammy's pretty, high yellow face was the last thing G saw before the small screen went blank.

"Damn, this lil' sexy bitch got a nigga open," G said, as he dialed Tammy's number.

"Hey big G," Tammy stated.

"What's up, girl? You got a nigga's dick hard."

"Oh yeah? So, you liked my video, huh?"

"You know it."

"You know what I told'cha. I'll put it down every time it pop up." Tammy giggled.

"Well, it's up."

"Okay, when can we meet?"

G looked at his watch. "It's four-thirty, come to my crib in an hour."

"I'll be there."

"Don't keep me waitin'."

"Oh, I won't."

G closed his phone. He grinned, thinking about Tammy. She was getting under his skin. *I know she's a gold digger, but her pussy and suckin' game ain't no joke, so a nigga like me don't mind breakin' her off with some money from time to time.*

G's thoughts were broken as door of the truck swung open.

"Damn, it's gettin' cold" Roc uttered, slipping back into the Escalade with a black backpack in hand.

Roc placed the backpack into G's lap. "Two hundred fifty g's in there."

G unzipped the bag, glanced in it and looked at Roc. "Slim, you got paper. How come you ain't move out of your apartment yet?"

Roc smiled. "I like this spot. Plus, I'm not even a block from the 7th District Police Station. I got all the protection a nigga need. Niggas will think twice before comin' at me 'round here."

G shook his head. "Let me find out you scared."

"Nah, never that, slim." Roc patted his jacket. "You know I keep that thang on me. I might be a lil' fat nigga, but I ain't scared."

"You a lot fat," G joked. "I'll holla at'cha." G gave Roc a handshake as Roc stepped out of the truck.

G made it to his $350,000 Mitchellville, Maryland home in no time. He drove into his two-car garage. Before entering the house, he surveyed his rides, an Escalade, Bentley and his red on white Yamaha R6 chromed-out bike. He smiled, thinking about how great life was for him.

As he made his way upstairs, he entered his walk-in closet, revealing clothes that hung on an electronic hanging system and shelves of shoes and sneakers. Standing in front of a huge floor to ceiling mirror, he slid it over as if it were a sliding glass door, revealing a medium size safe. G triggered the combination and the door opened, where he placed the money he had just gotten from his worker. As he stared at the stacks of money totaling some 4.1 million, he thought to himself, *I gotta get another stash spot. If a nigga try to come up in here, they gon' feel like they hit the damn lottery. But, then again, I ain't worried 'bout that cause I ain't beefin' wit' nobody.*

As soon as he walked out of his closet, he heard his doorbell ring. When he opened the door, a smiling Tammy stood in a $50,000 Chinchilla that G got for her for $30,000 and a pair of sixteen hundred dollar Charlotte Olympia shoes; a designer she'd never even heard of. She opened her fur coat, revealing nothing but a matching white lace bra and thong set.

"Damn, girl, get on in here so I can dig your back out," G said.

"Anythin' you say." Tammy sashayed past G and into his domain. "I'ma do somethin' new to you," she said, grabbing his hand and leading him to his bedroom.

# THIRTEEN

Tyra walked along Division Avenue as she waited for her ride. Jack Frost was nipping, not only at her nose, but at her body as well.

"Where the fuck is he!" Tyra cursed. Her eyes scanned each car that rode past when see finally spotted the Corvette making its way up towards her.

She stepped into the Corvette and shut the door.

"Everythin' good?" Def asked.

Tyra looked over at him with a stare that could kill. "No, you had me out in that cold freezin' my ass off. Where you been?"

Def didn't respond.

"So, you ain't gon' answer me?" Tyra snapped.

Def continued to drive in silence.

"You know what? You a silly ass nigga and you be on some bullshit!"

Def allowed a few seconds to past before he spoke. "I hope you finish talkin' all that shit." He waited for her to respond, but she didn't so he continued. "The reason you ain't see me as soon as you stepped on the Avenue, is because I was makin' sure you wasn't bein' followed. Now, like I asked you before when you stepped in the car, everythin' good?"

Tyra turned and faced Def. "Yeah, everythin' good, but you didn't tell me his lil' ass was so little.

Def smiled, causing Tyra to do the same.

"So what he say?" Def questioned.

"He wants me to come work for him after he test me out."

"So, in other words, he wanna fuck you first before you start sellin' ass for him. I told'cha that word on the street is dat lil' nigga freaked out."

"I wish you were in that apartment to see what he doin' in there. He got young girls in there fuckin' niggas in front of everybody and niggas gettin' high off PCP. I even saw dudes in there baggin' up crack and everythin'." Tyra shook her head.

"Did he wanna test you in there?"

"Yeah, but I told him not today 'cause I was on my monthly cycle. So, he gave me his number to call him as soon as I go off. Before I could leave, he approached me and wanted to know how I knew about him. I made up a lie and stepped off. Oh, by the way, he had a gun in his hand."

"So, how deep was he rollin'?"

"Oh, it was a lot of niggas in there. I see why you need me to get him alone. I hope I can."

Minutes later, Def pulled up to Tyra's building.

"Let me ask you somethin'?" Tyra said. "How did you become a hit man for G?"

"Simple, he asked me did I want the job and I said yeah."

"Just like that?"

"Just like that. G been my boy since we was locked up together at Oak Hill, the juvenile detention center where we met. I trust that nigga wit' my life," Def stated.

"One more question." Tyra looked at him with a grin on her face. "Do you have a girl and how old are you?"

"That's two questions, not one."

"Just look at it as one big question."

Def didn't respond.

"You know what?" Tyra snapped, as she opened the passenger door to step out. "You an asshole! I'll talk to you after I talk to him. Bye!"

Tyra was met by Sam as soon as she made her way into her apartment.

"Girl," Sam said with a huge smile, displaying the gap between her two front teeth and her tongue ring. "You ain't gon' believe who Cherry locked up in her room wit'."

Tyra squinted up her face. She followed Sam over to the sofa and they sat down. Sam grabbed the remote control and turned the volume up on the television. Smiling, she uttered, "Me and Cherry were sittin' in here talkin', waitin' for you to get in so you could do my hair, and a knock came at the door" Sam paused, waiting for Tyra to say something.

"And," Tyra finally said.

"And when Cherry opened the door, guess who it was?"

"Who bitch!"

"You ain't gon' believe me."

Frustrated, Tyra spat, "Girl, who was at the damn door?"

"Okay, Tyra. It was Smoke."

Tyra threw her hands up to her mouth and muffled, "You lyin'."

"Girl, no I'm not."

Dropping her hands from her mouth, Tyra asked, "How the hell did he get out? I thought he had a ten year sentence in the Feds?"

"I did, too," Sam said.

All Tyra could think was how bad she had treated Smoke throughout her time staying with Cherry when he called. She knew if Smoke was home legitimately and wasn't on the run or anything, he would be moving in and they would clash. There was no way he wasn't going to try to get her back. She had dissed him far too many times.

"How long they been in the room?" Tyra questioned.

"Not long, 'bout fifteen minutes."

Tyra stood up from the sofa. "You know they gon' be in there for a while. That nigga's backed up. Let me get started on your hair."

Two hours later, Tyra was using a flat iron to put the finishing touches on Sam's twenty-two inch Brazilian weave. As she executed her art, Sam was doing her usual, talking about club gossip.

"I took his ugly ass to the VIP booth and guess what he wanted to do?"

"What?" Tyra asked inquisitively.

"Some shit he called t*ea baggin'*."

"What the hell is that?"

"Okay, let me tell you since I did the shit. I laid on the floor on my back with my top off, right. He took off his pants and just squatted down over my face, not restin' his ass on my face, but just inches from my face so that his balls were hangin' down, almost touchin' my lips. I opened my mouth and he bounced up and down, lettin' his balls drop in and out of my mouth, like you do when you dippin' a tea bag into hot water."

Tyra burst into laughter, but Sam continued.

"This part ain't a part of t*ea baggin'*, but while he was dippin' his balls in and out of my mouth, he was jerkin' off at the same time. That's why he told me to take my top off, so he could shoot his cum on my chest and stomach."

"How much you make for doin' that shit?" Tyra asked.

"Two hundred and fifty."

"That ain't bad for doin' some shit like that."

"Let me change the subject on your ass and ask you this, girl," Sam said. "Who is this nigga you fuckin' wit' that's settin' that paper out to you like that, and how come Cherry nor I haven't met him yet?'

Tyra smiled, she thought about G and Def. If she had to show one of them to the girls, which one would it be? Because she wasn't in a relationship with neither one of them, G, she thought, would be the best candidate for her perpetration. Def wasn't flamboyant, he was more of a introvert. But G, he definitely was a flamboyant nigga.

"I'll let you meet him one day, but not right now."

"'Sup Tyra? 'Sup Sam?" Smoke said entering the kitchen. He was shirtless with a pair of jeans and untied Tims on. Sweat covered his brown face and defined torso that was invaded with jailhouse tattoos.

Both women eyed his ripped chest, stomach and arms. The last time they had seen him, he was tall and skinny, resembling rapper Snoop Dogg. Now, he was tall and twenty to thirty pounds heavier, with a cut-up body, cornrowed hair and busy goatee.

"Hey Smoke," they both said in unison.

"I see you hookin' Sam's shit up," Smoke stated.

Tyra locked eyes with Smoke. "Yeah, I am."

*Listen to this arrogant ass bitch. She sound now just the way she sounded on the phone*, Smoke thought, then said, "I like the way you hooked Cherry's hair up. That joint tight, slim."

Tyra wanted to say thank you, but instead she said, "As long as y'all been in that room you probably fucked her hair up."

Sam giggled.

*Man, I told myself I was gon' forget all that cruddy shit this bitch was doin' to me over the phone, but nah, fuck that shit! This lil' pretty bitch got too much mouth*, Smoke was saying to himself.

"You ain't kill her in that room, did'cha?" Sam said jokingly.

Ignoring Sam's remark, Smoke exclaimed, "I came in here to get a glass of juice for us. Tyra, Cherry told me to tell you to get it for me," Smoke lied.

Tyra looked at him and hissed, "The cups are in the cabinet and the jug of juice is in the frig. Help yourself."

Smoke made his way over to the cabinet. He had to squeeze past Tyra in order to do so. He intentionally made his hand graze her ass.

*Oh, I know he didn't just feel my ass*, Tyra said to herself. She looked at Smoke, who had a smirk on his face as he poured juice into two cups. He squeezed past her again and did the same thing. Tyra was about to say something, but she held her tongue. She watched him walk out of the kitchen.

"Girl, you see all those tattoos on him," Sam said. "What the fuck those niggas in prison be doin' to get they bodies to look so good? Cherry gon' have problems wit' him."

Tyra took a step back from Sam and sprayed her hair with oil sheen. Moments later, Tyra was walking Sam to the front door after being paid.

"You know if he move in here, y'all not gon' get along, right?" Sam uttered as Tyra opened the door to let her out.

"I know," Tyra replied.

"So, all that money that nigga givin' you, you better find a place and get'cha self a ride."

Tyra didn't respond, she simply nodded her head.

"You think Smoke got a big dick?" Sam questioned, from out of nowhere.

Tyra gazed at Sam crazily. "I don't know and I don't care. You just make sure you don't try to find out. You know Cherry got strong feelings for him."

"I'm a freak, but I wouldn't do that. Bye, see you later."

Two days later, around six o'clock in the evening, Tyra sat on the side of her bed with her cell phone in hand. She was draped in black leather from head to toe. She dialed a number and waited.

"Yeah," Def's voice shot through Tyra's phone.

"Is that how you answer a phone?" Tyra spat.

"Nah, that's how I answer my phone. Now, what's up?"

"I gotta ask you a question before I make that call to him."

"Go 'head."

"I be watchin' this cop show called *First 48*, and I was just wonderin' if I call him and that go down, can they get in touch wit' me if they find his phone?"

"G didn't tell you?" Def uttered.

"Nah, tell me what?" Tyra inquired.

"The phone he gave you, when you call someone, your number comes up "p" as an unpublished number. Let me put it like this, me, you, G and Roc have cell phones that the police can't break through. Don't ask me how G got that done but he did. So, for real, we safe to talk about anythin' we want."

"Okay, that's what I wanted to know."

"So, you gon' make that call today?" Def asked.

"Yeah."

"Hit me back and let me know what's up and make sure you're not persuaded to meet at that apartment."

Tyra hung up and dialed the number of the lil' man she'd met the other day. On two rings someone picked up.

"Speak," a male voice said.

"This BeeBee," Tyra said. "Can I speak to Lil' Stink?"

"This me. Who this?"

"BeeBee, the girl that came by your spot the other day to work for you. You wanted to test me out before you let me start, but I told' cha I was on my period."

"Ooooo. Yeah, yeah, you that broad wit' that phat ass, pretty face and hair."

"Mmm hmm. That's me. I'm ready for my test."

"Meet me in the Heights then."

"It's the spot where I met'cha?" Tyra asked.

"Yeah."

"Why can't we do our thing somewhere else so I can feel comfortable? "

"If you start workin' for me, it's spots like that where you gon' be sellin' ass. I got like ten spots like the one you visited."

"I understand all that but I'm a lil' nervous," Tyra said, making her voice sound like that of a child.

"I tell you what. Meet me in an hour in Ivy City. You know where that's at, right?"

"Yeah."

"Look for the only buildin' in the neighborhood that don't have any Christmas decorations up in any windows. Oh…by the way, I hope your face drop game tight, cause you know some niggas can't get enough of that. Includin' me."

"Face drop game," Tyra echoed, "What the hell is that?"

"Suckin' dick."

Tyra uttered a low, "Oh."

"See you in an hour," Lil' Stink piped.

Tyra immediately dialed Def's number

"Yeah," Def answered.

"He wants me to meet him in the neighborhood of Ivy City."

"Okay. I know where that spot is. He just use that spot to bag up coke and chill. He usually have no more than two niggas wit' him, but hopefully tonite he rollin' by himself since he gon' meet you there."

"So, his lil' ass is a full time pimp and a drug dealer?"

"Yeah," Def replied.

"I really want his ass dead now," Tyra mumbled.

"What'cha say?"

"Nothin'. You on your way, right?"

"Yeah, I'll be there in twenty."

Tyra closed her flip phone and placed it in her Michael Kors tote bag. She peered into the tote bag to make sure her can of mace and leather gloves were in it. As she sat and waited for Def, her mind wandered. *I damn sure hope this hit goes off without any complications. Dread was an easy target but, I ain't no fool to think they gon' all be that easy.*

Tyra's phone rang bringing her out of her trance. "Hello."

"Be out front. I'll be there in three minutes," Def said, before hanging up.

Five minutes later, Tyra was in Def's Corvette. He was schooling her on the dos and don'ts as he drove. By the time he turned into Ivy City, he had conveyed to Tyra all she needed to know in order to do her job.

Def dropped Tyra off two blocks from the spot Lil' Stink had indicated. Arriving in front of the building, she saw no sign of him. Just as she was about to call, a thumping base line roared from a navy blue Grand Cherokee that trailed up toward her. She not only distinguished the style of music, but she also came face to face with the passenger, Lil' Stink. He lowered the window just as the Go-Go music was turned off.

"You ain't been out here long, have you?" he asked, his eyes looking Tyra over.

"Long enough," Tyra replied, looking at him, but at the same time, averting her eyes on the driver of the truck. "Let's go in. It's cold out here."

When Lil' Stink rolled his window back up and started talking to his friend, Tyra shifted her body weight to one leg and recited a silent prayer that the driver of the truck wouldn't tag along into the apartment. If so, she would have to result to plan B that Def concocted and that consisted of her not entering the apartment at all.

The passenger door opened and Lil' Stink hopped down from the truck. When he shut the door, the truck pulled from the curb, leaving him standing in front of Tyra.

"Damn shorty, you fatter than a ma'fucka," Lil' Stink uttered, circling around Tyra and standing behind her. He reached out and squeezed her butt. "You got a big soft ass, too."

"You like it, huh?" Tyra questioned as she turned around to face him. She didn't want to give him another opportunity to feel on her.

"Hell, yeah! Let's go inside."

Entering Lil' Stink's apartment, Tyra wasn't surprised to see a well furnished living room. But what she was surprised to see was a big brick of crack and some powdered coke that sat on a plate in plain view on the glass coffee table. A few Ziploc bags and a small white digital scale set next to the plate.

"You into sellin' drugs, too?" Tyra posed to Lil' Stink.

"Yeah, I'ma pimp and a drug dealer and if you work for me, you gon' sell both, your ass and some of my coke."

Tyra thought, *I ain't sellin' shit nigga, my ass or your coke. If I can help it, your lil' ass gon' be dead tonite.*

Lil' Stink removed his jacket and skullcap and tossed them onto his sofa. He removed a black .380 from his waist and placed it on the coffee table. Tyra looked at the gun and instantly became uneasy.

"What's up? You want me to hit that on the couch, or in the bedroom on the bed?" he questioned.

"Let's go in the bedroom," Tyra replied, following the plan she and Def agreed upon.

Lil' Stink swiped his gun from the coffee table. He held it in his hand as he bent down towards the table and sniffed two lines of coke from the plate.

*Damn, this lil' nigga, not only a pimp and a drug dealer but, he get high on his own supply, dumb fucker,* Tyra thought to herself. Lil' Stink led the way to the back of the apartment and into the bedroom.

"You jive tall, girl," he said, while his eyes roamed all over her.

"I'm five six, but wit' these boots on I'm five nine." Tyra managed a smile, although she was nervous. "Plus, I just look tall to you cause you short."

Smack!!!!!!!!!!

"Bitch, don't you ever try to belittle me!" Lil' Stink roared after smacking Tyra hard across the face, causing her head to snap back. He reached out with his right hand, gripped her neck and choked her as he backed her up against the wall. Her back hit the wall with a thud. "Bitch, if you gon' work for me, you betta' learn to respect me."

Since Tyra's tote bag was in her right hand, she used her left to grab at Lil' Stink's wrist. She looked frantically into his face while gagging. He let go of her neck and took a step back. He watched Tyra hunch over, trying to catch her breathe.

"Now, start takin' off your clothes so I can see that bangin' ass body I know you workin' wit'." He stepped over to the king size bed, sat down and began taking off his boots.

Tyra stood erect with tears falling down her face. She wasn't actually crying though, the tears were an after effect from her being choked.

"Bitch, didn't you hear me tell you to take off your clothes!" he piped.

"Yeah, but since you choked me, I gotta take a leak. So, can I go use the bathroom? I'm only gon' be a minute."

"Go 'head, but hurry the fuck back. I want'cha to put those pretty lips around this dick," Lil' Stink said, rubbing his dick through his pants.

Tyra heard Lil' Stink mumbling to himself as she made her way down the long hall and into the bathroom. She quickly slid her leather gloves on and retrieved her cell phone to dial Def's number.

"What's up?"

"Apartment six."

"I'm in the buildin' so come open the door."

"And yeah, he has a gun in the room wit' him."

"You got your gloves on, right? And you didn't touch nothin'?"

"Yeah, to both questions." Tyra dropped her phone back into her bag and exited the bathroom. She walked quickly to the front door and let Def inside.

"You took longer than a minute," Lil' Stink said when she came back into the bedroom. Tyra could tell by the pace of his words that he was starting to feel the affects of the coke he had snorted earlier.

"So what, nigga?" Tyra snapped.

Lil' Stink gazed at Tyra with a puzzled look on his face. "Bitch, what'cha say to me?"

"You heard what the fuck she said, nigga," Def said, as he stepped into the room with his 9mm aimed directly at Lil' Stink. Def saw Lil' Stink's eyes bounce in the direction of the dresser where his gun rested, and said, "Yeah, go 'head, try your hand."

"Bitch, you good," Lil' Stink said, looking at Tyra. "I would've never thought this shit was gon' happen. Now who sent y'all here?"

"G, nigga. Now where the fuck is his dough?" Def barked.

Lil' Stink smiled. "Look, I got G's hundred and fifty g's, but it ain't in here. I got like fifty g's worth of crack and powder in the living room."

Def walked up to the bed and placed his gun up to Lil' Stink's forehead. With no words expressed, he pulled the trigger. Pffft! The once white sheets that covered the bed were now adored with red blood. Def turned and looked at Tyra, who was surprisingly smiling. At that moment, he saw something wicked about her smile, but didn't bother to ponder on it.

"Let's go," he said.

Riding in Def's car, Tyra asked, "Why didn't you take his gun from off the dresser?"

"The gun might have bodies on it," Def said, looking over at her. "I see this killin' didn't affect you like the other one did."

Tyra shook her head. "You didn't blow his brains out all over me. I didn't tell you this, but his lil' ass smacked and choked me."

"I know, I saw his hand prints on your neck and your face as soon as you opened the door for me. You a'ight?"

"Yeah, but I think I might need me a gun to carry in my bag when I do these set ups. This hit tonite taught me somethin'."

"You sure cause I can give you one now?"

Tyra nodded yes.

Def reached on his waist and pulled out a chrome, bubble gum grip, snub nosed .38 and passed it to Tyra. "You can have that. It's six bullets in there, I'll give you more before we do our next hit. Although that's a revolver and the shell cases don't pop out when you fire it, make sure you wear gloves when you handlin' the bullets."

"That's what'cha do?" Tyra inquired. She stared at the gun. "You wear gloves when you put'cha bullets in your gun?"

"Yeah, always. My shells pop outta my gun."

"This gun don't have any bodies on it, do it?"

"I never killed wit' it. It was given to me 'bout two years ago. I doubt if it have any bodies on it. The person that gave it to me said it was clean."

"You think I can get a silencer for my new gun like you have for yours?" Tyra smiled at Def.

"I'll get'cha one."

Tyra was about to put the .38 in her tote bag, when she noticed the letters C+T carved under the bottom of the handle. "You know what C+T means that's carved on this gun?"

Def shrugged his shoulders. "It was there when I got it, but I say it stands for Cruel Treatment."

Tyra let the gun fall into her bag. She leaned back in her seat and grinned. She was fifteen thousand dollars richer from the money Def had handed her a minute or so after they had entered his car. Her life was really moving forward, she thought, and who was to say that what she was doing was wrong. She was doing what the law was doing in the urban community anyway, eradicating drug dealers. They were doing their extermination for their reasons, and she was doing hers, but the question was who would be punished for their actions?

# FOURTEEN

Several months went by and Tyra's life moved in a direction that she would've never imagined. She was grateful that life was being good to her especially after what she'd been through. But no one could've told her after the love of her life was taken away that she'd be living a life of luxury.

Tyra had only one set back that occurred Christmas day, when she tried to visit her mother to give her the gift she'd purchased for her. When her mother didn't answer, she left the gift and a piece of paper with her phone number on it in front of her mother's door and departed. She vowed to keep trying to patch things up with her.

After that day, she brought in the New Year by moving out of Cherry's apartment and into a townhouse in Rockville. G had allowed her to use his porno store as a job reference. She moved out of Cherry's place for two reasons, one she needed her own space and two, she wasn't getting along with Smoke, who had managed in just a few days to take total control of Cherry's life. While she knew the goodness in Cherry's heart, she resented the situation and couldn't stay around to bear witness to it. Furthermore, she knew Smoke was up to something and although she hadn't figured it out yet, she had every intention of getting to the bottom of it.

The month of February rolled around, and Tyra's 20th birthday came with a big surprise. G bought her a silver convertible, Benz SL55 AMG that sat on twenty-inch chrome Capone rims. When G tossed the keys at her and stated that she had earned it for the jobs she had done, Tyra was in shock. It took her a couple of days to get use to driving a $140,000 vehicle.

One day during the middle of February, Tyra felt it was time to elevate her status so, she made a surprising move. She called G up and asked him for help in purchasing a hair salon.

"You sure you ready to make this move," G asked her.

Answering, yes, within three short months, G managed to get her a management, owner and cosmetology license. Plus, he found her a good area to open up the shop, which she named, *Laced Hair Salon.* It was located among the best hair salons in Washington, DC. With G's flamboyant demeanor, he got everything Tyra need to plush out her shop. The walls, ceramic tiled floors and all of the furniture were pink and white. Two T.V.'s hung in the corners so that everyone could see, except for Cherry whose receptionist station was located near the front door of the salon. But that didn't matter, because she had her own 13-inch DVD/TV combo on her desk. For protection, G had installed a high class security system operated by computers with two monitors to view both inside and out. To top things off, the waiting room chairs came equipped with full body massages.

Tyra didn't know how she would ever repay him for his generosity. The night before the grand opening, she invited G to come by and have one final look at how she had laid out the place.

"G, I don't know how a sista gon' ever repay you for this," she stated as they sipped on a glass of Moet.

"Just continue to do a good job takin' care of business with Def without gettin' yourself hurt," he responded. "Oh and by the way…,," G stated, as he finished the last of the champage, "Def gon' be your contact on the assignments so you'll be dealin' wit' him more than me."

After G left, Tyra thought on his words. *Six jobs down and so far so good, except for when Lil' Stink slapped and choked me. But, that nigga Def laid his ass to rest, so it's all good.* G's last comment instantly brought a smile to Tyra's face because she had no problem spending more time around Def. She just wasn't ready to let him know it quite yet.

On his last note to make sure everything would be alright with Tyra's endeavor, G introduced her to Jill, who schooled her on owning a business. She taught Tyra everything she needed to know on banking, taxes and hiring. The same knowledge Jill had given her for three weeks straight, was equivalent to what she would've learned had she taken classes at school. On the day Tyra opened her salon, she had four licensed cosmetologist working for her on a monthly commission basis, one nail technician, one shampoo girl, and Cherry, who was on Tyra's payroll as a receptionist.

When the month of August rolled around, Tyra's salon was in full swing. Her entire staff had clientele out the ass and everyone seemed to get along fine. The fact that she was the owner of a hair salon, gave Tyra a sense of pride and dignity. Yes, while it was true that G had been the ring leader behind the deal, opening the salon was her idea and it was her money that she used as the down payment to purchase the building. Life was going sweet and she secretly felt forever in debt to G for all that he'd done for her. So, when Def entered the shop with his camcorder in hand, indicating to Tyra that it was time to do a job, she stopped doing her client's hair and walked straight to the back of the shop and into her office with Def in tow.

"Is it hot enough outside for you today?" Tyra asked, as she took a seat behind her desk.

"Yeah, it's hot as hell," Def replied. He placed the camcorder on her desk. Out of the corner of his eye, he caught her eyes wondering all over his body.

Tyra flipped the small screen to the camcorder out, pressed play and began to view the contents.

"This ain't in DC, is it?" she asked.

"Nah." Def stepped from in front of the desk and stood beside Tyra. "That's Queens, New York."

"When do we have to go up there?"

"In two days."

Tyra looked up at Def from her seat. "That's where you been for the last five days, huh?"

Def grinned. "Yeah. Why? You were lookin' for me?"

"Don't flatter yourself. Cherry and Sam asked where you been since they hadn't seen you around. You know how broads are. They think we beefin' or somethin' bein' that they think we're a couple." Months ago, Tyra became fed up with Cherry and Sam asking her why they hadn't met the man that had been spoiling her. So she introduced Def as her man after literally begging him to play along to her song. Focusing her attention back to the video, Tyra asked, "So, what's his name?"

"Allah," Def said. "He one of them niggas that came down to DC, got cool wit' niggas for 'bout a year or two and borrowed some money off the strength of niggas sayin' he cool. But he ended up jetting back up to New York without payin' back what he borrowed."

Tyra frowned up her face. "What kind of name is that he have?"

"Five percent. A lot of New York niggas call themselves God Body. That's what the shit stands for."

"How long you think we gon' be up there and which of 'em loaned Allah the money, G or Roc?"

"We might be up there for a day or a week. I don't know, just pack some clothes and this is Roc's."

"How come I haven't met Roc yet? I've been on the team for a minute now," Tyra questioned.

Def shrugged his shoulders. "I don't know. What, you wanna meet him?"

"It don't matter if I do or don't. He don't pay me, G does. I just asked."

Def snatched up the camcorder and said, "Be ready in two days."

"I will." Tyra watched him walk out of her office.

She stayed seated. She pondered on her sex life that was pretty much nonexistent. She hadn't been with a man intimately in two and a half years. Since she'd become a part of society again, there were plenty of men trying to get at her but she would either shut them down right away, or get their phone numbers and never call them. *I don't know why I'm still holdin' on to my goodies. It's not like Cash coming back from the dead to hit this and a bitch got needs.* The more she thought on it, she realized that Def was the reason she wouldn't give a man a chance. He was in her head even though they hadn't even slept together.

"I'm sorry, Cash," she mumbled, as she rose to her feet, "I have to move on wit' my life all the way. I have to have sex wit' Def. I won't fall in love because I still love you. I will continue to get rid of drug dealers just for you. I love you baby!!!!!"

# FIFTEEN

The bright light from the ceiling, cast a shine onto the two naked bodies that lay in unison after a solid half hour of unadulterated sex. Smoke and Cherry had pleasurable smiles planted on their faces. They hadn't said a word to one another since they'd unlocked from each other's grasp.

Deciding to break the silence, Cherry looked over at him and said, "Smoke, you changed. You ain't the same."

"What'cha mean?" He didn't take his stare from the ceiling.

"It wasn't as if you wasn't sexin' me good before you went to jail, but now…now you an animal. You be fuckin' the shit outta me. You a beast."

Smoke took his gaze from the ceiling and looked at Cherry.

"You've been home eight months and you been beatin' the pussy up like it's gon' be your last piece. But I like the way you been hittin' it though. " She smiled.

"What else you think ain't the same about me?"

"To be real, you a lil' short tempered now, and more demandin'. That's about it."

"You sure that's it?"

Cherry nodded her head. "Yeah, that's all I can see that's different."

"Okay. While we talkin' let me ask you somethin'," Smoke began. "You like workin' at the salon?"

Cherry looked at Smoke strangely. "Why you ask me that?"

"Because like I told'cha, I like to take care of you without you havin' to work. You know how I am. If I'm gettin' it, you ain't gotta work."

"What'cha mean if you gettin' it? Are you tellin' me what I think you tellin' me?"

"Yeah, I'm gettin' back on today." Smoke grinned proudly.

Cherry rolled off the bed. "I'm goin' to take a shower."

A couple of minutes later, Smoke entered the steamy bathroom. He stepped up to the shower curtain and slid it back. "You mad?"

Cherry looked at him and rolled her eyes.

"Cherry, I'm tryna put you back in a house and all that good shit," he said.

She stared at his tall, ripped body. "You gettin' in or you stayin' out there?" She looked down at his feet. "Smoke, when you gon' stop wearin' those shower shoes to take a shower? You ain't in jail no more."

Smoked laughed as he stepped into the shower. Washing Cherry's back with a soapy washcloth, he asked her, "You like to see your girl, Tyra, livin' like a queen in a house, pushin' a Benz and ownin' a business, while you still livin' in this apartment and pushin' that Sentra?"

"Why you puttin' Tyra in this?" Cherry barked.

"Cause you act like you mad that I told'cha I'm gettin' back on today. You act like you don't wanna live like your girl livin'. Like she better then you or somethin' and she deserves what she got and you don't. She ain't better than you!"

"I never said she was," Cherry shouted.

"Then act like you want a nigga to get his dough up and have you livin' like a queen."

Cherry turned around and smiled at Smoke. She reached up and hooked her hands behind his neck. "You think Tyra better than me?" The shower water splashed down onto Cherry's back.

Smoke frowned and sneered. "Nah, she ain't better than you. That smart mouth ass bitch ain't better than my boo." He ran his hands down her back and onto her ass. "That's the same bitch that was livin' off you when her life was off track. Ain't nothin' different 'bout her, she just came up on a nigga that's holdin' bread."

Cherry pulled Smoke's head down and kissed him on his lips. "Let's not talk 'bout Tyra, that's still my girl. I love her."

*Man, fuck that bitch*, Smoke thought to himself.

"Smoke, let me ask you this since you haven't told me yet. Why you lie and tell me you had ten years when you didn't?"

"That's not important," he said. "I'm out now."

"I know, but I wanna know anyway," Cherry whined. "Please tell me."

"Okay. I wanted to see if you was gon' bounce on a nigga immediately after I told'cha. You hung in there, although you could've came and visited a nigga a lil' more."

"When you were in DC jail, I did come and see you a lot, but you gotta understand, when you moved to the Feds in Otisville, New York, that shit was like five hours away. But I did come up there a few times."

"Yeah, like eight times in the three years and two months that I was up there. It's all good though. You ain't move on wit'cha life like a lot of other bitches did to some niggas I know. Ole fake ass bitches; they only wit' a nigga when he up. But as soon as a nigga down, they step on 'em." Smoke shook his head with a distressed look on his face.

Cherry slid her hands from behind Smoke's neck and onto his face. "Baby, even if you had ten years, I still wouldn't have left you."

*Yeah right, bitch*, Smoke was thinking, *what makes you so different from another broad. None of y'all bitches have what it takes to hold a nigga down while he in.*

"What time do you think it is?" Smoke asked.

"It's 'round twelve noon."

"Uh, go lay my gear out on the bed and roll me up two blunts from the weed that's on the dresser." Smoke grabbed Cherry's hands from his face and placed them down by her side. "Make sure you put enough weed in the blunts, too."

She rolled her eyes at him, and stepped out the shower. "You just gotta smoke weed to live up to your name, don't you?" Cherry wrapped a white towel around herself.

"Just go take care of that for me." Smoke pulled the shower curtain shut.

Half hour later, he was exiting Cherry's apartment and driving towards his destination in her Nissan Sentra. Smoke was finishing off his second blunt when he parked in front of an apartment building on Jasper Street. He reached into his pocket for the cell phone Cherry bought him a month ago. He dialed a number and received an answer in two rings.

"Yeah," a male's voice barked.

"'Sup nigga? I'm out front," Smoke said.

"This Smoke, right?"

"Yeah nigga."

"Okay. Come on up."

Smoke closed his phone and stuck it back into his pocket. He stepped out of the car and headed into the building. When he reached the apartment door, it was already open. His eyes were drawn to a deep chocolate, big boned girl. *Just the way I like my women,* he thought to himself. The young girl who he immediately concluded couldn't have been older than sixteen was dressed in nothing but a black bra and thong set. She wore clear high heeled slides on her feet. She smiled seductively up at Smoke.

"Frog in here?" Smoke questioned, looking down at the young girl.

"Yeah, he in here," the girl said. She watched Smoke shoot a glance at her big breasts that bulged out from the top of her bra. "You high?" she inquired.

"Yeah," he replied.

The girl walked away from the door, giving him a good view of her thick legs and large plump ass.

"Frog, your boy here!" Smoke heard the girl yell, as he walked into the apartment and shut the door. He stood in front of the door, looking down the hall at the girl who stood in front of the closed bedroom door.

"He comin'," he heard her say as she waved at him with a smile on her fairly pretty face. She disappeared into the bedroom.

Smoked looked around the apartment and liked what he saw. The apartment had Italian leather furniture, a marble dining room set, a big screen television and an entertainment center with all the latest Sony stereo equipment.

"What's up, nigga?" Frog barked, making his way into the living room.

"'Sup Frog?" Smoke embraced Frog with a handshake and a bump of his shoulder.

"You, dawg. It's time for me to hit'cha off."

Smoke looked into Frog's huge bubbled eyes, which was why he was known as Frog. He also saw that he was under the influence. "You high?"

"You know it, nigga." They walked over to the sofa and sat down beside each other. "I'm sorry a nigga had to wait months to hit'cha off. I just didn't have enough shit to go around but now that one of my connects got bagged, it's all good."

"We been knowin' each other for years, so I ain't mad at'cha. I wasn't in no rush," Smoke explained.

"Yeah, I hear you, but it's been like what? Seven…eight months since you been out. At least you stashed enough bread to get back on." Frog looked into Smoke's face. "Let me ask you this, slim. How much time did'cha have? Cause the word was you had ten years, and you ain't do nothin' but about three, right?"

Smoke nodded and sucked his teeth. "I didn't have ten years. I just put the word out that I had ten to see if some of the bitches I was fuckin' wit' was gon' roll out on a nigga."

"Did they?"

"Nah, them bitches stayed loyal."

Frog stood up from the sofa. "You want'cha shit in powder or rock? I got both."

"Rock, cause I ain't in a position right now to have it cooked up," he said.

"You got that on you, right?" Frog asked.

"Yeah." Smoke sprung to his feet and reached into his pocket, pulling out a knot of money. "You said I can get that for ten, right?"

Frog smiled. "I ain't gon' go back on my word." He took the money from Smoke. "I'll be right back."

In a flash, Frog reappeared with a white plastic, mini grocery bag in hand. He passed it off to Smoke. "It's all there, and not a gram short, a whole kilo. But I gotta tell you this," Frog and Smoke were standing almost face to face, "I can't give you no deal like this again. A nigga gotta get full payment."

"I feel you." Smoke shook hands with Frog.

"Anyway, how you gon'get rid of that stuff? The strip y'all niggas used to have young'uns pumpin' on is dead."

Smoke grinned. "I gotta new spot not far from where my girl, Cherry live. You know where Hechinger Mall at right?"

"Yeah, I know where that's at."

"Well, while I was waitin' on you I was recruitin' some young'uns from around 21st Street that I'ma be fuckin' wit'."

Frog nodded his head.

"Oh yeah," Smoke began, "When I get my paper back up, I can get some keys from you, right?"

"If it's one, yeah. But anythin' over that, I can't help you."

"Say I wanna cop two or more birds, who can I get that from?"

Frog dropped his eyes to the floor. "I don't know if I can help you wit' that, dawg." He raised his eyes. "Nah, you know what? I can do that. The nigga I get my shit from like to get rid of his shit as soon as he gets it so when you ready, I'll make somethin' happen for you."

"That's what's up," Smoke said, excitingly. "That's keepin' it real wit' a nigga. So, what's your connect's name?"

Frog had a hesitant look on his face. "Tell you what, dawg. I'll let him tell you that if everythin' go good and you hook up wit' him."

"Bet. I can go wit' that." He took a step back and looked Frog over. "Slim, what's up wit' that young broad that opened the door for me? She look like one of them young girls that be on The Maury Povich Show, talkin' 'bout they want a baby and they only fourteen or fifteen years old."

Frog laughed. "Nah, slim, she eighteen. Matter of fact, she turned eighteen yesterday. That's the only reason she still over here. I took her out yesterday and she ain't left my side yet."

"So, what's up wit' her?" Smoke inquired. "That's you or what?"

Frog frowned his face up. "Nigga please, Chocolate one of my young freaks."

"That's her name?"

"Yeah. Nigga, check this out. If you wanna do somethin', just say the word. We can DP the bitch. She down for whatever, I guarantee you that."

"What the fuck is DP?" Smoke asked.

Frog giggled. "Double Penetration. I know you were lookin' at pussy books while you were in."

Smoke shook his head. "Oh yeah, I used to see that DP shit in those butt flick  magazines while I was in. That's when a bitch gettin' hit in her ass and pussy at the same time.

"So, you tryin' to get down or what", Frog quizzed.

"Yeah." Smoke nodded.

"Come on." Frog led the way towards the bedroom.

When they entered the bedroom, Chocolate was seated at the foot of Frog's king size bed, naked.  She held two sealed condoms in her hands.

"I was wonderin' what was takin' y'all so long," she said, placing the condoms next to her on the bed.

Smoke glanced over at Frog, who was already taking off his sneakers and sweatpants. Seeing that, he dropped the bag he was holding to the carpet and began undressing.

"Frog, your friend got a nice body. Damn, you have a lot of tattoos," Chocolate said to Smoke, as she waved them over.

They walked up to her, standing side by side. Both of their dicks were semi-hard and inches away from her face. She took both of them into her hands and began stroking them. When they were fully erect, she stuck her tongue out and flicked at the heads of their dicks.

"Which one of y'all want me to put it in my mouth first?" she asked.

Frog looked to his left at Smoke. "Hit my man off first."

Chocolate smiled up at Smoke and quickly engulfed him into her mouth. The pleasure he was receiving caused him to tilt his head back and let out a deep grunt. When he tilted his head back forward, he stared down at Chocolate and watched her work him with pro hooker type skills. He got so much into it, that he reached out with his left hand and palmed the back of her head, his breathing intensified.

All he thought about at that moment was all the brothers that were locked down. *Those niggas would kill to be in this position.* He remembered telling a couple of dudes before he was released that when he got some head or pussy that it would be in the memory of them and since he'd been out, he hadn't thought about that until now.

Looking down, he pushed Chocolate's head further into him, causing her to gag. But surprisingly to him, she didn't stop her attack. She slid her mouth swiftly up and down his shaft causing saliva to escape from the corners of his mouth.

"She a beast, ain't she?" Frog said, while grinning over at Smoke.

"You ain't never lied," Smoke stuttered, as he sat down on the edge of the bed to catch his breath.

After giving Frog head, Chocolate tore open both condoms and rolled them onto their dicks. She stepped over to the dresser and grabbed a bottle of KY Jelly.

"Which one of y'all plan on enterin' my ass?" Chocolate asked.

"I'ma let my man Smoke penetrate that", Frog stated boldly.

Chocolate walked over to Smoke and rubbed some of the jelly onto Smoke's dick. Frog crawled up on the bed and laid on his back. As Chocolate straddled him, Smoke pulled up behind her and immediately began working himself into her warm, tight ass. Within seconds, they all were in a world of bliss. Chocolate made sounds that could be heard throughout the apartment, while Smoke and Frog growled like animals until they exploded into their condoms, bringing the episode to a halt.

Half hour later, Smoke was heading to his next destination. He pulled into a McDonald's parking lot and turned off the car's engine. He looked over at the passenger seat where he had placed the kilo of crack. When he saw who he was waiting for pull into the lot and park next to him, his body tensed up.

He grabbed the kilo, got out of the Sentra and into the passenger side of a bright yellow Range Rover.

"Hola Poppi!" the Puerto Rican man that sat behind the wheel of the truck said. He displayed a huge smile on his face.

"Sup Rico?" Smoke replied weakly. He scanned Rico's five foot nine, stocky frame. It amazed Smoke to see the Puerto Rican man dressed like a young'un in the streets. He wore a navy blue Hugo Boss shirt, jeans, the latest pair of Jordans, a diamond stud in his right ear and a platinum chain around his neck.

"That's it right there, Poppi?" Rico eyed the bag that sat in

Smoke's lap.

Smoke nodded and passed the bag to Rico. "Yeah, a whole kilo."

Rico looked into the bag then looked over at Smoke. "Ooohh baby," he sang! "We got a whole key of that raw. It cost you the whole twenty, right?" He smiled even harder.

Smoke looked dead in Rico's face and lied. "Yeah."

"Did you see what he did wit' the money?" Rico questioned.

"Nah," Smoke replied. "That money was straight, right?"

"You mean was it tagged?"

Smoke nodded.

"Not this time, but when it go down again, it will be." Smoke thought on Rico's words. *Good thing his bitch ass said no since I kept 10g's of their money. That could'a been ugly.* Smoke's thought was broken when Rico reached into his pocket and pulled out a roll of money. "You signed on for 5 g's for every transaction, so here you go." He handed the money to Smoke then reached on the side of his seat, retrieving a small clipboard. "You gotta sign this every time you receive a payment." Rico shrugged his shoulders. "The Feds like accountability. Welcome to the life of a paid CI."

Smoke resented being called a CI, but that's what he was, and had been since he was released from prison. He couldn't stay in prison for another five years and a couple of months. So, when the law approached him with an ultimatum of finishing off his ten year sentence or working as a confidential informant he chose to work for them and narcotics agent, Rico Santos, who was only twenty-six was his contact.

"You find out who supplin' him?" Rico questioned, after Smoke passed him back the clipboard.

"Nah, not this time. But I will once y'all give me more money to re up. Frog said he'd hook me up wit' his man if I'm buyin' two or more keys."

"He give you a name?"

"Nah," Smoke said. "He said he'll let his man tell me his name when I meet him. So, since I supposed to be gettin' my money up, y'all have to wait at least a couple of weeks to give me dough to buy more shit."

"You right, so in a couple of weeks we'll do it and by the way…,," Rico pulled out a business card and handed it to Smoke. "Go to that address and get you a ride. They have nice cars. I got this Rover from there. Show them that card and you'll get an up-to-date car for little or nothin'. The cars there are seized cars. Besides, you don't need to be pushin' your girl's whip."

Smoke stared at the agent surprisingly. "How you know who car that was?"

Agent Santos smiled. "That's Miss Cherry Moore's car. We might not watch you all the time, but we do sometimes. We won't disrespect you in no way, so don't worry. Won't nobody know you're workin' wit' us and yeah, if you gon' sell on the side, be discreet about it."

It was Smoke's first time smiling since he'd got in the Range Rover. The Agent Santos giving him the okay to do his thing made his day, and he planned to capitalize on it.

"I'll be in touch wit'cha Poppi. Adios," Agent Santos said.

Smoke stepped out of the truck and back into the Sentra. He started the car, and seconds later, pulled out of the McDonald's parking lot. As he drove, he thought about what he was expected to do in his current profession. Agent Santos had told him if he could bring down at least two big dogs in the game, his agency would cut him loose and big dogs to them were any dealer that sold ten kilos or more a month. The agent also told him that if he could give them one key player that was supplying to numerous dealers and they could draw up a big conspiracy case, he'd be cut loose on that.

Smoke hoped Frog's connect was a key player in the game far beyond what Frog thought he was. That would count for one of the two deals he needed under his belt. Smoke had one other person in mind that would make it two big dogs for the Feds and that person was linked to a person he didn't like. Although he wasn't certain, he was sure that person was involved somehow in the drug game. The question was, just how involved?

# SIXTEEN

Def clung on to every word Old Man Bootney spoke. Even though he had somewhere to be in the next half hour, he felt obligated to listen when the old man would drop knowledge on him about diverse, worldly matters.

"What does extortion mean to you?" Old Man Bootney asked Def, without giving Def time to answer. "It means to obtain by force or improper pressure. In street terms, give me my money or I'ma do somethin' to you. Who does that and have to spend time in jail for it? Civilians. Who does that and it's considered legitimate? Government. They do it in the form of taxes."

Def nodded in agreement.

"When I was in Vietnam in 1968, a priest anointed me and told me it was okay for me to kill for the sake of my country. I did, and when I made it back, I was told to put that habit behind me. I did, but I say that to say this. Why wasn't I jailed for takin' lives over there? If I had done the same over here, in this country, wouldn't I've been put in jail?"

Def nodded.

"So, is killin' really wrong or is it wrong only if the powers that be say it's wrong?" Old Man Bootney stared into Def's face.

"What's up?" Def asked from the look the old man was giving him.

"Do you think what'cha doin' is wrong, young soldier?"

Def shrugged his shoulders.

"Let me give you an example of something'. A police officer takes the life of a person, whether armed or unarmed. You do the same. You're jailed for your actions. The officer is suspended wit' pay while the matter is being investigated. Later, the officer's actions are called justifiable. Why? Didn't he take a life? Isn't one of God's Ten Commandments, *Thou shall not kill*? It didn't say if you're an officer of the law you can. It says, *Thou shall not kill* and that's it. So, why is a man of the law exempt from that most of the time? You know why? Because the man that holds the gold makes the rules. It has nothin' to do wit' God. If so, every man that takes a life, whether of the law or not, would be put in jail for their actions."

"That's makes a lot of sense," Def agreed.

"So, what I'm sayin' is this. You're gettin' paid to kill. An officer of the law, in some ways, is gettin' paid a salary to kill because we all know that's what they out in the ghetto doin'. Killin' inner city young boys. Shootin' 'em down and sayin' they thought he was reachin' for a gun. So to me, what you're doin' isn't wrong."

Def nodded his head. He looked down at his watch. "Sorry, old man." He stood up from the sofa. "I gotta go. I gotta take that ride back up to New York."

"You and that gal gonna take care of a lil' business, huh?" The old man smiled.

"Yeah. You gon' be straight, right?"

"Yeah, Kelly comin' over. How long you plan on stayin' up there?"

"Until the job is done," Def replied, while strutting up to the front door.

"You gon' bring that gal by to meet an old man, right?"

Def nodded up and down. He opened the door and stepped out of the apartment.

In no time, Def was in a black rental Dodge Caravan, en route to Tyra's townhouse. When he pulled up in the parking space next to Tyra's Benz, she was coming out the front door with her luggage in hand.

Def got out of the Caravan and went over to help Tyra with her things.

"Thank you. Aren't you a gentleman today?" They exchanged smiles.

"You want me to drive?" Tyra asked.

"Yeah. You know those state troopers be racially profilin' a nigga."

As Tyra climbed behind the wheel, she stated, "I'm black, too."

"Yeah, but they'll pull me over before they pull a beautiful, black woman over." Def cursed himself as soon as his indirect compliment left his mouth. He'd been avoiding saying things like that because he didn't want Tyra to know that he'd been lusting for her since he'd met her.

Tyra smiled broadly. "You just called me beautiful," she said, backing out of the parking space.

"No I didn't," Def quickly fired.

"Yes, you did."

"No, I didn't," Def fired again.

"You did. If you think I'm beautiful ain't nothin' wrong wit'cha sayin' that." Tyra was smiling the entire time she was talking. "Sayin' that ain't gon' kill your tough guy image." She shot her eyes over to Def. "So, you don't think I'm beautiful?"

Def looked over at Tyra. He wanted to tell her she was beautiful from head to toe, but instead he said, "You a'ight."

They both laughed as Tyra took off towards the highway. Def glanced down at his watch and then over at Tyra whose head moved back and forth to the sounds of the music from the radio.

"It's four-thirty. It ain't gon' get dark until 'round nine, so take your time. We want it to be dark by the time we get there," Def coached.

"Why?" Tyra asked.

"Cause it's Monday and the nigga don't come out 'til late on Mondays for some reason."

"So, do you want me to go after him as soon as we get there?"

"Don't you wanna get this over wit' as soon as possible, so you can get back to your shop?"

"Yeah, but I gotta change and all that good stuff. I can't go at him dressed like this."

"Don't worry. I already reserved a hotel room."

Tyra wanted to ask whether one room was reserved for them or two separate rooms, but she didn't, she told herself she'd simply wait and see.

Four hours after getting on I-95 North, Tyra was driving along the Triborough Bridge, heading for Southside Jamaica Queens, New York. Fifteen minutes later, she pulled into the hotel's parking lot and parked.

"I got us one room wit' twin beds. I hope you don't mind," Def said.

"What'cha mean you got us one room?" Tyra piped, playing as if she was appalled by Def's statement. But, in reality, she was happy to be shacking up with him.

"We need to be together at all times on this shit," Def uttered calmly. He pushed his door open. He didn't care to hear her reply. "I'm goin' to get the room key." He shut the door and walked in the direction of the hotel entrance.

By the time they entered the room, it was about nine o'clock in the evening. Tyra noticed he didn't have any luggage of his own.

"Where your stuff at?" she questioned.

"I didn't bring nothin' but what I have on."

"Why?"

"Don't plan on bein' here long. But if I do, I'll just grab some gear from the Coliseum on 165th Street."

"Where your gun at?"

Def pulled up his shirt, but did so a little too high and exposed more than the 9mm that was tucked on his waist. Tyra got her first look at his small waist that connected up to his eight pack abs.

"You want me to start gettin' ready?" Tyra asked grinning. The sight of Def's abs played with her mind.

"Yeah, and while you gettin' ready, I'ma go check somethin' out real quick."

Tyra watched him walk out the door with the Caravan's keys in his hand. When he made it back to the room a half hour later, Tyra was seated on the bed, talking on her cell phone. When she spotted him, she said a few more words to Cherry, who was holding down her shop, before hanging up.

"I just came back from the spot he be at and he's out there," Def informed.

Tyra stood up from the bed. "I'm ready." She placed her phone into her tote bag and grabbed it by its straps.

Def looked her over. Tyra wore a black bustier top that exposed her entire torso except for her breast, a pair of jeans that fit her like a glove, and suede Prada boots.

Tyra lifted up her arms and spund around in a circle. "You think this good enough to catch his attention?"

Def wanted to tell her to turn back around so he could get another peek at her ass, but he didn't. Instead, he said, "You good. He'll bite. Now, let's go."

Minutes later, Def pulled up and parked on 110th and Guy R. Brewer Boulevard.

"You ready?" Def asked. He was staring at the side of Tyra's face.

Tyra inhaled deeply. "Yeah," she nodded her head, "I'm ready."

"You got'cha gun in your bag, right?"

"Yeah."

"The silencer on it?"

"Yeah."

"Go do your thing then. If anythin' go the opposite of how we planned it, bounce. I'll be watchin' everythin'."

"Okay." Tyra stepped out of the car with her tote bag in hand and headed up the fairly crowded block to 109th.

She looked straight ahead as she strutted up the block, with her hips swaying from side to side. She could hear catcalls coming from men who stood in front of storefronts as she walked along. She even heard the sound of car horns honking, trying to get her attention. But none of that broke her focus on what she was in New York to do, and that was to do her part in helping take the drug dealer, who went by the name of Allah, out.

Only a hundred feet or so away from Allah who stood with a few other men in front of a pizza joint, Tyra prepared herself to begin her role playing.

"Excuse me," she said to a young, dark brown, skinned woman that was walking down the sidewalk. "Have you seen…,," Tyra dug into her tote bag and pulled out a picture of a young girl who looked similar to her, who Def had given her a picture of, "this girl."

The woman took the picture from out of Tyra's hand and

looked at it. "Nah." She handed the picture back to Tyra. "Who is she, she's cute?"

"My lil' sista. She missin'."

The woman ran her eyes over Tyra. "Shit, if she dressed anythin' like you, she gon' stay missin'." She walked off giggling.

"Bitch!" Tyra mumbled. As she proceeded up the block again, she stopped another woman and ran the same game past her. The woman said she hadn't seen the girl on the picture, so Tyra kept it moving. She didn't bother to stop anyone else. Instead, she walked up toward Allah and his crew. They all stared at her as if she were prime meat, ready to be devoured. She placed the picture out before her and asked, "Have any of y'all seen her?"

Allah, who stood around six feet, even with a lanky build, stepped forward, grabbing the picture from Tyra's hand. He wore a plain white t-shirt, an iced-out chain sat around his skinny neck, dark blue jeans that matched the Yankees fitted cap, which he wore tilted on the side of his head, and dark blue Nike sneakers. A Jacob the Jeweler watch was clasped around his left wrist, to seal off his hood look.

"Who this, ma?" he questioned.

Tyra peeped over Allah's shoulder at the four men who stood behind him. They all had envious expressions on their faces as if they were mad they weren't the one who had approached her first.

"That's my lil' sista," Tyra said, taking her attention off the men and back to Allah.

"She missin'?" he asked.

Tyra squinched up her face and was briefly distracted after noticing Allah's teeth. Although it was dark outside, she could see that they were jacked up. *Damn, he got a handsome ass face and his teeth look like that? Why doesn't he use some of his drug proceeds and see a damn dentist* she thought to herself. Coming out of her brief trance, she responded, "Yeah, for a month now."

Allah looked down at Tyra's exposed navel. "You sure she ain't just out havin' a good time? I can only see her face in this flick, but if she have a body anythin' like yours, she might be out wit' a nigga havin' fun. No disrespect."

Tyra snatched the picture out of his hand. She gave him a fake smile. "That's my lil' sista, boy. She ain't nothin' but sixteen."

"How old are you?" Allah smiled, showcasing all his teeth.

Tyra placed the picture into her bag and her hand on her hip. "Why?"

Allah motioned for Tyra to step off to the side with him. She did, and all the men made disapproving sounds with their mouths.

"What's up?" Tyra inquired.

"You. Where you and your lil' sista from, ma?"

"We from Chesapeake, Virginia."

"What'cha lil' sista doin' all the way in New York?"

Tyra threw an exasperating expression on her face. "She came up here, followin' after this lil' nigga who moved up here with his folks."

Allah stared at Tyra. "You know where the dude be at?"

Tyra shrugged her shoulders. "I was told by some people at home that he hang out 'round here. His name Moe, but he go by Lil' Moe sometimes."

Allah thought on Tyra's words for a moment before he stated, "Nah, ma, I ain't seen her and there ain't no nigga named Moe playin' these streets."

Tyra looked Allah up and down. She looked directly into his face and asked, "How you know that?"

"I'm that nigga 'round here, ma. Trust and believe, I know."

Tyra's face transformed into a sexy grin. "What's your name?"

"Allah, ma. Allah the God. What's your name?"

"Debbie," Tyra quickly said, extending her hand out for a shake. Allah took it but lifted her arm above her head and spun her around, as if they were dancing.

"Damn, ma! You a dime hands down," he said, when Tyra's turn was completed and she was facing him. "If you don't mind me sayin', you got ass and hips for days. Plus, you got a tiny waist wit' a cute face." He let go of her hand.

"Thanks for the compliment."

"Since you from out of town, where you stayin'?"

"Boy, I can't tell you that," Tyra replied, shy like. "I don't know you."

"You wanna get to know me?"

"I'm leavin' to go back to Virginia tomorrow if I don't find my sista. So, if you wanna get to know me, it gotta be tonite. I got a man down in Virginia, and when I'm home, I don't mess around on him. If you know what I mean." Tyra winked at Allah.

"Damn!" he cursed. "I got some important shit to handle tonite."

"Well, don't worry about it. Maybe we'll meet up in the future."

"Ma, what time you leavin' to go back home tomorrow?" Allah uttered promptly, not wanting his chance to get with her to slip away. "You know, if you don't find your sista tonite?"

"What time you want me to leave?" she smiled, devilishly.

"Can we hook up 'round eight tomorrow?"

Tyra reached into her tote bag and pulled out her cell phone. "What's your number?" she questioned, coming to grips that the hit wasn't going to happen tonight.

Allah uttered his cell number to Tyra, which she punched into her phone.

"Ma," Allah said, looking into Tyra's face, "Don't bullshit. Get at a nigga."

"I will. Don't worry." Tyra dropped her phone back into her bag. "I need some money anyway." She winked at Allah for the second time.

"You know what?" He dug into his pocket and whipped out a bankroll. He peeled off two fifty dollar bills and five twenties. "I'll double this if I see you tomorrow." He placed the money into her hand. "You'll go back to Virginia wit' six hundred extra."

Tyra dropped the money into her bag. "I'll see you tomorrow, even if I find my sista tonite." She started to back away from Allah.

"Hit me 'round seven-thirty," he said.

"Okay, I will." Tyra spun around and strutted back in the direction of 110th.

After stopping at a liquor store to buy a bottle of Grey Goose, Bleu, Def and Tyra headed back to their hotel room. Tyra explained to Def what the deal was with Allah then she excused heself and slipped into the bathroom with her small suitcase in hand. Def was surprised to see Tyra exit the bathroom ten minutes later draped in a red, silk pants pajama set, with red furry, high heeled slides on her pedicured feet. He watched as Tyra sashayed around her bed and over to him.

"So," Tyra began, "You gon' have a drink wit' me or what?" She looked into Def's face.

Def's eyes shot down towards Tyra's feet. He wanted to tell her how beautiful her toes were peeking out from the front of her slippers. But as usual, he kept his mouth shut. He looked up at her and said, "I told'cha I don't do no whole lot of drinkin', especially when I'm on a job."

"Def, don't act up tonite. Just have a drink wit' me and then you can go back to being on your job," Tyra said.

Def looked at the bottle of Grey Goose. "I'm only gon' drink a lil' bit." He grabbed one of the two small plastic cups that sat beside the bottle.

Tyra twisted the top off the bottle and poured their drinks. She smiled.

"Why you smilin'?"

She shook her head. "No reason."

"Nobody smiles for no reason," Def stated.

"Okay, I was just thinkin' I bet you can't hold your liquor. That's probably why you wanna drink a lil' bit. It don't have nothin' to do wit'cha being on your job. You ashamed a girl might out drink you." Tyra held her cup out in front of her for a toast. "To our success in not arugin' like we used to."

Def grabbed the bottle by the neck and filled his cup up to the brim. "You didn't pour me enough," he said, placing the bottle back and holding his cup up to Tyra's. They touched cups then gulped away, but Def downed his in one shot.

Tyra stared at him and grinned. Her words to him about him not being able to hold his liquor caused his male ego to get the best of him. She watched him pour himself one drink after the other, and by the time she was on her second drink, he was on his fourth. His state of intoxication became apparent.

"Why you ain't got no man?" Def stated from out of nowhere.

"Excuse me," she snapped.

"You heard me. Why you ain't got no man?"

*Yeah*, Tyra thought to herself, *this nigga can't hold his drinkin' just like I thought.*

"I don't have a man because I don't want one and why you don't have no girl?"

"Cause I don't want one." Def poured himself another drink.

"How old are you, Def?" Tyra asked quickly. She wanted an answer to an old question that she'd asked him a while ago that he never responded to.

"I turned thirty-one last month," he said, taking big gulps of his drink.

Tyra smiled inwardly. She had gotten answers to two questions that she had wanted to know for months and now she knew the only device that could get him to open up was alcohol so she pressed him for more answers.

"Def, your moms and pops still alive?"

Def shook his head sadly. "Nah, they both dead. My…my pops died when I was around nine, at least that's what I was told. My moms was killed by by stepfather, who I killed in the same place he had killed her after he bragged to me about how he killed her and was gon' get away wit' it. The dumb ass police really believed that an intruder broker into our apartment and killed her. Tyra, I did eight years for killin' that faggot."

Tyra's right hand went to her mouth, covering it. "I'm so sorry about…"

"Ain't no need for you to be sorry, that's how my life was. Anyway, it's this old man that used to be my real father's best friend that I want you to meet. He like a father to me."

"Okay," she said.

"So, is your moms and pops still alive?" Def poured himself another drink.

"My father OD'd off heroin a long time ago. My moms still alive, but she ain't speakin' to me. But I think it won't be too long before we speak though. I say that because her number showed up on my phone." Tyra beamed. "I called it back but she didn't answer, but I know she gon' come through." Tyra stood up. "I'll be right back, I gotta use the bathroom."

When she made her way out of the bathroom Def was stretched fully out on his back, sleeping like a baby. She gazed down at him and was pissed. Her hidden intention to get him drunk, which she had succeeded in doing, and then have sex with him was ruined. She had hoped tonight would've been the night they became one. She was sure that he wanted her just as bad as she wanted him. Although he tried to hide it, she knew. Not only was it written all over his face, it was in his eyes.

Tyra slid out of her high heels, flicked the light off, and climbed into bed. She fell asleep with an itch between her legs that needed to be scratched with a vengeance. Def, she believed, was the only one who could assist her with this dilemma.

# SEVENTEEN

Her eyes flickered a few times before they opened. It took her fifteen seconds to gather her vision completely, and when she did, she saw that Def's bed was empty and the hotel room was partially dark.

Tyra laid on her back with the pillow under her head. Her eyes roamed around the room when she heard a deep grunt followed by a hissing sound.

As she sat up she noticed Def doing push-ups on the floor near the window. The sun that broke through shined down on his bare, muscular, well-defined back. She immediately became excited. Tyra reached into her pajama pants to touch herself, and sure enough, she was moist.

"You finally woke up, huh?" Def exclaimed, after rising from the floor.

"What time is it?" she asked.

"It's 'round twelve-thirty."

Tyra took her eyes off Def and looked over at the table. "Where those bags come from?" she asked, referring to two shopping bags that sat on the table.

"I went to the Coliseum and picked up an outfit. We here for another day, so I had to get somethin' to wear."

Tyra watched him drop to the floor and began doing push-ups again. She climbed out of bed and walked over to where he was, standing over him.

"Def, do you find me attractive?" she questioned, as he was rising up from the floor. He brushed his hands off on his jeans and stared into her face.

"Why you ask me that?" Def asked.

"Just answer the question," Tyra spat sternly.

"Yeah," Def replied. He made sure his face didn't reveal how the question had instantly aroused him.

Tyra ran her eyes over Def's ripped torso. The tattoo of a woman's face rested on his upper left chest.

"That's a picture of my moms," Def said, watching her scrutinize the tattoo.

She spun around, walked to the bathroom, and shut the door. Def sat, puzzled by her questions and actions. He thought about knocking on the door but decided against it.

Just as he was about to drop back down and continue his workout, Tyra exited the bathroom draped in nothing but her birthday suit. He was immediately taken back by what he saw, Tyra naked, strutting in his direction. When she made her way up to him, she grabbed him by the hand, walked him over to the bed and said, "Show me how attractive you think I am." She unbuttoned his jeans and pushed them down around his ankles. She was surprised to see that Def wore boxer-brief underwear, instead of plain boxers. *Not what I envisioned,* she said to herself. But what she wasn't surprised to see was the huge hard on in his underwear.

"You sure you wanna do this?" Def inquired, looking at Tyra.

"Why wouldn't I?" she replied.

"Cause now we'll be mixin' business wit' pleasure."

"Sometimes that can be a good thing. Just hope in our case it is."

Def took a step back and took off his jeans. His boxer-briefs fell to the floor.

Tyra gasped at the sight of Def's penis. She wasn't sure if her shock was the huge size of Def's dick or the fact that she hadn't seen one since Cash. But, whatever the reason, she wasn't going to be scared away.

As Def stood in front of Tyra, she grabbed his throbbing dick with her right hand and began stroking it. She eyed it with an intense look on her face. Tyra noticed it wasn't that long, maybe six or six and a half inches. But what it lacked in diameter it definitely made up in circumference. It was fat, fat as in the size of her wrist, and the head of it resembled the head of a mushroom.

Tyra passed the condom to Def that she had in her left hand. "Open that," she said to him. He did and passed it back to her as she rolled it down onto his dick. It was a tight fit. She looked up at him. "I hope you didn't think I was gon' suck your dick." Tyrasmiled and crawled backwards up to the head of the bed. Def followed her and stationedhimself between her parted legs. "I haven't done this in awhile, so take your time," she said.

Def heard what she said, but he didn't believe her. How could she not have had sex and what did she mean by awhile? Every nigga and their father would want to get with her. If her words were true, Def pondered, something wasn't right with her, but for now, he decided he'd put finding out what that was aside and enjoy what he'd been craving for.

Tyra took hold of Def's thick dick and rubbed the head up against her clit slowly, before she allowed the head to slip inside her.

"Ahhh!" she moaned. She let go of his dick. "Go 'head, but take your time."

He slowly started working his way into her. With each thrust he took, she moaned and each thrust he took, he felt closer to heaven. Though he wore a condom, he felt every bit of her wetness. The way her insides feel, maybe she hasn't had sex in a while, Def thought to himself, as he continued to work his way into Tyra and she willingly gave Deffull access of her pleasure nest.

"Ahhh! Ahhh! It feels sooo good!" Tyra cringed in delight. "Oh my God!"

"Oh yeah." Def's hands gripped Tyra's calves, while he pushed himself in and out of her. "Why you make me wait so long to get some?"Def watched his thickness disappear into her then out. He tilted his head up toward the ceiling savoring in the moment.

"Why you make…Ahhh! Why you make me wait so long to get some?" She threw his question right back at him. Tyra stared into his face with a twisted expression on her face."Oh my goodnessss, it's so thick. It feels so fuckin' good. Oh my goodnesss, Def your dick is so good!"

Just as Def was about to turn the question back around to Tyra for her response, he noticed a slight twitch in her body. "Oh!" Tyra stretched out her arms, as if she were reaching out for a hug. "Ahhh!

Ahhh! Let go of my legs and come down here and kiss me. I think I'm 'bout to cum. Oh God!"

Def freed her calves and fell into her embrace. His hips thrust rapidly back and forth, even as he and Tyra french kissed.

He pulled his lips from hers and grunted, "I think I'm 'bout to cum too."

"C'mon, cause Ahhh! Ahhh, I'm cummin' now!"

"Oh shit! Me, too!" Def said, as they both yelled out like dogs in heat.

As they laid there locked in each other's embrace, Tyra could-n't help but to let her mind wander. That was da' bomb. I could get addicted to that shit. I hope I didn't come off like an amateur. I know I've been out the game for awhile but a girl still got some tricks up her sleeve. Next time, I'm gonna give him a lil' more, but I have to break him off slowly. Make him earn the pussy. She looked up at Def who had fallen off to sleep. She smiled and positioned herself closer to his chest.

"Sweet dreams," she stated softly.

Later that day, they were riding to the spot where Allah told Tyra to meet him when she phoned him around seven-thirty.

"I told him whatever we gon' do together had to be done tonite because I was leavin' tomorrow," Tyra explained to Def. "I also asked him what was the deal once we met up. He said he'd let me know when we saw each other."

Def shot his eyes over at Tyra and gave her an assuring look. "Whatever he got planned, don't worry, I'll be watchin' everythin'. Ain't nothin' gon' happen to you."

Tyra smiled. Hearing his assurance of her safety brought a se-cure feeling over her. Def pulled to the curb, parked, and looked over at her.

"You good?" Def asked.

Tyra nodded. "Yeah." She pushed the passenger door open.

"Hold on," Def said. He leaned over towards Tyra. "Gimme a kiss before you go."

Tyra grinned from ear to ear. Def asking her for a kiss surprised her. It just wasn't his character to initiate anything outside of doing his job as a hired killer.

After they kissed, Tyra uttered, "Lettin' you dive into my sea got'cha open, huh?"

"You want the truth?"

"Yeah."

"Nah, I ain't open." Def grinned.

"Yeah right." She got out of the car with her tote bag in hand.

In no time she was walking up to Allah who stood with the same group of men in front of the same pizza joint from the night before.

"What's up, ma?" Allah said with a smile, as Tyra stood in front of him.

"You," Tyra replied dryly.

Allah turned to his associates and said, "I'll see y'all niggas later." He threw his right arm around Tyra's neck and walked off with her. They walked to a brand new pearl white Navigator truck with Lamborghini doors that flipped up from a push of a button on his key ring.

Tyra smiled and thought to herself, *this what he spent some of G's money on.*

Before Allah could pull off, one of the men that had been standing with him ran up to the driver's side of the truck. "Dawg, you sure you don't want me to tag along?"

"Nah son, I'm good. I'll get up wit'cha later on." Allah stuck his hand out the window for a shake. "Peace, God."

When the Navigator pulled off and made a left turn, Tyra noticed a sign that read, The Cross Island Parkway.

"Where we goin'?" She looked out her side view mirror and saw Def two cars behind them.

"To my spot in Long Island." Allah reached into his pocket, while he drove. "Here go six hundred. That's triple what I gave you last night. I'm gettin' paper so why not spread the wealth." He smirked arrogantly and passed the money off to Tyra.

She dumped the money into her bag. "Thank you."

"You ever find your sista, ma?"

"Nah, I guess she'll come back home when her lil' pussy gets worn out." They both laughed.

A few minutes later, Allah was pulling into a one-car garage of a nice middle class home in the residential district of Elmont, Long Island. Tyra turned and faced Allah, who was dressed in hip-hop attire.

"You don't know me like that, and you takin' me to your crib. Niggas that's gettin' it don't do shit like this."

Allah smiled, showing all his teeth. "How do you know if this is my crib, ma?"

"I don't know, but I have a good idea it is."

"And you're right. This is my spot. Well, at least one of my spots. I can trust you, right?"

Tyra threw her hand up to her chest and batted her eyes. "Who, lil' old me? Of course you can, I'm harmless." *But Def ain't*, she thought.

Inside the house in the upstairs bedroom she stood between his legs staring down into his face while he sat on the side of his water bed. He slid his hands up and down her ass.

"Damn, ma…" Allah squeezed both of Tyra's butt cheeks, "You got a soft ass."

Playing along, Tyra replied, "I know, so when we gon' do what we came to do?"

"Oh, you want some dick, huh?" Allah stated.

"I'm just tryna give you what'cha already paid for."

"Oh, I'm gon' get that, ma, and more." He grinned wickedly.

Tyra became nervous; his words didn't fall on deaf ears. She instantly knew that he was up to something that she might not like; something that she and Def hadn't planned for.

"Before we get started, let me go use the bathroom and freshen up a little bit." Tyra took a step back.

"It's down the hall on the right."

"I'll only be a few minutes."

Tyra hurried out of the bedroom and was on her cell phone before she could make it downstairs.

"Tyra," Def said, receiving her call.

"I'm openin' the door now.

"Tyra, I'm fucked right now. I got pulled over. The police are runnin' my tag number and license in. I'm only a block away from the house, I saw y'all pull into. If you look out the front window you might see me."

"Def, please tell me you playin'." Tyra frantically ran to the front window and pulled the white curtain back. She looked down the block. "I don't see you."

"Don't worry, just hold on. She should be comin' to give me my shit back in a minute."

"Please hurry. I don't wanna have to fuck him."

"Try to hold him off."

"Okay, I gotta go." Tyra tossed her phone into her bag and made her way upstairs and into the bathroom. She wasn't in there thirty seconds before Allah knocked.

"You a'ight in there, ma? You got a nigga waitin' too long."

Tyra stood in the middle of the bathroom staring at the door. "I'll be out in a minute," she said. She didn't hear him walk away, so she knew he was still there. She took a deep breath and opened the door, using a piece of toilet paper to touch the doorknob.

"Damn, you took a long time in there." Allah ran his eyes over Tyra. He was shirtless.

She saw something in his eyes that didn't look right. She couldn't figure out what it was, but she knew his eyes depicted something menacing. She walked past him and headed toward his bedroom. He walked behind her.

When Tyra walked into his room, everything in her gut told her that something was wrong. The same man that had asked Allah did he want him to tag along was stark naked, sitting on the side of Allah's bed. He stroked his hard dick slowly with a sinister grin on his face.

"Let me get that." Allah swiped Tyra's tote bag from her hand and placed it on the dresser, without even looking into it.

"You should just go 'head and take your shit off cause I didn't pay you eight hundred for nothin'," Allah uttered.

"That's right and where you say she was from God? Virginia, right? Yeah, a thick, country bitch. I know how y'all bitches love us New York niggas," Allah's buddy stated.

Tyra stood in a daze. She didn't say a word. She just looked from Allah to his boy then to her tote bag. She had to find a way to get to it because there was no way she was going to have sex with two drug dealers.

"Take that shit off!" Allah came up behind Tyra.

Tyra quickly moved to the side, avoiding being touched. She was about to ask how did the naked man get in the room, but she thought better of it. She knew how. She'd been set up.

Allah and his buddy planned for things to go just the way they were. The naked man must've raced to the house, beating them there in his car. He took the short route, while Allah took the long way, giving his friend sufficient time to enter the house before them and hide in the bedroom closet.

"I can take my own clothes off," Tyra stated as she threw a fake smile on her face. She knew in order for things not to get out of hand, she had to play the game accordingly.

"Okay, ma, then take that shit off," Allah's buddy stated. He stroked his dick vigorously, while staring at Tyra. "I'm tryna get up in those guts fo'real."

"Do y'all have any condoms?" Tyra asked.

"You don't have none in your bag?" Allah said.

*Right answer*, Tyra thought. "Yeah." She moved to the dresser and dug into her bag. Her back was turned to the two men, and when she did an about-face, she held her .38 in her right hand.

"Yo!" Allah's buddy shot to his feet, his dick no longer in his hand. It was deflating rapidly from the sight of Tyra's gun.

Allah had a nervous expression on his face. "Ma, what's the gun for?"

"Y'all was gon' try to rape me, right?" She waved the gun between both men. She hadn't noticed it, but the gun was shaking in her hand, and Allah saw it.

"Ma, you ever fire a gun before?" He beamed. The nervous expression that was on his face vanished, because he believed it would be simply a matter of time before the .38 with the silencer on it would be in his possession.

"Yeah, I fired a gun at a shootin' range," Tyra replied truthfully, being that Def had taken her to a range twice since he'd given her the gun.

"Yeah, but have you shot anybody before?"

She glanced at the shaking gun. "Nah, but y'all might be my first." She grinned faintly, hiding the fact that she was somewhat petrified.

"This bitch fakin'," Allah's friend snapped. "Look at her hand. That shit can't stay still. Bitch, let me get that up off you." He motioned towards Tyra and Pfft! Pfft! Two bullets entered his naked body, causing him to drop to the floor. Blood made its way from his neck and chest where he'd been shot.

"Oh shit, bitch!" Allah hollered. "You shot my dawg!" He threw his hands up in the air, while looking down at his friend, who'd just taken his last breath.

When it registered with Tyra that she had shot a man dead, the gun in her hands shook even more. Fire was in Allah's eyes. He wanted to get at Tyra in the worst way. If he could get the gun from her, he could make something happen.

"Ma, let me get that gun. You don't need to catch another body. You a girl, you don't wanna do no life bid."

Tyra suddenly remembered the reason why she was even in Allah's presence. "Do you have Roc's money?" she said, in the same manner Def would have.

Allah's face froze up. Hearing Roc's name puzzled him. "How do you know Roc?"

"Never mind that, where is his dough?"

Allah caught on to what was happening. He'd been set up. Roc had sent a bitch to get at him. A bitch that had ran game on him to get him alone so that only meant one thing, she came to kill him. His man, Ronni, who lay dead in his own blood, was just in the wrong place at the wrong time.

"Tell that nigga Roc he a smart ass nigga. He got a bitch doin' his killin' for him. Niggas ain't gon' suspect a bitch to do him dirty. But anyway you can go 'head and shoot me cause I ain't givin' you shit!"

Pfft! Tyra fired one single shot to Allah's head, dropping him instantly. Tyra was startled when she heard footsteps approaching the bedroom door. A sense of relief came over her when Def appeared, making his way into the room.

"Damn, what happened?" he quizzed, staring at the two dead

bodies.

"They was gon' try and rape me so I shot 'em. The other one was here, hidin' in the closet," Tyra said.

Def came over to Tyra and threw his arms around her. "Let's get outta here and get back to DC. I don't think it's no money in here anyway."

"Def," Tyra said, as they walked out of the bedroom, "Don't tell G or nobody else what I done. You did this, okay. I wanna make like this didn't happen."

"Okay," Def said. As they made their way out the house, Def noticed that Tyra wasn't a bit shaken by what had taken place and that concerned him. *Damn,* he thought, *she just shot two niggas dead and don't seem fazed by it. Nothin'Personal, but I gotta watch this chick. She might become dangerous.* For now, he decided to let his concerns go as they headed towards the highway.

# EIGHTEEN

He slid the razor into the pile of coke that sat on a small, square shaped mirror on top of the coffee table, transforming the white substance into six thin, three inch lines. Satisfied with his arrangement, he placed the razor aside and picked up his three inch *Red*, what he called his coke straw.

Plopping down onto the sofa, he quickly sniffed two of the six lines up his nose.

"Aw, baby," he barked! Daddy sat up on the sofa with his head held back. He pinched at his nose rapidly. "Mmm hmm. This some good shit here," he said, as if he hadn't snorted the same quality of coke just hours ago. He kept his head tilted back to savor the sour taste that ran down his throat.

The sound of his cell phone broke the pleasure of his high. He let it ring a few times before he picked it up. "Yeah?"

"Hey Daddy, what's up?" a woman said.

He immediately knew who he was talking to, not just from caller ID, but from being called Daddy.

"What's up, twins?" he uttered, knowing both of the women were on the line.

"You. "What's up? "What'cha doin'?" Rita asked.

Daddy placed the phone between his ear and shoulder and swiftly sniffed two more lines of coke.

"Rita, you hear that?" Cita said to her sister.

"Uh huh. That nigga sniffin' that white girl."

"That once a month thing he started wit' is gone, huh." The girls were talking to each other as if Daddy wasn't still on the phone with them.

"Y'all called to see if I'm comin' to cop tomorrow, right?" Daddy asked. Beads of sweat formulated on his forehead and a sense of paranoia started to kick in after he had taken in a few more lines.

"Yeah," they both stated in unison.

"I'll be there. I gotta go."

"Nigga, you ain't gettin' paranoid on us again, are you?" Cita asked.

"Nah, nah," Daddy uttered, lying.

"Yeah you are," Rita snapped. "A five hundred or so dollar a day habit, uh, do that to a ma'fucka."

"I'll see y'all tomorrow." Daddy hung up the phone. "Bitches," he said, then sniffed the last two lines of coke.

He sat back on the sofa and allowed the coke to travel throughout his system. He grinded his teeth together, another side effect his drug of choice had been having on him for the last two months. The sound of his phone interrupted his mellow moment.

"Yeah?"

"What's up, slim?" the man on the other end of the phone said.

Daddy sat up straight. "Oh yeah, I'm on my way. I almost forgot." He sprung from the sofa and headed to his bedroom to get his Glock 40 before he exited the apartment.

It didn't take Daddy long to reach Jasper Street since he didn't' live too far away. He parked in front of the building and turned off the engine. He looked into his mirrors to make sure he wasn't being watched before heading into the building. When he reached the apartment door, he suddenly felt his paranoia kick into high gear. He didn't know the reason for it, but he sure as hell felt it. *Damn, this white girl really got a nigga trippin'*, he muttered to himself, while knocking twice on the door. Standing there, he told himself that he would count to ten, and if no one opened the door, he'd leave. He was only on four when the door opened.

"What's up, slim?" the owner of the apartment said, allowing Daddy into his domain.

"Hey. What's up, Frog?" Daddy replied, his eyes roaming around the living room. "You here alone?"

"Nah, the dude I told'cha about is in the bathroom. That nigga in there takin' a shit." Frog grinned.

Daddy walked over to the sofa in the living room and sat down. Frog followed suit and sat down across from him.

"You said you've been knowin' this dude for a while, right?" Daddy questioned.

Frog nodded his head. He stared at Daddy and saw that he was coked out. He'd seen that look in his eyes many times. Plus, he noticed that Daddy pinched his nose almost every minute or so, which he'd picked up on the last time they met.

"Yeah, I've been knowin' him for years," Frog said.

"So, you said he wanna cop two birds?"

"Yeah. When I cop my eight, he gon' get two.

Daddy nodded his head up and down. "Yeah, okay. But you responsible for this nigga."

"Chill, slim. He good."

When Daddy heard the man come out of the bathroom and toward the living room, he rose to his feet. When the man appeared, Daddy looked him over. The nigga stood around six feet two, with long cornrowed hair and a bush goatee. Daddy couldn't help but notice how built the man was.

"Smoke, this my connect I was tellin' you about," Frog said.

Daddy watched as Smoke walked up to him. Not only did he feel somewhat physically intimidated by the tall man, who stood eight inches taller than him, but his gut told him to get the hell outta there because something wasn't right.

"'Sup dawg?" Smoke said, extending his hand out to Daddy. "Like Frog said, my name is Smoke."

Daddy shook Smoke's hand. "Yeah," he replied, not really sure if he should reveal his name to Smoke, since he wasn't getting a good vibe from him. But then he thought, *why not*? He was sure Frog had already told him his name. "My name Roc, dawg," he said, sitting back down on the sofa. He didn't take his eyes off Smoke.

Frog sat back down and Smoke sat next to Roc.

"So, what's the deal? Are we straight on that?" Smoke asked, looking from Frog to Roc.

"Yeah," Frog said, as he looked over at Roc. "You gon' hit us tomorrow wit' those ten birds, right?"

Roc sat motionless and quiet, while staring adamantly into

Smoke's face. His eyes didn't budge. It was as if he was peering through Smoke instead of at him. Then abruptly, Roc popped to his feet and produced his Glock 40 from his waistband.

"Slim!" Frog called out. "What's up?" He stood up from his chair.

"Somethin' ain't right about this nigga!" Roc piped, with his gun pointing down on Smoke.

"Hey Frog, get'cha man, dawg!" Smoke barked, with his hands in the air.

"Hey Roc, everythin' good, dawg! You just sniffed a lil' too much of that shit and it's made you paranoid. I put my word on him dawg, he good."

Roc reached down and flipped the coffee table over. "Hell nah," he shouted! "This nigga ain't right."

"Roc, you lunchin'," Frog exclaimed. "I wouldn't bring no hot nigga to you or no stick-up kid. I don't fuck wit' niggas like that."

"You know what? Fuck this shit." Roc walked backwards all the way to the front door. He took his eyes off Smoke and onto Frog. "You remember a while ago when I told'cha I don't know how much longer I'ma be hittin' you off?"

Frog nodded.

"Well, I'm done. That's it for me." Roc peered at Smoke. "And if I were you, I'd pay that nigga wit' a ten foot pole."

Roc made it out to his BMW and drove off quickly. His mind was going faster than his car was. He made up his mind to do something that he'd contemplated and planned to do months ago, quit his drug hustle. He knew that it would be the end to not only his drug game but his sex with the twins; but just like the saying goes, all good things must come to an end. He was willing to accept the end to his hustle, but not giving up sniffing that highly additive white girl.

# NINETEEN

Smoke sat behind the wheel of the burgundy Lexus LS 460 that he got from the seized cars impound lot that Agent Santos hipped him to. While Smoke sat waiting for his two young runners to exit the liquor store, he thought about what happened to him just a week ago. He was still angry about the whole ordeal that went down with Frog and Frog's connect. But, Smoke had to admit to himself that even though Roc might've been coked up and tripping, the fat nigga was on point about his accusations.

That night, Smoke had been wearing a wire that the Feds concealed on him. He was there that night to take Frog's connect down but nothing went as planned for the Feds or for Smoke.

For five days after that night, the Feds tailed Roc. During those days, he didn't showcase any illegal activities, nor did their investigation result in any illegal prior activity. Although he had pulled a gun out on Smoke and Frog, that wasn't enough to make a conviction stick. Besides that, the only thing the Feds had on tape was Roc's declaration saying that he was giving up selling cocaine so the Feds eradicated him altogether.

The Feds turned their attention to Frog, and four days after that night, they raided his apartment and confiscated two guns and one kilo of crack. But what they didn't know was that Smoke had purchased two kilos from Frog the next day after that night. Frog didn't like the way things went down with Roc, so to show Smoke how sorry he was about what happened, he went out and got three kilos from some other nigga he knew and sold two of the three to Smoke. In turn, Smoke distributed it to two youngsters that he recruited from 21st Street.

The down side to the entire ordeal was that Frog had gotten locked up and would probably due some time; he had to give the Feds their money back since the drug deal went bad; and lastly, he had to find someone else to bring down in the game.

The passenger door of the Lexus opened, and one of Smoke's seventeen year old young'uns hopped into the car, breaking his thoughts.

"Smoke, that nigga Lil' Ant in there fuckin' wit' a bitch. I told that nigga to come on," Scoop, his older worker said.

Smoke squinted up his face. "That nigga lettin' a bitch hold him up, huh?"

"Yeah," Scoop's faced beamed, "But I ain't gon' lie. She phatter than a ma'fucka, slim."

Smoked nodded his head. "Oh yeah?"

"Yeah, she gotta be about twenty though."

Changing the subject, Smoke inquired. "Y'all get the bags to bag up y'all shit?"

"Yeah." Scoop patted his pocket.

"I got that bitch number," Lil' Ant said, entering the Lexus.

Smoke looked into his rear view mirror at the sixteen year old youngster. Lil' Ant was the wildest of the two. Smoke had met him first, and the way he did so was memorable. Smoke had been taking out the trash one night from Cherry's apartment, and in the hallway of the building he bumped into Lil' Ant getting his dick sucked by a woman, who he later found out was a crack head. Lil' Ant and Smoke made eye contact, and Smoke went back into the house without even dumping the trash.

The next day, he spotted Lil' Ant and they talked. He put him down with his game and Lil' Ant agreed to work for him, but not without informing Smoke that if he put him on he'd have to put his homeboy Scoop on too. He did.

Smoke pulled in front of a building on 21st Place, where Lil' Ant lived with his mother. "Listen, we got a key left after y'all push that on. So, don't be out here bullshittin', rollin' up in these hoodrat bitches cribs, smokin' weed, playin' X-Box and all that shit that ain't gon' put no money in y'all pockets." Smoke made eye contact with Lil' Ant from the rear view mirror. "Go 'head and get that money."

As soon as Lil' Ant stepped out of the car, Smoke looked over at Scoop and said, "I know it's only one-thirty and the sun out this joint, fryin' a ma'fucka, but Scoop make sure y'all try to push that whole ounce today. Don't let that nigga lure you into none of those bitches cribs. Fuck them hoes, they only fuckin' wit' y'all because y'all gettin' money. If y'all were to get locked up and have to do time in Oak Hill, them bitches wouldn't even write y'all or nothin'. Y'all would be out of sight out of mind."

Scoop nodded his head in agreement. "I know you tellin' the truth. If anybody know the deal about being locked up, shit it's you. You did time in the Feds, right?"

"Yeah, young'un. I was in the Feds in New York and believe you me, bitches dog a nigga out when he in."

Lil' Ant crawled back into the back seat of the Lexus after running out of his building. He handed Smoke a rubber band, wrapped wad of cash. "It's all there, $9,950."

"Y'all niggas fifty dollars short, but y'all my young'uns. Y'all good." Smoke smiled at him. "I'll see y'all tomorrow."

He watched his two workers climb out of his car before he pulled off, heading to Cherry's apartment. As soon as he got there, he gathered all his money up and counted it. He had $50,000 cash, plus one kilo and an ounce left worth $35,000, after paying his young'uns off.

He put all his money into a small safe and placed it under the bed and stared up at the ceiling. He thought about what his next move would be. He knew he was going to move Cherry into a house and his mind was already made up about her quitting her job at Tyra's salon. As a matter of fact, he was planning on telling her he was giving her one month tops to quit when she came in from work. But there was one move he hadn't really thought about much but he knew he had to; doing his job as a CI and getting the Feds one more, big dog in the game.

It would be easy for him to get the dude he was now going to purchase his shit from since Frog was locked up, but he couldn't do that, he needed him. So, the only person that came to his mind was that bitch he hated. He had to get to Tyra's man but first he needed to find out what the nigga was into; the first person he had to question for a lil' more info was his baby girl, Cherry.

# TWENTY

Tyra stood behind her station finishing up her customer's hair. Although the salon was filled with voices, her face displayed a radiate smile probably because she was getting pipe laid to her on a regular basis by Def.

Breaking out of her thoughts, Tyra took a step back and sprayed Jill's hair.

"I'm done, girl," Tyra uttered, as she spun the chair around so Jill could look at her hairdo in the mirror.

"I like it," Jill said, with a kool-aid smile. "Tyra, everybody knows you are the bomb, but girl, please make sure you hook up my friend that came here with me. I've been bragging about you for two months. She's even dissing her regular hairstylist to come see you."

Tyra peeped over in the waiting area at the lady Jill was referring to. "She's cute. I see she has short hair, so I know I'ma lace her up."

"She's into that novel she's reading so let me go over and tell her it's her turn," Jill said, rising from her seat.

Tyra greeted the woman that came up to her with a handshake and a warm smile.

"Hi, I'm Tyra. Welcome to Laced Hair Salon." She allowed the woman to sit in her chair before throwing a black cape around her.

"My name is Glory," the woman said. "Jill has told me so much about your shop that I just had to try it out."

"Thanks for givin' my salon a chance. I hope I can satisfy you," Tyra said.

"You don't mind if I read this novel while you do my hair, do you?"

"No, not at all. How do you want your hair?"

"It's short, so do it in any sleek style that you think will fit my face."

"Okay. By the way, what's the name of that book you readin'?"

"*Double Life*. I swear this book is a replica of my past. One of the characters even has my name."

"That's how those books are," Tyra said, preparing to start on her client's hair. "They have a lil' bit of everybody's life in em'."

Fifty minutes later, Tyra was almost finished with her hair. If it wasn't for the sexual conversation that consumed the shop, which had the attention of every woman in attendance, she would've been done.

"I don't care what none of y'all say, I think havin' a man wit' a big dick is better," Alisha, the youngest hairstylist said. She was sassy and five two, but the most noticeable, physical thing about her was the deep dimples that exploded when she smiled.

"I agree," Brandy, another stylist, exclaimed. She was the fattest of all the women, but everyone liked her. She was the type of woman that found beauty in everything and everyone. "Y'all know wit' all the fat I have on me, he has to have a big one to reach my sugar."

The shop erupted with laughter.

"A lil' one or a big one, I don't care. As long as I can get one," Ms. Cat, who was a hairstylist said. She was every bit of 49-50, and a mother figure to all the girls. She wore her hair partially bald. Her body was slender and tight for her age.

"I don't really like a big one or lil' one. I like a medium one," Tonya said, who was the last stylist Tyra had hired. She was only twenty-five, and already was the mother of five kids, ranging in ages from four to eleven. Having all those kids cost her once petite body to transform into a thick one.

"Girl, you shouldn't even be lookin' at no more dicks, cause every time you look at one you end up pregnant," Shonda uttered from across the room. Shonda was the only nail technician Tyra had hired. She was what some women called a fake bitch and that's what she was literally. She had fake breast, had fat injected into her lips to make them fuller, and had a nose job. She even had green contacts in her eyes. She had liposuction done to her waist and thighs and it was also said, but not proven, that she had an ass implant. That was the only surgery she denied she had and when someone would bring that up, she'd let them know they were just jealous.

"Shonda, don't start no shit up in here today," Lil' Nikki, the shampoo girl, piped. The lil' before her name represented her four foot eleven inch height. Though she was in her twenties, she looked like a teenager.

"Well, I'll tell y'all this," Alisha began, "If you lay your man on the bed on his back, and grab his dick and bend it back towards his stomach, and the head of it don't land on his navel, your man got a short dick."

The shop exploded into ear piercing laughter.

Five minutes later, Jill and Glory paid their bills and headed out the door satisfied with their services.

After the girls completed their last customers for the day, they all paid Tyra their monthly commission fee and left for the night. As usual, Tyra and Cherry were the only two left inside to close up the shop.

Tyra moved her mouse around, staring into her computer screen when Cherry walked into her office to hand her the day's receipts. She quickly tallied them up and logged them into her computer.

Looking up from the screen, Tyra stated, "I'm a'ight, Cherry. You can go 'head home. Just make sure you lock the door on your way out," Tyra uttered, as she watched her friend walk up toward the front of her desk.

"Tyra," Cherry muttered. "I wanna ask you somethin'. I don't mean to be all in your business or nothin' though."

Tyra noticed Cherry's face had turned beet red. "What's up, girl?"

"Um…you told me a while back Def got you this salon, right?"

Tyra shook her head.

"Well, you never told me what he does for a livin'."

Tyra stared at Cherry with a shocked look. She saw that Cherry wasn't looking her in the face. "What'cha mean?"

"You know. How did he get the money to buy you this shop? Is he in the drug game or do he have a legit job?"

Tyra leaned forward in her chair. "Cherry, why you askin' me this?"

Cherry shrugged her shoulders. "I just asked that's all. I don't mean nothin' by it."

Tyra looked at Cherry with a strange expression on her face. She couldn't figure out why Cherry was asking her about Def's line of work. Besides, she had sensed all day that something else was bothering her friend.

"Cherry, what's botherin' you girl? You've been actin' strange all day. Is there somethin' else you wanna tell me?"

Well, what I really wanna tell you, I know you ain't gon' like it."

Tyra frowned. "And what's that?"

"Don't be mad, but I'm quittin'."

"What?" Tyra shouted.

"I'm sorry, girl, but I just don't feel like workin' no more."

"Cherry, you gotta be kiddin' me, right?"

"Nah, I'm serious," she whined.

"Sorry, you…" Tyra became mute, something came to her. There was no way Cherry would just up and quit on her. It had to be something wrong, and the more she sat and pondered she knew why her friend was quitting. "It's Smoke, ain't it? He put'cha up to quit, huh?"

Cherry shook her head. "No, I'm doin' this on my own. I…"

"You lyin', Cherry. You don't think I know that Smoke back in the game? He must be tellin' you he got'cha, huh?"

"No. No. Well."

"Well what? I'm right ain't I?"

Cherry nodded her head.

"Cheerrryyy!" Tyra slurred her friend's name. "The whole time he was in jail, you were doing for yourself. Ain't nothin' wrong wit'cha continuing to do that."

"I know, but I don't have'ta no more."

"Cherry, we should never let a man do everythin' for us. If we do, then we make ourselves handicap, and when he's gone, our handicap becomes apparent to the world. Trust me, I know and you should, too."

"I'm sorry, Tyra."

"That you are."

"What's that suppose to mean?" Cherry had a hurt look on her face.

"You know what it means!" Tyra snapped.

Cherry stared at Tyra coldly. "You know what? It's easy for you to tell me to do myself and all that other stuff. But I ain't the one right now who owns a salon, drive a Benz, and live in a beautiful townhouse. You are! Your man did good by you, so why can't you let my man do good by me?"

"Cherry, our situations are different."

"What, you can't stand Smoke and y'all don't get along and me and Def cool and we get along? You know what, Tyra? I love you and you always gon' be my girl, but right now I'm gon' make my own decisions." Cherry handed Tyra a piece of paper. "You already have my cell number. That's the number to the house me and Smoke moved into yesterday and the house address. I'll be here later in the week to pick up my last check." Cherry walked out of the office.

Tyra sat stunned. All she could do was shake her head and say to herself, *That nigga got her fucked up.* Then the phone on her desk rang. She picked it up and read the number. She smiled and said, "Hi Mom."

"Hey baby," Tyra's mom, Jada said.

Two days after arriving back in DC from New York, Tyra's mom had phoned her. That phone call permitted them both to express their hurt to each other. They shared tears and laughter, telling one another all they'd done in the time they weren't speaking. But most of all, they reconciled and were now back in their rightful positions as mother and daughter.

"Did you lock up the shop yet?" Jada inquired. She made it a habit of checking up on Tyra between eleven-thirty and twelve, the time she knew her daughter would be closing her shop.

"Not yet," Tyra replied, as she began gathering her things to leave. "I'm doin' it as we speak."

"Okay, call me when you get in."

"Oh Mom!"

"Yeah baby?"

"Remember you were tellin' me about your friend that got fired from the nursing home y'all work at?"

"Yeah."

"Well, tell her I'll hire her tomorrow if she shows up. Tell her to come at twelve noon."

"That's good baby. Carolyn was just tellin' me how bad she needed another job. Okay, I'll tell her first thing in the mornin'."

"Bye Mom. I'll call you when I get in."

Tyra locked up her shop and headed home. As she drove, listening to the sounds of old school Whitney Houston, she thought about Smoke.

She couldn't believe he was still controlling Cherry's life in the manner that he was. Boy, did she hate that nigga. It was no secret that they didn't like one another. The question was who didn't care for one another the most? If someone would've asked Tyra that, she would've answered, *I hate him more*. He was taking away from her the one and only true friend she had, and she didn't like that. So maybe, it was time to do something about her dislike for him?

Tyra snapped out of her train of thought when she looked into her rear view and spotted a car behind her with its high beams on. There wasn't any fog out, so there was no reason for the person to have them on. The lights were so bright she couldn't see what make the car was. Deciding to ignore the obnoxious driver, she turned her music up a notch and continued to drive. Then, five minutes later, she looked into her rear view again and the bright lights were still there. She now became concerned. It was possible that she was being followed, but by who?

She glanced over in her passenger seat at her tote bag, where her .38 rested. Looking back into her mirror again, the bright lights were now gone. There was no car directly behind her. She shrugged her shoulders and focused back on the road. Ten minutes passed and she was pulling into the small complex where her townhouse was located. But, before she could pull into the parking space in front of her home, flashing radiant lights shined from behind her. Someone was trying to get her attention. She quickly pulled into her parking space, turned off the car, retrieved her gun from her bag, and held it up against her leg.

She took a closer look at the car that was flashing its lights at her and saw that it was Def's Porsche. She smiled, placed the gun back into her tote bag, and locked her ride. She watched him as he headed in her direction. She was feeling him to the tenth power.

Ever since they'd become intimate, she couldn't get enough of him. She craved him more than she wanted to admit. No more pretending they were a couple; it was official, they were a real item now, although neither of them actually told one another they were.  A man and woman couldn't have sex with each other three times a week and not consider themselves a couple. It wasn't ethical. Plus, they were going out on dates when Tyra wasn't working. They were either in love or on their way to falling in love, yet, the question still lingered in Tyra's mind; how long would it be before one of them deterred from what they were feeling and lashed out like a poisonous snake?

# TWENTY-ONE

Smoke sat in the front seat of his Lexus talking with his two young runners about business. "Y'all know I moved, so shit changin' just a lil' bit. Instead of me givin' y'all an ounce at a time, I'm givin' y'all an eighth of a brick at a time. I can't be goin' back and forth to my spot to hit y'all off. Y'all already know how much to bring back." Smoke reached under his seat and pulled out a ziploc back of crack. He passed it to Lil' Ant. "Do y'all thang. Call me in two days and let me know how y'all doin'. I gotta go take care of somethin'."

A half hour later, Smoke climbed into the passenger seat of Agent Santo's yellow Range Rover.

"'Sup Rico?" Smoke said.

"Hola Poppi." Agent Santo ran his eyes over Smoke's clothes. "I see you doin' good for yourself, huh'?"

Smoke nodded his head. "I'm doin' a'ight." He looked down at his white t-shirt and platinum chain.

"Okay, what'cha got for me buddy?"

Smoke shook his head. "Nothin' right now."

"Nothin'. C'mon Poppi. You with this for a reason. You supposed to be gettin' us one more big dog. Now give me somethin' to tell my boss."

Smoke wanted to reveal to Agent Santos what he'd been brewing, but he couldn't. He didn't' have anything on the nigga yet. Shit, from the way things were going at the moment, it looked as if he wouldn't' find out anything on him at all. It seemed to him that what he'd done the other night turned out to be a waste of time. Well, mostly a waste of time. At least now he knew where his girl laid her head. He had followed Tyra home that night and the way he had tailed her, she likely didn't have a clue who was behind her with high beams on. He had even seen when the Porsche pulled behind her and tailed her home. For the first time, he had seen her boyfriend, who Cherry told him went by the name Def.

"So, what's up with the dude you buyin' your stuff from now since you got'cha man Frog bagged?" Agent Santos smiled.

Smoke didn't find what he said amusing. He wondered whether Agent Santos was speculating about him buying coke from some dude, or did he really know. Not wanting to antagonize the agent, Smoke said, "I have somebody I'm lookin' into right now, and it ain't who I cop from."

"So, when you think you gon' have somethin' for us?"

Smoke shrugged his shoulders. "Soon I hope." Smoke opened the passenger door. "I'll get in touch wit'cha when I have somethin' for you."

"I hope that's real soon!"Agent Santos yelled, after Smoke walked away from the truck.

Smoke had already smoked two blunts before he parked his ride in front of a building on Chesapeake Street. He punched a number into his phone and waited.

"Hello?" a woman answered.

"Can I speak to Chocolate?"

"This me. Who this?"

"Smoke."

"Oh, what's up Smoke? You finally called me, huh'?"

"What's up? I'm in front of your buildin'."

"Stop playin'," Chocolate barked!

"I ain't playin'."

Chocolate's phone beeped, and she said, "Come on up. You know my apartment number." Click.

It was only moments before Smoke made it to Chocolate's door where she stood dressed in nothing put a pair of white thongs and a bra. Her hair was pulled back into a slick pony-tail that accented her chocolate, young face. As she talked on the phone, she held her index finger up to her lips signaling Smoke to be quiet.

He walked into the apartment. Chocolate locked the door behind him, pointed to the living room sofa, and motioned for him to sit down.

Smoke's eyes roamed over her body as she chatted on the phone. He licked his lips partially because Chocolate looked like her entire body had been dipped in a pot of fudge, but mainly because his mouth was dry from smoking weed.

"I swear, I sent that visitin' form out about two weeks ago. I wouldn't lie about that, you betta holla at your lazy ass counselors.They ain't doin' their fuckin' jobs. Anyway, Cumberland, Maryland ain't that far from the city," Smoke heard Chocolate say to the person on the phone.

Smoke's antennas went up. *She must be talking to Frog,* he thought

"Who you talkin' to?" Smoke mouthed silently, when she looked his way.

"Frog," she mouthed back.

Smoke's heart dropped. Since Frog had gotten locked up, Smoke often wondered did he have any idea that if it weren't for him, he wouldn't be in prison. There was only one way to find out what Frog thought or knew, and that was to talk to him.

"Let him know I'm here," Smoke whispered.

Chocolate shook her head, no.

"Why not?"

"Hold on for a sec, Frog," Chocolate said, and placed her hand over the mouth of the phone. "What's up? Why you want him to know you here?"

"That's my man? I'm tryna holla at him. I haven't talked to him since he been in."

"Hello, Frog. Somebody wanna holla at you." Chocolate passed Smoke the phone.

"'Sup nigga?"

"Who this?" Frog asked.

"Smoke."

"Smoke? Oh, what's up nigga?" Frog piped excitedly.

Smoke instantly knew he didn't have a clue he was behind

him being arrested. If so, he wouldn't have sounded so thrilled to hear from him.

"What the fuck you doin' over Chocolate's crib? No, hold up. You ain't gotta tell me, it don't matter anyway. We both know how broads are especially when a nigga locked down. So what's up? How you doin' out there? Shit a'ight for you?"

"I'm good, slim," Smoked said, as he watched Chocolate rise from the sofa and prance towards the back of the apartment.

"Shit fucked up in here, dawg. And a nigga got fifteen years to do in this ma'fucka."

"Damn, slim, they hit you wit' fifteen?"

"Yeah, and that was a plea. You know a nigga had a few felony priors."

"What's up? You need some money?"

"C'mon, you know niggas always need money."

Beep!

"I know what that sound means," Smoke said.

"Yeah, this phone is about to hang up. Slim, give that to Chocolate to send to me. She good for it, she'll send it and give her your number to give to me. I know you gon' fuck her, so make sure you fuck the shit outta her for all the niggas that's…"

The phone went dead. Just as it did, Chocolate walked back in the living room and plopped back down on the sofa. She held a lit Newport in her hand.

"You smoke them cancer sticks, huh'?" Smoke said, placing the cordless phone on the coffee table.

Chocolate giggled. "Boy, you don't smell that?" She took a puff of the cigarette.

"Smell what?" Smoke frowned up his face.

"This ain't just a cigarette. This a Newport dipped in water. This the dipper, angel dust, love boat, whatever you wanna call it. It's a cigarette dipped in embalming fluid. Where the hell you been?" She took another puff.

"I heard of that shit, but I don't fuck wit' nothin' but that hydro." Smoke grinned.

"That shit weak compared to this." Chocolate pulled hard on the cigarette.

With a wide grin still on his face, he said, "You know why I came over tonite?"

Chocolate grinned sexy-like at Smoke. "I know why you came over. You want some ass."

"You right, but I literally want some ass."

"You ain't said nothin' but a word. I can cum gettin' hit in my ass just like I can my pussy."

Smoke stood up and reached into his pocket. "Frog wanted me to give you some money to send him. He told'cha how much time he got, right?"

"Yeah, five years."

"He told'cha five years, huh." Smoke thumbed through his bankroll. "He lied to you. Dude got fifteen years. He just told me that. You know niggas gon' keep it real wit' niggas. He gon' lie to a bitch cause he don't want you to bounce on him."

Chocolate gazed at Smoke crazily.

"Now that you know he lied about his time, cut him off. Get a block on your phone and get what'cha was gettin' from him from me. You know you was only fuckin' wit' him cause he was holdin' some bread." Smoke handed her some money. "That's six hundred. Do you, but if he call before you get the block on and ask about the money, tell him it's in the mail."

Chocolate pulled on her dipper, inhaled, then slowly blew smoke out though her nose. She smiled and said, "Y'all niggas ain't shit!"

Smoked placed his money back in his pocket, unbuttoned his jeans, and allowed them to fall at his ankles. "Bitch, come suck this dick and get him hard, so I can run up in that ass."

Chocolate put her dipper out in the ashtray then dropped to her knees. She pulled his boxers down and took his dick into her right hand. She stared up into his face and said, "I want'cha to fuck me in my ass hard too."

"Bet," Smoke assured, as he watched his dick vanish between her lips.

An hour and a half later, Smoke entered into the door of he

and Cherry's new house on Wisconsin Avenue. He was immediately greeted by a happy-go-lucky Cherry, who threw her arms around his waist and smiled into his face.

"Hey Poo," she uttered.

Smoke threw his arms around her and smiled. "What's up? You real happy today, huh?"

Cherry squeezed his waist tightly and pressed her face against his chest. "Yeeaahh," she said.

"Why?" Smoke asked.

She let go of him and took a step back in her playful mood. Cherry looked real good to him, even though less than two hours ago he had his dick deeply rooted in another woman's butt hole.

"I'm happy because we live in a house, you takin' care of me, and we got all this." Cherry pointed in the direction of the well furnished rooms.

Smoke surveyed the living room. He had gone all out and bought every piece of furniture Cherry had picked out when they had gone furniture shopping. He had to admit he loved her, and it probably wasn't anything he wouldn't do to please her. But, at the moment, he had something on his mind and he needed answers. As he sat down on the sofa, he motioned for her to sit on his leg as though she were a child. She did.

"What's up, baby?" Cherry questioned.

"I know you told me Tyra didn't give you no info on her man the night you quit, but I need to know somethin'."

Cherry rolled her eyes and sucked her teeth. "Smoke, you startin' that again. I told you she didn't tell me nothin'."

"Yeah but I need to know what that nigga livin' like."

"Anyway, you never told me what exactly you want from him."

"Cherry, that ain't none of your business. You don't need to know all that."

She gazed at him with an evil eye. "Why you gotta talk to me like that, Smoke?"

He huffed. "Look, I wanna find out what Tyra's man is into, so I can get some coke from him. I was just thinkin' maybe I can get a cheaper price from him bein' that I'm your man and you and Tyra are friends."

"Well, I don't know what he's into, Poo. Plus, me and Tyra haven't really talked since I quit. When I picked up my last check, she acted like she had an attitude wit' me."

"So, what'cha think I should do cause I gotta find a cheaper price then what I'm gettin'."

Cherry shrugged her shoulders. "I don't know, but I have an idea."

"And what's that?"

"I know you and her don't get along, but just call her and tell her what's up. All she can say is her man ain't into sellin' drugs or you have to talk to him about that. Her number is pinned in the corner of the vanity mirror on a piece of paper in our bedroom."

"I can't talk about that over the phone."

"You don't have to. Just call and ask her can you stop by the shop to holla at her."

"Nah, I ain't tryna holla at that bitch." Smoke shook his head.

"Well, that was just my suggestion."

Smoke sat and thought for a second. *I might just do what my Boo suggested. What do I have to lose? I'll just call her up and not tell Cherry. She has no idea about me followin' Tyra home the other night and she doesn't need to know about this either. Hopefully, if they talk, Tyra won't reveal it to Cherry, no matter which way things go down.*

"So, that's dead. You not gon' do that?" Cherry asked breaking Smoke out of his thoughts.

"Nah, I'll just have to get wit' some other nigga. Anyway, I don't wanna put no more money in that nigga pocket so his girl can continue to outshine my girl." Smoke grinned broadly. He ran his hand along Cherry's meaty thigh.

Cherry smiled. "So you gon' make it whereas she ain't gon' keep outshinin' me, right?" She placed her hand over his bulge that grew rapidly within his jeans.

Smoke nodded his head. Then he thought to himself, that if Tyra did decide to tell Cherry about what he was up to, by the time Cherry found out, Tyra's man would be behind bars somewhere in the Federal pen.

Before Smoke could emerge from his thoughts, Cherry had already unzipped his jeans, taken his dick out, and was lying flat on her side. She massaged him with her hand. "Why your dick smell like Dove?" She ran her nose along Smoke's shaft.

Taken back by Cherry's question, Smoke thought, *this some psycho shit. How she know what the fuck different brands of soap smell like?*, although he knew she was right. With a puzzled expression on his face Smoke replied, "I went to the gym to workout. I don't know what type of soap they have in their dispensers. What, you questionin' a nigga now?"

Without another word, Cherry slid Smoke into her mouth and worked him good like she always did. So good that she had him moaning her name as if it were a hit song.

# TWENTY-TWO

Tyra stood antsy in front of her mother's apartment door. They had reconciled their differences over the phone but had not met face to face. They spoke yesterday and decided that they would meet at her mom's place where she grew up.

Tyra placed her royal blue Celine handbag on her right arm and looked down to check her appearance one final time. Seconds later, she knocked on the door.

"Hey baby!" Tyra's mom walked up to hug her before she could say a word.

Tyra stood there with her arms clenched to her sides. With her chin over her mom's left shoulder, her eyes became glassy. She hadn't felt her mother's embrace in over five years. It felt good, so good that she didn't mind if her mother's embrace lasted all day.

Jada pulled back, her hands grasping Tyra's arms. "Look at you, baby. You're so beautiful." She embraced Tyra again. "I'm sorry, baby. I miss you so much."

"I miss you, too, Mom," Tyra retorted. Tears started to drop from her eyes, and when her mom pulled back again, Tyra saw that her mom was crying also.

"Look at us," Jada uttered, smiling. "We out in this hall cryin' like two fools. It's a good thing we don't wear a lot of make-up or we'd be lookin' like two goblins. C'mon in here, baby."

Tyra stood stunned as she looked around the living room. It looked nothing like it did when she lived there. The ugly, raggedy flannel sofa that was the only piece of furniture in the living room was replaced by a butter soft leather sofa and matching love seat. There were also new curtains and the carpet was super clean. The apartment actually smelled of fresh fruits.

Jada walked up beside her daughter, who still had tears rolling down her face. "I know, it looks nothin' like it used to. It even smells good in here now." She threw her arm over Tyra's shoulders. They both giggled from the truth of her words.

Tyra wiped her eyes and said, "It's a far cry from what it used to look like in here. You did a good job, Mom."

"Thank you, baby. I just wish I could've done this a long time ago."

Tyra gave her mother the once over for the first time since she stepped foot into the apartment. Jada had put on between ten to fifteen pounds in the last five years. But that didn't hinder her good looks. She still possessed that cocoa brown skin and long wavy hair, just like her daughter. Frankly, if Tyra hadn't known first hand that her mother was an ex-dope fiend, her mother's appearance would've never told her so.

"Mom, you put on a lil' weight, I see," Tyra said.

Jada ran her hands along side her hips. "Yes, I did and it all went straight to my ass." She turned around and smacked her ass with both hands. "I had a little trouble gettin' my tail in these jeans I have on now."

Tyra hadn't expected the visit to go so well. Not that she thought it would be a disaster, but she had no idea, judging from the strain of their past, that ten hours later they would still be together. By eleven o'clock, they had danced, cooked a meal, ate dinner, and watched two movies.

Before Tyra departed, she peeked into her old bedroom, which she hadn't done the entire time she was in the apartment. She couldn't believe the room hadn't changed. The same bed she slept in before she left was there, but had brand new linen on it. A small radio sat on top of an eight drawer dresser that she used to listen to 'til the wee hours of the morning, even when she knew school was only hours away. Posters of R&B singers and rappers were plastered on the walls around the room.

"Baby, your Mama loves you," Jada said to her daughter, as Tyra stood at the front door, preparing to leave. "I'm so sorry for not accepting you in when you needed me the most." Jada stood in front of Tyra with her hands holding the sides of Tyra's face. "Please tell me you forgive me." A single tear found its way down her face.

"Mom, don't cry, I forgive you. I understand. Anyway, you should be all cried out. Both of us have been cryin' all day." They laughed.

Tyra drove home in a state of bliss. She couldn't stop smiling even if she wanted to. She and her mom were now fully reconnected, something she'd wanted for years. As she drove, she wanted to share her excitement with someone else. So, she pulled up to a stop light, whipped her cell phone out, and dialed Cherry's cell phone. Allowing it to ring only once, she hung up. She knew Cherry wouldn't have known it was her who called because her number was unpublished. She could thank G for that.

Though she wanted to share her happiness with Cherry, they weren't on speaking terms. As a matter of fact, the last time she had seen Cherry at the shop when she had come by to pick up her last pay-check, Cherry acted as if she didn't even know her. But, Tyra thought as she dialed another number, she and Cherry would be speaking again soon. That was her friend, and no drug dealing ass nigga was going to prevent that.

"Def," Tyra uttered, once her call was answered.

"Tyra, what's up?"

"I'm just leavin' my Moms."

"How'd it go?"

"You can't hear it in my voice?"

"You sound happy."

"I am. We hit it off good. Everythin' went good. I'm so happy, Def."

"I'm happy for you."

"Happy enough to stop what'cha doin' and come over to my house?"

"I can do that. I ain't doin' shit but watchin' some old throw back boxin' matches."

"Okay, come in about forty minutes."

"A'ight.

When Tyra got home, she called her mom to let her know she made it in safely. After making herself an apple martini, she proceeded upstairs to take a shower, slipping into a see-through, flaming red negligee with matching silk thongs.

As she stood in front of the mirror, she admired her beauty. Her Brazilian features were undeniable.

The sound of her doorbell ringing startled her. She quickly smeared cherry lip gloss over her lips and headed downstairs.

When she made it to the front door, she stood in front of it and fixed her hair in such a way that it sprawled out over each side of her shoulders. She looked through the peephole to make sure it was Def.

"Damn, you look…"

"Shh." Tyra hushed Def by placing her index finger up to his lips. She grabbed him by the hand and drew him into the house. "Don't talk," she said as she pushed his back up against the door. She could tell that Def was confused by the look in his eyes. Tyra raised his shirt and slid his gun from his jeans, passing it to him. "Hold that."

Tyra dropped to her knees. Def couldn't believe that she was about to do something she hadn't done in the time they'd been having sex. The thought made his dick expand rapidly.

"I'm feelin' generous tonite," Tyra said, with a smirk. She looked up at Def from her knees. As she fondled with his sagging balls, she saw that he was about to speak. "Shh, don't talk."

She let her left hand continue to fondle his balls while her right gripped his manhood. While working her magic, she glided her tongue from the bottom to the top and back, finally expanding her mouth to accept his dick in full force.

Def moaned for seven minutes straight! Tyra sucked him off as if she were trying to prove a point and when she suddenly stopped and rose from her knees, Def stared at her in bewilderment.

"Tyra, please don't…"

"Shh!" She stuck her finger up again. She smiled broadly. "Don't talk, I said."

Tyra took a step back, reached under her negligee, and slid off her thongs. She sat them on top of Def's throbbing dick. She giggled, causing Def to do the same.

"I'm goin' upstairs. I want'cha to come up in a minute, and have all your clothes off, too." Tyra turned and sashayed towards the stairs.

When Def made it to her bedroom, they both were naked. She sat at the foot of her bed with her legs parted, showcasing her goodies. Def moved up to her and fell to his knees. He knew what she wanted; something he hadn't given her since they'd started sexing. Def spread her legs further apart, bent his head down, and begin to feast.

"Oooohh Def! Oh my God! Your tongue is so hot," Tyra sung, just before Def raised his head.

"Shh!" He looked at Tyra saying, "No talkin', just enjoy." They both smiled.

Def pushed Tyra back and threw her legs in the air. He did this so that he could use both his hands and tongue to work her over. She got the hint and ten minutes later, she was having convulsions from a powerful orgasm that shot through her body. When her turbulence ended, she pushed Def's head away from her drenched pussy and begged for him to enter her.

Confused, Def asked, "You don't want me to put on a condom?"

"No, just put it in me, please," Tyra begged. "Please Mr. William Davis." Tyra smiled because she knew Def didn't like to be called by his government name.

Def shot to his feet, his dick in his hand. As he drove it into her slowly, she squealed. He was so warm, thick, wide and broad, filling her up to capacity.

"Do you…you feel that heat?" Tyra asked.

Def heard bits and pieces of what she said, but her insides had him traveling out of space. She felt so warm, so slippery, yet tight. So damn good. It was as if his dick and her pussy were meant to be.

"Ah! Ah! I'm 'boutta cum again, Def. Oooohh! Oooohh! Oooohh!"

Def felt her walls constricting around his penis. When he was sure her orgasm was complete, he slid out of her. He looked down at her limp body.

"Are we done?" he asked smiling.

Tyra sat up. She didn't say a word. She took him into her mouth, sucking away her juices. When she was done, she stood up, and turned around placing both knees on the bed. Def placed his hands on Tyra's ass cheeks, spreading them apart. He moved his pelvis forward letting his body guide him into her soaked pussy. She grunted when she felt his thickness invade her. She looked over her shoulder at him and saw that he was watching himself go in and out of her. That turned her on, so she thrust her ass back, meeting his strokes.

Def took that as a challenge and sped his strokes up, causing Tyra to try to keep up with him. She couldn't, he was moving at the speed of a jackhammer and before long, he exploded inside her after she yelled out to him that he could. Afterwards, they showered together and spooned under Tyra's fluffy comforter. They both fell asleep to the sounds of *Fantasia*, playing softly in the background.

# TWENTY-THREE

The sex had been so good that hours later, it was still having an effect on Tyra. Def had worked her over, not just last night, but an hour before she had opened up the shop. She could still feel his hot tongue lapping away at her kittycat. Tyra was glad she didn't have any clients right now because her mind was in pleasure land, and if it wasn't for Alisha breaking her out of her thoughts, she would've continued to savor their sexual escapades.

"Let's get Tyra's opinion. Tyra, what'cha think about Lil' Kim goin' to jail a few years ago and not snitchin' on her friends? You think she should've told?"

Tyra looked around the shop. It seemed as though all eyes were on her, even the eyes of three women that had their heads under dryers.

"I don't think nothin' about her goin' to jail. I don't really care, but I like the fact that she didn't tell though. That's big for a girl. Niggas can't even keep their mouths shut these days. You see how all those so-called gangsta ass niggas ratted on her. So no…no, I don't think she should've told. She represented for the ladies. And now we got one up on the fellas wit' they tellin' asses."

The shop exploded into applause.

The ringing of Tyra's cell phone interrupted her laughter.

"Hello."

"I have reservations for us to stay at the Wynn Hotcl in Las Vegas…you game?"

Tyra scanned the salon sneakily, she didn't want the women who were still laughing at her last comment to notice the huge blushing look on her face. "Well hello, to you too," she said to Def, who was on the other end of her phone.

"The shop closed tomorrow and Monday, right?"

"Mmm hmm."

"We leave tonight. I already have plane tickets. Hey, you think you can get Ms. Carolyn or one of the girls to close up for you? We gotta be at the airport at six, our flight leaves at seven."

"Yeah. That shouldn't be no problem." Tyra looked at her watch.Ten after two. "So, you'll be pickin' me up from my house at five?"

"Yeah, in a cab."

"Okay."

"See ya."

The moment Tyra closed her phone it rang again. "Hello."

"Um…um. Can I speak to Tyra?"

Tyra frowned. She didn't recognize the masculine voice. She took the phone from her ear and scanned the number. She wasn't familiar with it.

"Who is this?"

"Um…Tyra, don't hang up."

The raspy voice came to her at once. It was Smoke, her enemy.

"This is Smoke. I'm tryna holla at'cha."

"Holla at me about what?" Tyra barked. "And how in the hell did you get my number?"

"Calm down. You…"

"You don't tell me to calm down, niagga…" Tyra sprung to her feet and headed toward her office. Out the corner of her eye, she could see the women in the shop staring at her. "You might be able to tell Cherry what to do but not me." She made it into her office and plopped down in her chair behind the desk.

Smoke huffed. "Look, I ain't tryna make trouble."

"You called here didn't you?" Tyra snapped.

"Yeah, but I called in peace."

Tyra sighed heavily. "How you get my number, Smoke and what do you want?"

"I got'cha number from off a piece of paper and I wanna ask you somethin' 'bout your man."

Tyra frowned. "Ask somethin' 'bout my man. What about him?"

"I don't wanna talk about it on the phone. I wanna meet'cha somewhere."

"Meet me some…" Tyra stopped what she was saying when something crossed her mind. Her opportunity to do something about her dislike for him was present.

"Tyra, you still here?" Smoke asked.

Tyra took a deep breath to calm herself down. She was angry that Smoke was on the other end of her phone. But now, she had to suppress her anger if she wanted her opportunity to get at him.

"I'm here," she said calmly.

"Okay, I thought'cha had hung up on a nigga."

"Do Cherry know you callin' me?" Tyra shut her eyes, hoping to hear what she wanted too.

"Nah, she don't know I'm callin' you."

Tyra smiled. "So, where you wanna meet at?"

"I can come to your shop."

"Nah, let's meet somewhere else."

"Okay, how about we meet up at the Farmers Market? That's not too far from your salon."

"Okay, by the way. How is Cherry doin'? You know me and her haven't talked in a minute."

"I know. She a'ight. That's my baby, she good."

Tyra rolled her eyes. "I'll see you in what?"

"Twenty or thirty minutes," Smoke said.

"Bye." Tyra hung up and sat back in her chair. She knew what she wanted to do, but she wasn't sure how or where to carry out her plan. She leaned up, grabbed her tote bag from off the desk, and sat it in her lap. She dug into it, pulling out her .38, which she carried just about everywhere she went. Def had told her to do so just in case someone tried to retaliate on her for being a part of G's team.

As soon as she locked everything up in her officc, she made her way to all the stations, telling each person that she'd see them on Tuesday.

When she got to Ms. Carolyn, the woman who had taken Cherry's place, she said, "Hey, Ms. Carolyn." She stood in front of the counter, looking down on the heavyset, brown skinned woman who sat in a rolling chair.

Ms. Carolyn looked up with a smile. “Hey, Ms. Young.”

“C’mon now Ms. Carolyn, I told’cha you can call me Tyra. You one of my Momma’s best friends.”

“I know. I know, I know.”

Tyra handed her the keys to the shop. “I need you to close up for me tonite. Is that a’ight?”

“Sure. I can do that.”

“Okay, I’ll see you Tuesday. Have a good weekend.”

Tyra walked out of the shop headed to her car. While she walked, she thought about Ms. Carolyn. She liked the middle-aged woman from the second she had hired her. She was polite, kind, easy to get along with, and a hard worker. It had been plenty of times following the shop’s closing, that she and Ms. Carolyn would just sit and talk.

When Tyra got into her car, thoughts of how she would entrap Smoke came to her. She stared down at her clothes. She wore Stiletto heel thong boots, a blue jean skirt, and a scoop neck white shirt that exposed her entire neckline. She smiled into the rearview mirror. *I know how I’ll get him, seduction. S*he grinned as she sped off.

When Tyra parked her car about a half block from the outdoor market, she sat and watched. She hadn’t realized she was a tad bit nervous until she got out of her car.

With her tote bag’s straps snug upon her left shoulder, Tyra treaded through the hustle and bustle of the market. Although she had on her dark shades, she could see men of diverse races checking her out. Conscious of the fact, she popped up her swagger, hips swaying seductively.

‘May I help you?”an old, pudgy, gray haired white woman asked Tyra when she stepped up to her stand of raw vegetables and fruits. The old woman had a smile on her face as big as the state of Texas.

“Yes,” Tyra said. She picked up a peach that looked to have been injected with steroids. It was the size of a baseball.

“You like ‘em big, huh honey?” the old woman said.

Tyra smiled. “You can say that. How much is it?”

"One for seventy-five cents, but you can get two for a dollar twenty-five."

"She'll take two," Smoke stated standing behind Tyra. He handed the old woman a five dollar bill and picked up a peach for himself. "You can keep the change."

"Well, thank you, young fellow."

Tyra and Smoke walked side by side along the market talking.

"So, what were you sayin' on the phone?" Tyra inquired, while cutting her eyes over at Smoke. He sported a fresh new pair of Nike Foamposite sneakers and a platinum chain around his neck.

"You know I'm in the streets, right. So, I was thinkin' maybe I can get a better deal on my coke from your man than what I'm gettin' now. You know, since you and Cherry friends and all."

Tyra stopped, causing Smoke to do the same. She turned, faced him and looked up into his face. He looked at her, but he couldn't see her eyes that were hidden behind her dark Chanel shades. She raised her peach up to her mouth and bit slowly into it. Juice trickled over her bottom lip and onto her chin.

"Oops," she muffled with a seductive grin that she could tell moved Smoke. She wiped her mouth with the back of her hand.

"Maybe you should've taken a smaller bite," Smoke said grinning.

"I like to take big bites of shit…not small ones."

"I see." Smoke raised an eyebrow.

"Smoke…" Tyra chewed the rest of the peach in her mouth and swallowed it. "I'm sorry, but the dude you callin' my man ain't in the game. He ain't no drug dealer. He a boxer, a prize fighter. I don't know if you keep up wit' boxin', but that's what he is."

Smoke looked confused. "He ain't in the game at all?"

She shook her head. "Nope."

"Damn! You ain't lyin' to me, are you?"

"Don't have to. You know I don't fuck wit' drug dealin' niggas no more. Cherry didn't hip you?"

"Nah." Smoke threw his peach to the ground, which he hadn't even bit into.

"Let's walk to my car," Tyra told him.

She leaned up against the driver's door of her whip, while Smoke stood a foot or so in front of her, absorbed in her beauty.

"I don't know how you gon' take this, but the reason why I had so much animosity toward you was because I always liked you but, Cherry had you. Truthfully, I think you can do better than that. Cherry my friend and all, but you and I both know she ain't got shit on me." Tyra grinned wickedly.

Tyra's words hadn't registered to Smoke completely, and the expression on his face was an indication of that fact. He looked baffled and confused. He ran his eyes all over Tyra's body.

"Smoke." Tyra waved her hand in front of him. "Smoke to earth, Smoke to earth, come in."

"Yeah, yeah, yeah, I'm here."

"Did you hear what I said to you?"

"Yeah I heard'cha. I just can't believe you said it."

"Well, I did. So what's up?"

"What'cha want to be up?"

"Plain and simple. I wanna fuck you."

Smoke swallowed hard. "What'cha gon' do? Tell Cherry after we fuck?"

"I don't kiss and tell." Tyra looked at her Gucci watch that read three thirty-one. *Damn, I gotta make this shit quick. Def gon be at my crib to pick me up at five sharp,* she thought to herself. "I know this cheap motel we can go to out PG that's low-key. I'm not a motel type bitch, but I'ma do this one time."

Smiling, Smoke said, "I'll stay a few cars behind you."

They made it to the motel in under twenty minutes. The parking lot was relatively empty with a few cars parked sporadically throughout. Though they had come there together, their cars were parked quite a distance from each other. Smoke picked up his cell phone and dialed Tyra's cell. Recognizing the number, she answered the call without allowing him to speak.

"I know you use to dominatin' shit, but let me take control of this. I ain't Cherry," Tyra said into her phone. "I want'cha to go pay for the room, but I want'cha to get it for a day. After you get the room, I want'cha to call me up and tell me the room number. Go in the room and get ass naked. Leave the door cracked slightly so I can just walk in. As soon as you're naked, lay stretched out on the bed on your back."

Smoke chuckled. "You serious?"

"What, you think I'm playin'?"

"Cherry ain't tell me you was like this."

"Hmph, she don't know. Now go get the room." Tyra hung up and breathed a sigh of relief. She thought he would reject her orders, but he didn't. Tyra could see from where she sat in her car, Smoke get out of his Lexus and walk towards the check-in window.

"Room 21," Smoke uttered into his phone after paying for the room.

"I'll see you in a minute," Tyra said, before quickly closing her phone.

Ten minutes had passed before Tyra was slithered into Room 21. She pushed the door shut with the heel of her boot. She glanced around the hazardous looking room before directing her attention to the queen sized bed that Smoke lay naked on. She smiled nervously at him, while she moved up to the foot of the bed. Her eyes moved in the direction of his dick that stood stiffly in the air at full attention.

"I hope you like what'cha see, cause what'cha lookin' at is what got'cha girl doin' anythin' I tell her to do." Smoke smiled confidently.

Something clicked in Tyra at that moment. She felt a surge of anger go through her body from Smoke's comment. Her face, no longer depicted nervousness, but rather ruthlessness. She reached into her tote bag and whipped out her .38. She aimed it down at Smoke.

He instantly sat up. His face showed concern. "Tyra, what's up wit' the gun?"

"Cherry don't need a nigga like you in her life. You wanna control her and keep us from bein' friends. Plus you a drug dealer! I know wit' you bein' dead, she gon' be crushed, but she'll get over it in time."

Pfff! Her first shot hit him in the stomach, causing him to grab his abdominal area. Smoke panicked when he held his head down and noticed the blood. Pfff! Tyra let another bullet loose, hitting the top of his head. She watched his body slump forward, then on its side. Wasting no time, Tyra quickly found Smoke's jeans and took his cell phone from out his pocket. She used a napkin to remove the phone from his pants. She didn't want to chance anything. Def had trained her well. She made her way out the room with her head held down low. She was confident she wouldn't be fingered as the last to be seen leaving Room 21 because the cheap motel didn't have cameras.

But something strange happened just before Tyra reached her Benz. She heard her name being called; she didn't dare turn to acknowledge the voice though. She swiftly hopped into her ride and sped off. She reached her townhouse around twenty minutes before five. She would've made it home a minute or so sooner, but she stopped on the highway and tossed Smoke's cell phone off the bridge and into the water.

By the time five o'clock rolled around, she had taken a quick shower, dressed, and packed three different outfits. When Def showed up in a cab, he made Tyra leave her cell phone, as well as her bag behind. He told her the two day vacation was for them and he didn't want it interrupted and as far as outfits went, they would buy what they wanted on the Vegas strip.

# TWENTY-FOUR

When Tyra made it home a little after eleven on Tuesday from her trip to Sin City, she knew she wouldn't make it to the salon to open up for business. She decided to phone Ms. Carolyn and ask her to open the shop. After that, she checked her messages on her cell. There were messages from her mom, G and Cherry. She dreaded calling Cherry back because she knew what her song would be. By now the death of Smoke had likely reached her. She purposely procrastinated on returning any calls. Instead, she put away her many bags of pricey attire she brought home from her trip, undressed, took a hot bubble bath, and a well needed nap.

It was three o'clock when Tyra was awakened by the hip hop ringtone of her phone. "Hello," she murmured.

"You sleep?"

Tyra smiled. It was Def. "I was. What's up?"

"Nothin'. I thought you was goin' to work?"

"I was, but I changed my mind and got Ms. Carolyn to open up."

"So, you free all day?"

"Why?" Tyra grinned.

"I just asked."

"Is it that good?"

"Is what that good?"

"That thang that had'cha spendin' all that money on me in Vegas." Tyra chuckled.

"You got jokes, huh?"

"The truth hurts, huh?"

Beeep!

"That's your phone," Def revealed. "That might be G. I'll hit'cha back."

"A'ight," Tyra said, then clicked over.

"Chile, you're hard to get in touch with," Jada barked.

"Hey Mom."

"Hey baby. Where you been?"

"Vegas."

"You went to Sin City and didn't even take your Mama?"

"I went wit' a man, Mom." Tyra blushed.

"Oh."

Suddenly, Tyra's other line beeped.

"Mom, that's my other line. Hold on."

"No, that's not necessary. I'll just call you back."

"Okay, Mom," Tyra said as she clicked to the other line.

"Hello."

"What's up Vegas show girl?" G piped as soon as he got through to Tyra.

Tyra frowned. *Hell no! I know Def's ass ain't tellin' my business out*, she thought. "Why you call me a Vegas strip girl?" Tyra asked, inconspicuously. She hoped that Def hadn't told G that she dressed up for him.

"Cause you a girl and you were in Vegas. Why you ask? What's up?"

"Nothin'," Tyra quickly retorted, believing by G's reply that Def hadn't told him squat. "You was tryna get in touch wit' me while I was gone?"

"Yeah. I wanted to invite you to the birthday party I'm throwin' for my sis' next Saturday at this new club called *GO*."

"It must be real new cause I ain't never heard of it. I heard of clubs like Lux Lounge, The Park and Café Asia, but not *GO*."

"It's new.  It's in Bethesda, Maryland. You'll be there, right? At ten."

"Of course."

"Oh yeah, it's over. No more hits. Your job is done until somethin' new comes up. Hopefully it won't. You a business woman now." G stated. "So, you gotta live a business woman's lifestyle. Oh, before I go, you know I gotta fuck wit'cha, right?"

"What?" Tyra chirped. She sat up in bed.

"You know what's up. I remember a while back you tellin' me you wasn't feelin' Def. Now y'all goin' to Vegas like a couple and shit. Let me find out you in love."

Tyra exploded into laughter. "Boy, I know you didn't just go there. I ain't in love wit' nobody."

"Yeah, I hear you, but you can tell that shit to somebody that don't mind hearin' it."

Tyra was still laughing after G hung up. What made him make that kind of statement was beyond her. She wasn't in love with Def. She would admit that she did feel something strong for him, but she wouldn't call it being in love.

It was more like, *Yeah, that's who I enjoy fuckin' and I don't wanna fuck nobody else. He's good for me sexually but* being in love she wasn't and how could she? She was still dangerously in love with a dead man.

Tyra pushed each number into her cell phone slowly, as though she didn't want to make the call. She placed the phone to her ear and listened. It rung once, then twice, then three times.

"He…hello," a soft voice said in a muffle.

"Can I speak to Cherry?"

"This…this me."

"This Tyra, Cherry. You…"

Tyra's words were cut short from an earsplitting sob that shot through her cell. She took the phone from her ear and looked at it. When she placed it back to her ear, the sobs continued. Her heart dropped and guilt filled her body. Hearing her friend in such pain struggling to get her words out crushed her.

"Cherry, ca…calm down," Tyra coached.

"Tyyyrraa! Heee goonnee!" Cherry bawled.

Playing dumb, Tyra questioned, "Who gone, Cherry? Who gone?"

"My baabbyy! My baabby! Smoooke! Thcy took him! They tooook him! They took him away from meee!"

"Cherry, I'm gon' hang up now. I'm on my way over, okay."

"Okay, okay."

Tyra dressed quickly and ran out her house with her keys and cell phone. In minimum time she made it to Cherry's house. She stood uneasy on the porch of the house she had never visited until now. In her heart she knew that she was the cause of the sorrow that Cherry was feeling. After taking a deep breath and composing herself, she tapped on the door.

Cherry swung the door open and rushed to Tyra falling into her arms. With her head buried into Tyra's bosom, she cried her eyes out.

Sliding her hands along Cherry's back, Tyra uttered, "It's gon' be a'ight, Cherry. He's in a better place now. God will take care of him."

Cherry removed her head from Tyra's chest and looked at her with a puzzled stare. "I…I don't remember tellin' you he was dead." She licked her dry lips. "I told'cha they took him away from me."

*Shit!* Tyra cursed herself inwardly. Cherry was right, she hadn't told her Smoke was dead. Acknowledging her slip of the tongue, she swiftly countered with, "You didn't have'ta tell me he was dead. I knew. You wouldn't be cryin' the way you are if he was just locked up."

Cherry nodded her head in agreement to what Tyra said. "You…you right. They killed my baby." Cherry buried her head back into Tyra's chest and howled away.

It took Tyra almost an hour to calm Cherry down so she could talk to her about what she knew pertaining to Smoke's death and when Cherry, whose face was blood red and eyes puffy from crying, finally talked, Tyra found out that Cherry didn't have a clue as to what happened to her man. All that had been told to her by Smoke's relatives was that he'd been killed in a motel room out in Maryland.

Two days later, Tyra sat clothed in an all black Prada dress in the third row of pews at Smoke's wake. She sat two rows back from Cherry, who sat in the first row along with Smoke's family. Tyra listened to the mournful cries of family and friends throughout the funeral home. Strangely, out of all the cries it was one particular one that stood out to her, Cherry's.

Her friend had just sat back down from viewing Smoke's body. While doing so, she had even attempted to crawl up into the casket beside him and had to be restrained. Not even Smoke's aging mother could compare to Cherry's uncontrollable sobbing which caused Tyra to wish she hadn't taken Smoke out. But as she stood and followed behind the line that was making their way up to view the body, she told herself she had done the right thing. What was Smoke? A drug dealer, and he had received what a drug dealer was supposed to, death.

When Tyra stepped up to the black casket where Smoke lay, a feeling of accomplishment washed over her. It was her that had put him where he belonged. She wished she could open the white dress shirt he wore to witness where she had shot him in his stomach. So, she settled for looking at the good job they had done by patching the top of his head up where her fatal shot had landed.

Seated again, Tyra watched others tread up to the casket to view the body. At times while she sat, she wanted to go console Cherry, who was still crying her heart out and screaming Smoke's name at the top of her lungs. But just when she made up her mind to do so, Sam approached Cherry, bending forward hugging her. She hugged Cherry she and Tyra locked eyes. Tyra gave her a faint smile, and Sam gave her nothing. Tyra's eyes followed Sam as she walked back down the aisle. As they locked eyes again, Tyra smiled not faintly, but briskly with a wave of her hand. Still, Sam gave her nothing, not a wink, wave, nod, or smile. Tyra watched her strut out of the funeral home without glancing back and wondered what that was all about?

# TWENTY-FIVE

It was nine-thirty at night, and G stood with his back toward the grill of his Bentley. He stood proudly in the parking lot, gazing up at the gigantic, bright yellow banner that read: *Grand Opening*. He took his eyes off the banner to observe the crowd of people that were waiting in line behind the velvet rope to enter the new two story club. G nodded his head with a gratifying grin on his face. He'd done it. He was now the owner of a club. A club he name *GO* after the first letter of his first name and his sister's. What would his parents say to him if they were alive today? He could only imagine.

He glanced down at his Versace suit then tapped the hood of his car, signaling the woman that sat in the passenger seat to step out and join him.

"Tammy, I made it happen," G said, looking at the line of people making their way into his club.

Tammy grabbed his hand. She stared at the diamond stud in his right earlobe. "Yes, you did. And you should feel relieved after all that bullshit you went through just to get this club up and runnin'."

G shook his head and smiled down at Tammy. He smiled because she had become his number one, even though he hadn't planned on it. All of the women he was fucking had fallen to the wayside and now it was just Tammy. Someone he would've never thought would cause him to become a one woman man.

"You think you sista made it here yet?" Tammy asked G.

"Nah, I told her to show up at ten."

An hour and a half later, the VIP section of the club was jammed packed and off the hook. After revealing to Olivia, Def and Tyra that the club was his, G popped open over twenty $1,400 dollar bottles of Louis XIII de Remy Martin. He also showered his sister with expensive gifts, telling her they all were from the fifty or so friends and family members in attendance when they all were really from him. Hip hop blasted from hidden speakers throughout the room. Some people danced on the floor, while others sat along the silk-covered black sofas that gave the VIP section its casual appeal. The only person that was missing-in-action was Roc, who was an hour late.

G and Def sat slouched on one of the many sofas that filled the dimly lit VIP lounge. They both had drinks dangling from their hands. While they talked, they observed Tyra, Olivia, Tammy and Jill, who had Uncle Pete sandwiched on the dance floor.

"I'ma ask you this and keep it real," G began. "You in love with Tyra?"

Def grinned and shrugged his shoulders. "I don't know. I can't tell you I am or not."

G grinned. "You know if you in love or not. I have to admit, I'm in love wit' Tammy. Never thought that would happen, but it did."

"I hear you, slim. I just don't know. But I'll tell you this, I feel somethin' strong for her. But it's somethin' about her that's dark and vicious." Def squinted up his eyes, while he peered at Tyra, who was still dancing along with the girls and Uncle Pete. For a moment he was lost in his thoughts until G interrupted him.

"Let me skip the subject. Man, it's somethin' up with Roc. I don't know what the fuck it is, but that nigga is startin' to bug out. It's like he's paranoid or some shit."

"I noticed that, too," Def concurred.

"Matter fact…" G drew the sleeve back to his suit jacket to check the time on his diamond infested watch. "That nigga almost an hour and a half late. Where the fuck he at."

He'd gone all day without having his fix and the fact that he hadn't wasn't a big deal until now. It was bad enough it had become a part of his everyday routine, and now at a time when he wanted to suppress his urge for it, he couldn't. He knew that he didn't need to be under the influence when he showed up at the party, but he couldn't fight the urge much longer. He was no match for the psychological or physical hold it had on him. He knew that it would be better if he waited until he got to his destination to snort some coke so he quickly got dressed and headed out to meet up with his crew at Club Go, arriving there in record time.

Inside of the men's restroom, he inhaled the white girl up his nose while sitting on the toilet bowl. He held a piece of aluminum foil with coke in it in his left hand, and in his right, he dipped his pinky finger nail into the coke and scooped some up. Without a blink of an eye, he placed the coke up his right nostril and sniffed.

Roc threw his head back and pinched his nose rapidly. "Mmmm," he hummed.

Within a few minutes, he stood in front of a tall brown skinned man dressed in a black suit, before the threshold leading up to the second level of the club where the VIP section was.

"This part of the club isn't open tonight, sir," the man informed Roc.

"The VIP section is up here, right?"

"It is, but only this level that we're on is opened for patrons tonight."

"Check that clipboard in your hand and see if my name is on it."

The tall man ran his finger along the board. "And your name is?"

"Roc, nigga. Roc."

Smiling, the man said, "Oh, it's right here. I'm sorry for holding you up." He moved to the side and gestured for Roc to climb the short flight of steps.

When he made it into the VIP lounge, he noticed the music that was being played downstairs wasn't the same as upstairs. He also noticed several familiar faces on the dance floor. Roc spotted G and Def on the sofa and joined them.

"Where the fuck you been, nigga?" G shouted, handing Roc a drink as he sat between him and Def.

"Aw man, I got caught up wit' this bitch," Roc replied over the thumping music. He turned to his right and bumped fist with Def. "What's up, nigga?"

"You," Def said coldly, looking tipsy.

Roc grinded down on his teeth. The side effect of his coke usage was kicking in and he knew it. He took a gulp of his drink.

G stared at Roc strangely. He squeezed his eyes together tightly, then reopened them. He stared at the white speck on the tip of Roc's nose.

"G ain't tell you this was his club, huh?" Def boasted to Roc. "That nigga doin' it big."

Roc looked to his left at G. "This your club for real, dawg?"

G nodded his head yeah. "What's that white shit on your nose, slim?"

Roc's paranoia kicked in just as G finished with his question. He brushed at his nose as if his life depended on it.

"Hey y'all," Tyra shouted, leaping into Def's lap. She wrapped her arms around his neck and planted a kiss on his lips. "You drunk?"

Def nodded. "A lil', but I'm a'ight. Hey, here's your chance to meet Roc since you never met him face to face," he said, tapping Roc to get his attention.

Roc stopped brushing at his nose and looked Def's way. When he did, he and Tyra fastened eyes. Flashes of memories flooded his coked-out mind. Memories he hadn't thought about in years.

"I finally get to meet'cha face to face," Tyra piped, extending her hand out to Roc.

He leaped to his feet, quickly shook Tyra's hand, shouted that he had to take a bad leak, and briskly stormed out of the VIP lounge. G, Def, and Tyra sat looking at one another with strange looks on their faces; none of them able to get a read on what the fuck had just gone down with Roc.

Turning to G with Tyra still on his lap, Def said, "Damn, that nigga act like he just saw a ghost or some shit!"

Tyra smiled and stated, "Yeah. I guess a sista have that kind of affect on niggas."

Without thinking any further on the incident, they went back to drinking and partying.

Ten minutes later, Roc sat in his BMW, sniffing more coke. Beads of sweat covered his forehead. He kept swinging his head around, looking out his car window and into the club's parking lot. He was paranoid, and to him, he had a right to be. He was seeing things. He was seeing ghost that could actually talk. Coke wasn't known to do that to its users, PCP was. So why was it affecting him like this?

"I gotta get that ghost outta my life! I gotta get that ghost outta my life," Roc recited over and over, wide eyed. He started his car and recklessly zoomed out of the lot, but not without sideswiping a few cars along the way.

# TWENTY-SIX

Both she and Def were intoxicated but they made it into Tyra's townhouse safely from the club. It was a little after one o'clock in the morning, and Tyra and Def were stark naked, wallowing around on Tyra's bed playfully.

"Okay. Okay, you win," Def said, surrendering. He lay under Tyra who sat on top of his stomach.

"I told'cha you had more to drink than I did," Tyra chanted, grinning down on Def. She had her left hand pressed down on his chest, while her right rambled through his curly hair. "Now, you wanna answer my question?"

Def nodded. "Yeah."

"Okay." Tyra smiled briskly. "How many niggas have you killed and what's some of their names?"

Def stared blankly at Tyra, as if he was thinking. "I'll say around twenty."

She bit down on her bottom lip. "That's sexy, and just about all of 'em were drug dealers, right?"

"Yeah, just about all of 'em except for maybe two or three."

"What was some of their names, if you can remember?"

Def had that blank look on his face again. "I…um. I…um. I don't know if I can remember all of their names. Same of 'em I killed over eight, years ago."

Tyra started grinding her pussy on Def's stomach. He smiled. "Just name the one's you can remember." She leaned forward and tongue kissed him then sat back up.

"You gettin' turned on by this, huh?" Def asked.

Tyra nodded her head. Smiling devilishly, she said, "Mmm

hmm. Sure am."

"Uh…let me see. Don, Lil' Stink, Dread, Kevin, Steve, Red's, Chris, Roochy, Luke, David, Paul…that's all I can remember."

She bent down and tongued Def with intensity, and without forewarning, she slipped his hard dick into her soaked pussy. When she drew back from kissing him, he said, "Oh, I remember one more name."

"Who is that?" Tyra gyrated on top of Def slowly. Her eyes were shut and she had a pleasurable expression on her face.

"Dre."

Tyra's eyes popped open, but she continued to gyrate on his dick. "Who?"

"Dre. One of the niggas I killed named was Dre."

Tyra stopped moving. Her face had concern written on it. "Dre. Dre who?"

"I don't know. Just Dre. Some nigga that owed money that I had to put to sleep." Def grinned wickedly.

Tyra dismounted Def and sat on her knees next to him. "Dre from where?"

"Dre from here, DC." Def gazed at her.

Tyra said a quick silent prayer before saying, "What hood was he from? And what did he look like?"

"Hold up." Def sat up. "What's up?"

"Please Def. Just answer me," Tyra said sternly.

Def shrugged his shoulders. "Uh…I don't know. I'll say the nigga was 'bout five eleven or so, light skinned, and kind of stocky, with a lot of acne on his face. I believe he used to hang 'round Trin…"

"Shh!" Tyra placed her fingers up to Def's mouth. Her chin dropped to her chest. She shook her head. When she lifted her chin from her chest, she asked, "Whose hit was it on Dre? G or Roc's?"

"Definitely Roc's."

Tyra sprung from the bed and whisked toward the bathroom, with Def calling after her. She burst into tears before she could even reach the door. In a quick moment, she slammed the bathroom door, locked it, then sank into the corner next to the toilet. Tyra cried and cried. Though she could hear Def shouting her name, she ignored him.

The information he had just given her was life altering. The man she had been fucking for the last couple of months was possibly the one who had killed her first and only love. Though she wasn't sure, she knew Def was connected in some way to Cash's murder. Instantly, Tyra remembered she and Cash talking about Dre the night he was murdered. Her mind raced. G, Roc, nor Def were involved in selling drugs, she thought. Cash and Dre were drug dealers, and were both killed because of their association with drugs. So, why did Def have to take Dre out?

Tyra abruptly stopped crying. She knew that the questions she asked herself could only be answered by Roc. But in the meantime, she needed to start her investigation before she decided to kill who was responsible for Cash's death, and whoever was down with them.

Tyra scrambled to her feet and opened the bathroom door for Def, who was knocking on it. She threw herself into his arms and told him why she had locked herself in the bathroom. She lied, telling him that the dude Dre whom he had killed, was a childhood friend of hers. Def whispered to her about how sorry he was and Tyra let him know that she accepted his apology. But what she didn't let him know was that he would really regret it if he was the one who had murdered Cash.

# TWENTY-SEVEN

Cherry stood in front of the bathroom mirror in her panties and bra. She gazed into the mirror, as if she expected what she was looking at to change. Since the death of Smoke, Cherry had gone into a deep depression. So deep in fact, that she had thought about taking her own life. She had convinced herself that at least she would be closer to her man. Her physical appearance and mental state had been totally neglected as evident by the bags and redness of her eyes, along with her unkept hair and dramatic weight loss. She had barely eaten since the three weeks that Smoke had been deceased. Cherry hadn't even left her house since returning from Smoke's burial, and had no intention of doing so.

"Why?" she squealed at her reflection. "Why my baby!" Tears started rolling down her face. "Why when everythin' was…was goin' so good for us? Why?"

The sounds of someone knocking at the front door startled Cherry. She wiped the tears from her face and ran downstairs to answer the door. When she reached the door, she looked out of the peephole to see who it was.

"Give me a minute," she shouted! Cherry turned and made her way back upstairs to her bedroom. She slid on a pair of jeans and a t-shirt that read, 'We love you Smoke'. Stepping up to one of her dressers, Cherry stopped and pulled the first, second and third bottom drawers out completely and stacked them on the floor. The drawers were only partial drawers. The bottom and back of all three were missing, creating space for the safe that Cherry was triggering the combination to.

Click! The safe opened.

Cherry snatched the half kilo of crack from the top shelf of the safe that was packed in a ziploc bag. Before closing the safe, she eyed the stack of money that sat on the second shelf. After placing all three drawers back in place, she made her way downstairs to the front door.

"What's up, Cherry?" Lil' Ant and Scoop said in unison as they walked into the house.

"Again, like I told'cha at the funeral, I'm sorry about Smoke," Scoop uttered.

"Yeah, me, too," Lil' Ant concurred. His eyes shot down to the ziploc bag Cherry held. She had asked them for help at Smoke's funeral. While Cherry wasn't involved daily with Smoke's affairs, he had told her about his dealings with them in the event that something happened, she would know what to do. The only reason they hadn't stopped by sooner to pick up the package was because she had told them she'd call them when she wanted them to come.

"I don't really know anythin' about this stuff other than Smoke told me to get in touch with y'all." Cherry handed Lil' Ant the drugs which he quickly dropped into the brown paper bag he held. He smiled.

"Like I told'cha on the phone, we didn't owe Smoke nothin," Lil' Ant said, lying.

He cut his eyes over at Scoop who had a, *you lyin' ass nigga*, look on his face. "But we willin' to pay you for what'cha gave us."

Cherry shrugged her shoulders. "I don't care. I just want it out of here."

Scoop reached into his pockets and pulled out a knot of money. To be exact, the 10,000 that he and Lil' Ant owed Smoke. Before he handed the money over, he stared at Cherry, really noticing her sick look. So sick in fact that she looked like she was using the drugs herself. "You gon' be a'ight?" he inquired, passing her the money.

Cherry nodded her head sadly. "Mmm hmm. I'm just still grievin' that's all. I'll be a'ight, hopefully."

"What, you went on a diet after Smoke got popped?" Lil' Ant

blurted out.

Scoop tapped his boy to let him know that he was out of line for what he'd just said. He couldn't believe his boy was standing there like Smoke's death was a joke.

Cherry stared at Lil' Ant. Water built up at the rim of her eyes. Lil' Ant's words hurt her. His insinuation of her weight loss wasn't what stung. It was his last words that did it. *Smoke got popped.* Those were the words that had hit her the hardest. A single tear fell from her eyes. She raised her hand and pointed to the door. "Get out!"

Lil' Ant and Scoop shuffled to the front door.

"I'm sorry about that," Scoop said, while being first out of the door.

"I ain't sorry. Find you another nigga and move on!" Lil' Ant spat, before shutting the door behind him.

Cherry burst into a loud sob. She ran up to the front door and started pounding on it. The money she held fell to the floor, and was followed by her body. She sat lifeless, crying her eyes out.

At least an hour had passed and Cherry was still in the same position crying. If it wasn't for the hard pounding on the door, no telling how long she would've continued in her emotional state. She made it to her feet, wiped her face with her t-shirt, snatched the roll of money up from the floor and ran over to the sofa, placing it behind a pillow. She peeped out of the peephole and opened the door.

"Good afternoon to you ma'am. I'm Homocide Detective Sinclair, and this…" The dark skinned detective, who favored actor Samuel L. Jackson pointed to his partner and said, "Is my partner, Detective Brown."

"How are you doing ma'am?" The white detective extended his hand out to Cherry. "May we come in and have a few words with you?"

Cherry let go of the white man's hand and looked both men, who were dressed in black suits over. She didn't see any badges, so she said, "May I see y'all badges?"

Both men brandished their badges.

Cherry opened the door wider and allowed them in. She directed them to the dining room, where they all took a seat around the table.

"Ms. Moore, we're here to talk to you about Paton Washingon aka Smoke," the black detective said.

Cherry nodded her head.

"We tried to give you as much time as we could for you to grieve before we came over," the white detective said. Quickly, he pulled out a pocket size writing pad and pen from the inside of his suit jacket.

"We wanted to know if you've heard anything about his killing at all," Detective Sinclair questioned.

Cherry shook her head no followed by a crazed look.

"We have a few things we want to run by you. Is that okay?"

"Yes."

"Were you aware that Mr. Washington was a CI…Confidential Informant?"

Cherry shook her head with an even more confused look on her face. "What's that?"

"He was working for the Feds as a paid informant. He was what the streets call a snitch or a rat. He was released from prison early after only doing about three years of a ten year sentence. When he hit the streets, he was in contact with an agent by the name of Rico Santos. He was Mr. Washington's contact. That's who he gave his information to."

Cherry covered her face with her hands. She couldn't believe what she was hearing. Smoke, the man she had loved was working for the cops. The fact that he was didn't bother her. What bothered her was that she didn't pick up on it and he hadn't bothered to tell her.

"Ms. Moore, are you okay?"

Cherry dropped her hands from her face. Her eyes were glassy now. "So that's why y'all think he was killed?"

"We don't know, but it's possible."

"Do y'all have any type of leads?"

The detectives looked at each other. The white detective, Brown, spoke up, "Well, we don't really have anything of great significance, but we have something. You see, the agent that Mr. Washington was working with gave us a little information. He told us that since Mr. Washington was working for them, they made sure to sometimes tail his movements. It just so happens, the day he was murdered, he was tailed. Anyway, Mr. Washington was followed that day to a farmers market. There, he was seen talking to a young lady inside the market. But since the agent was stationed too far away, he didn't make out the woman's features. What he did tell us was that the woman had long hair and she was African-American or Brazilian. She was the last person seen with him.

Cherry looked at the white cop stupidly. "That's all y'all have?"

"Well, yes. Because the agent didn't stay around to witness anything else."

The black detective looked at Cherry. "No disrespect to you, but do you know if Smoke was faithful to you or not?"

"How many men are?" Cherry snapped. "I don't know, but if you say the agent saw him talkin' to some girl, then I guess he wasn't faithful."

"They were only talking. That doesn't constitute they were having sex."

Cherry stood up from the table. "Do y'll have anythin' else? If not, I have a few things I have to do."

Both of the detectives rose to their feet. They stared at one another.

"Oh yeah, and a man who worked in the market said he remembered seeing Mr. Washington and the woman standing by the driver's door of an expensive looking car, but he couldn't remember the make nor the color," the white detective said.

"So, what good is that?" Cherry questioned.

"None. No good at all." He handed Cherry a card. "If you hear anything, call us."

"Oh, and one more thing for the road," the black detective interjected. He stared Cherry in the eye. "And I'd like the truth on this. It's imperative. Was Smoke selling narcotics?"

Cherry dropped her eyes to the floor.

"We need to know in order to help our case Ms. Moore. We're homicide detectives. We don't give a shit about narcotics. Now help us out here, will you."

Cherry looked at the detective and nodded. "Yeah."

"Okay. Thanks for your time."

Cherry saw the men to the door. Afterwards, she stashed the money she had gotten from Lil' Ant and Scoop in the safe and grabbed her cell phone, which she had shut off three weeks ago, from her pocketbook. She dialed a number and the phone was answered on the second ring.

"Hello."

"Hey, Sam."

"Girl, it's about time you called me. I've been tryna get in touch wit'cha for weeks fo'real. You okay? How come you haven't been answerin' your phone?"

"I haven't been feelin' good. I'm still grievin'. I'm hurtin' so bad, Sam," Cherry said sadly.

"I know, but you gon' be a'ight. It's just gon' take some time. Cherry, now that I have you on the phone, I wanna ask you somethin'. Did any detective drop by to ask you anythin' about Smoke's death yet?"

"Yeah. Matter of fact, they just left."

"What did they say to you?"

Cherry explained to Sam what the detectives had revealed to her, and the one thing she had revealed to them.

"So, what'cha think about the girl? You know, like who was she, and what about the expensive car Smoke was seen talkin' to her in front of?" Sam inquired.

"I don't know. I don't know what to think about it. Most likely he was fuckin' her. I don't know, Sam."

"They said the dude that works at the market couldn't remember what kind of car it was or what color, huh?" Sam was saying more to herself than to Cherry.

"Mmm hmm. That's what they say he said."

"They told'cha the agent said the bitch had long hair and she was either African-American or Brazilian, huh?"

"Yep." Cherry squinted her eyes. "Sam, why does it sound like you know somethin' that I don't?"

It was a long silent interval between Sam's next comment. "Maybe I do, but the question is, are you gon' believe it?"

"I don't know. Maybe I will, maybe I won't. Try me and see."

"Okay, you asked for it. I hope you can handle it.

# TWENTY-EIGHT

Roc sat with his BMW idling. He glanced at the time on his Navigation screen that read eleven thirty-one. He pinched at his nose and made a hog's grunt with his throat. Less than one hour ago, he had danced with his white girlfriend, and she still had him high from her moves. He turned off the engine, surveyed the neighborhood, and made his way towards the house he had come to visit. There, standing on the dark porch, he surveyed the neighborhood again, and when he didn't see anyone, he banged harder than he should have on the door. In a minute or so the porch light came on and the door swung open.

"Nigga, are you fuckin' crazy?" one of the twins, Rita, snapped. She stood in the threshold of the door with one hand on her hip and a scowl on her face. She was barefoot, wearing blue jeans and a t-shirt. Her hair was braided in cornrows reaching her back.

"Why the fuck are you bangin' on the door like you the damn police!"

Roc didn't answer her. Instead, he turned and surveyed the neighborhood for the third time.

"Rita, who that at the door?" Cita barked from somewhere inside the house.

"Girl, you ain't gon' believe this. It's that nigga that sold us out. Daddy, he doesn't deserve to be called Daddy any more. It's Roc's black sellout ass."

Cita made her way beside her sister. She looked at Roc and smiled. "What brings you here, nigga?" she questioned, draped in a flower printed satin robe. It looked as if she had just gotten out of the shower. She had slippers on her feet.

Roc looked from one of them to the other. He hadn't seen

them in a while. And seeing the twins who favored the average rap video dancer, caused his nature to rise even when all the side effects of him using was at its peak.

"Nigga, we gon' shut this door on your ass if you don't speak up!" Rita snapped.

Roc pushed passed the twins and walked into the house with Rita cursing him out something terrible from behind. He cruised into the living room and squatted on the sofa. He watched the twins move in front of the coffee table. Rita was still cursing him out viciously.

"Your black ugly ass, dead wrong. You gon' sell us out then think you can just come up in here. You stay your ass right there!" Rita stormed off.

Smiling, Cita said, "You know she goin' to get a gun, right?"

Roc shook his head and stood up. He reached into his pockets and pulled out wads of cash, dumping them onto the table. "That's for sellin' y'all out. I know the last time I talked to y'all, I was supposed to cop some coke from y'all the next day." He pinched at his nose then continued. "But some shit jumped off and I decided to get out the game immediately. I…"

Clack! Rita pulled the hammer back on the chrome and black P89 Ruger. She extended her arm as she moved beside her sister. "Nigga, I'm not playin' wit'cha ass!" she piped, with the gun aiming at Roc.

"Rita, calm down," Cita said, pointing down at the money that covered the table. "How much is that, Roc?" she asked.

"Fifty thou. That's off the strength of not showin' up to pick that up."

Rita lowered her gun when she focused on the money.

"So, why you here if you out the game?" Cita asked.

"I need y'all help." Roc pinched at his nose and did that hog thing with his throat.

The twins stared at him strangely.

"Help wit' what?" Cita said.

Roc plopped down onto the sofa. He ran his hands over his head, in need of a haircut. "I um…I um. I got this problem, I need y'all to handle for me." He pinched at his nose. "You see. I got this um…this um…" He looked up at the twins, who were staring at him.

"I got this ghost that I need to get off my back."

The twins looked at each other and burst into laughter. "What the fuck are you talkin' 'bout, nigga?" Rita spat.

"Yeah, what the fuck are you talkin' 'bout, ?"Cita echoed her sister.

Roc sprung to his feet and paced along the length of the sofa. "It's after me. I'm tellin' you. I seen it again and it acts as if it's not after me when I know it is. It has to be. Why would it come back? Why?"

Sternly, Rita snapped, "Roc, what the fuck are you talkin' 'bout? You buggin' the fuck out now. What, you sniffed too much of that shit up your nose or somethin'?"

"Yeah, and can you please stop pacin' the floor like that. You givin' me a headache," Cita uttered.

Roc stopped in his tracks and eyed the woman. "Are y'all gon' handle my problem for me or what?"

"How we gon' help you if you up in here talkin' 'bout some damn ghost and shit?" Rita said.

Roc threw his hands over his ears, as though he didn't care to hear anything else the twins had to say. He shook his head vigorously, his hands still covering his ears.

"Uh-uh. Roc, what the fuck is wrong wit'cha, dawg?" Rita inquired.

Cita gazed at Roc and couldn't believe what she was witnessing. Roc had changed. He wasn't the same person they once knew and if she had to guess, she would say it was the coke that was doing this to him. Initially, when he appeared at the door, she smiled because she thought she would get some dick, but boy was she wrong. He was irrational, and what he did next really proved it.

He magically whipped out his Glock 40 and brandished it at both women. Rita reacted by doing the same to him by aiming her gun at him. "I'm tellin' y'all," he piped, it's after me! That's why it's on the team. Y'all…"

"Roc, get the fuck out!" Rita shouted. "Get out now and we gon' make like this didn't happen. Do you want a price over your head? If you don't get out now ma'fucka!"

"I'm tellin' y'all!" Roc was making his way out of the living room and to the front door, with his gun still aiming at the women. Rita was still aiming at him. "I thought y'all fucked wit' me!"

"Get the fuck out!" Rita fired a shot that she intentionally meant to miss. The bullet lodged into the wall, but it caused Roc to haul ass out to his car.

"I'll do this shit myself. But this time…this time ain't gon' be no comin' back," Roc was saying as he dipped from the curb and sped from the twins' block. His brake lights never flashed.

# TWENTY-NINE

Tyra had been cruising the neighborhood of Trinidad, for the past thirty minutes. She was determined that today would be the last day she went searching for him.

For a week straight she had been looking for a guy named TimTim, who at one time hung out with Cash and Dre. From the information she'd gathered from all of their street cronies, TimTim ws probably the only one who knew what had happened to Cash and why.

Tyra glanced at the time on her watch that read 7:15. She was becoming frustrated. She now felt that TimTim was ducking her. She knew that word had gotten to him that Cash's girl, Tyra, had been looking for him.

She pulled her Benz up to the curb, where a group of men stood. Two of the men approached the car.

"He ain't show up around here yet, huh?" Tyra inquired with a light smile, after rolling down her window.

"Nah, T. We told that nigga, what, two days ago, that you were lookin' for him. It seems like eery time you bounce, he show up," one guy said. He had the biggest nose Tyra had ever seen.

"Yeah, but like we told'cha, you know he got baby momma drama goin' on and that nigga duckin' 'bout three of 'em," the other guy said, who resembled *Flavor Flav*.

Tyra shook her head. "And none of y'all have his cell number or nothin'?"

"Nah," the men uttered in unison, then Flavor Flav said, "That nigga change his number like every two weeks."

"Hold up," big nose said. He was peering up the block. "You

might be in luck, that looks like his truck drivin' down towards us now. Yeah, that's that nigga."

The black GMC Yukon pulled up and stopped beside the two men who were now sandwiched between the truck and Tyra's Benz. The passenger window of the truck lowered revealing TimTim behind the wheel. Before stepping off, leaving TimTim and Tyra to converse, Flavor Flav turned to Tyra and said, "Let me get'cha card or somethin' so I can hip my girl to your salon." Tyra passed both men a business card.

Leaning over into his passenger seat in order to get a better look at Tyra and her Benz, TimTim smiled his approval. "Damn Tyra, you doin' it like that. I ain't seen you in a couple of years, and when I do you pushing a Benz sittin' on those thangs and rockin' the latest gear."

Tyra threw on a fake smile, but thought, *Nigga, I've been lookin' for you for days. I ain't got time for no small talk. I have questions to ask.*

I heard you were lookin' for me. What's up?"

Tyra leaned her head out of her window and peered up into the truck at TimTim. "I have some stuff I'm tryna find out and I think you have the answers."

"No problem. I'ma pull over and hop in your whip."

She watched him pull over and park. A brief second later, TimTim hopped his six foot, overweight, dark skinned body into Tyra's passenger seat.

"Damn girl, you lookin' good. Who that lucky nigga that got Cash's leftovers?"

It took all that Tyra had not to give TimTim a good tongue lashing. If it wasn't for the information she needed from him, she would've dug in his shit. But she couldn't do that, she needed to know what he knew. So she played along, smiling.

"Ain't nobody gettin' his leftovers. I ain't fuckin' nobody."

TimTim pushed a laugh out through his lips. "You can tell that shit to somebody else. Look what we sittin' in. You gotta be somebody's woman."

"I paid for this car wit' my money. I own a salon."

"You can drive while we talk," TimTim said, looking out the

window. "I don't want none of my crazy ass baby momma's to show up and see me sittin' in here talkin' to you." Tyra speed off. "So, you own a salon, huh?"

"Yeah, in Northwest. It's called *Laced Hair Salon*," she said proudly.

"How long have you had it?"

"Five or six months now."

"So, what's up? What'cha wanna talk to me about?"

"Cash and Dre," Tyra stated plainly. She was turning onto Florida Avenue.

TimTim stared out of the passenger window, as if he were looking at something specifically. "Damn, them niggas was my dawgs," he mumbled. "I miss those niggas."

"Who killed Cash and Dre?" Tyra questioned. She took her eyes off the road to look over at TimTim.

Gazing straight ahead out of the front windshield, TimTim began, "Man, I told Dre not to fuck wit' that nigga from the get go. But nah, he didn't wanna listen to me. It was supposed to have been me and him goin' in half to cop three keys for 40 g's. But when the nigga told him the deal came wit' gettin' fronted three keys and bringin' him back 60 g's, I backed out. I ain't never been into owin' a nigga money and since I backed out, I guess he hollered at Cash about it, and Cash went along wit' it. I had talked to Cash before they tried to get on from slim. He told me it was a sweet deal, so he was rollin' wit' it, even though he didn't know nothin' 'bout that chump."

"Did you know him?" Tyra quizzed, riding past Gallaudet University.

"Nah, I met him once before they copped from him."

Tyra felt a surge of waryness shoot through her. Since TimTim had revealed that he'd met the dude who Cash and Dre were dealing with, he had to know the man's name and what he looked like.

She asked, "What's his name and what does he look like?"

As if he hadn't heard her, TimTim continued to talk. "And I met him again after Dre didn't pay. That nigga kept comin' around askin' me had I seen him. I was like, I don't know where that nigga at. I ain't his partner. Then one day the word was out that Dre got slumped and when I heard about it, I knew that nigga did it or had somethin' to do wit' it."

"So, what was his name?" Tyra was becoming frustrated. Since she already knew that Def had killed Dre, she was eager to hear the guy's name who Dre owed money to.

Again, TimTim acted as though he hadn't heard her question and continued. "Then months later, that nigga approached me at a McDonald's and told me since I reneged on goin' in wit' Dre on that, I owed him 60 g's." TimTim turned and stared at Tyra. "Tyra, I ain't never been no go hard nigga and I knew I didn't have the money to pay him so I told him about Cash goin' in wit' Dre. He told me to let Cash know that he gotta pay up the 60 g's. I did. I told Cash. Cash told me fuck that nigga so I relayed what he said back to the dude, and after that, I ain't see him again." He took his eyes from off Tyra and gazed straight ahead. "Then a month later that shit happened to Cash."

Tyra's eyes were on the road but her mind was some place else. She couldn't believe she was sitting next to the man that had ratted Cash out to be murdered. If it ever was a time where she wished she had her gun with her, it was now, because she wanted to kill TimTim for giving Cash up.

She thought about driving him to her townhouse so she could blow his brains out. But for now, she needed to know the name of the man that fronted the drugs to Dre and Cash. She wanted to be one hundred percent sure before she took vengeance, because for some reason, she felt Dre and Cash were killed by different people. She didn't believe Def was responsible for murdering them both.

"What was the dude's name and what did he look like?" Tyra inquired, still traveling along Florida Avenue.

"The lil'…"

Those were the only words TimTim got out before the Benz abruptly jerked forward, giving him and Tyra whiplash. Someone had hit them from behind. Tyra quickly gained her composure and stared into her rearview mirror, slowing her car down and just as she did, the car that bumped her, pulled up to the passenger side. Before she knew it, the driver's window came down halfway, and out came a gun. Pop! Pop! That was the last thing she saw before the Benz skidded out of control, crashing.

When Tyra regained slight consciousness, she noticed she was no longer in her car, but she couldn't quite make out her surroundings.

Beep!...Beep!...Beep!...Beep! That was the sound Tyra heard right before her eyelids flickered a couple of times. As she regained her sight, she blinked twice, trying to adjust her eyes to the bright lights that were shining down upon her. When she felt her vision was steady, she allowed her eyes to survey her surroundings.

She looked to her left and spotted a woman, who looked to be her mother, asleep in a chair. Not accepting the fact, she closed her eyes then reopened them and still, she received the same results. She looked down at herself and noticed she was lying in a bed with tubes protruding from her arms. She raised her right arm and touched her nose, a tube was running from there also. Then it hit her. She was in a hospital, she had crashed her Benz.

"Mom!" Tyra said hoarsely, then looked at the machine that beeped. "Mom!" she said more clearly.

Jada's eyes popped opened. Though she was a little groggy, she could see it was her daughter who had called out her name. She and Tyra stared at each other for a hot second before Jada sprung from the chair and to her only child's side.

"My baby!" Jada piped while bending down, planting kisses all over Tyra's face. "You woke up!"

When Jada let up on some of her kisses, Tyra inquired, "How long was I asleep?"

"Baby, you were in a coma for three weeks. The doctor said you would pull through, but he didn't know when. He said he didn't know how you even got in a coma because you didn't rupture any-thin'. You came out of that accident with not even a scar."

"So, how did I get in a coma?"

"We don't know. The doctor said the only theory he could come up with is the pressure of the airbag hittin' your face must've packed a mean blow. Matter of fact, let me go get him."

Tyra watched her mother slide out of the room and re-enter with a short, Indian looking doctor. He smiled the entire time he examined her and when he finished, he informed her that she was okay and the tubes would be removed within thirty minutes or so and he'd sign her out tomorrow if her physical therapy went well.

"Mom, what's today's date and how is TimTim doin'?"

Jada's face saddened. "Baby, today is November 17th, and the guy that was in the car with you didn't make it…he died. He was shot. That was the reason why you crashed in the first place. Somebody shot at your car."

Tyra didn't smile outwardly, but she did inside. She wouldn't have to kill TimTim for ratting on Cash after all. *But who had shot at me*, she thought, then asked her mom, "You the only one been comin' to see me the whole time I was in a coma?"

Jada pointed to a chair to Tyra's right that was overflowing with cards, balloons, and small teddy bears. "All the girls at the shop stopped by. Oh yeah, and Ms. Carolyn kept the shop open because I told her to. And a few of your friends dropped by from time to time. Let me see if I can remember some of their names. Olivia, G and Tammy, Def and some other guy, I can't remember his name. He came by once, he was kind of strange too."

Tyra wondered who that could've been but thought little more of it. "Mom, my car totaled ain't it?"

Jada shook her head with a smile. "Nope, the police did their investigation on it, and released it back to G. He got it fixed, and I'm now drivin' it. Boy, is that car bad!"

"So, you gon' pick me up tomorrow in it, right?"

"Yeah, but don't be mad if I'm a little late doin' so." Jada smiled wickedly.

An hour later, all the tubes had been removed from Tyra and she was relaxing watching television. Jada had left over ten minutes ago. Just when she began to relax even more, she heard a tap on the door and in came two white men wearing suits. She immediately concluded they were detectives. Tyra was right; homicide detectives Stone and White, two men who looked too young to be enforcing the law.

They asked her a thousand and one questions. Most of their questions were about TimTim's murder. Questions like had she seen the shooter and things of that nature. But, of course, damn near all of her answers were no this and no that. But it was one question that one detective had asked before they departed that had Tyra thinking. Stone had asked her did she have any enemies that she knew of. That question had her pondering for several minutes after they left. Did she? Maybe she did, but the only person she really considered her enemy was dead. Smoke and dead men can't shoot at you. So who could that have been?

Although she believed TimTim had been the target, she wanted to know who was behind the shooting. So at that moment, she decided that she'd continue her own investigation into Cash's murder, and at the same time, find out who shot at her. But finding out who killed Cash would be her primary goal.

Tyra thought back on some of the names her mother had called out to her that had come to visit. She didn't recall hearing Cherry's name. She knew at least one person in the shop had phoned and told her what happened and yet Cherry hadn't shown up or called. As she thought on it further, maybe the dectective had asked a valid question. Did she have any enemies that she knew of?

# THIRTY

Tyra passed the physical therapy test with`flying colors and just as the doc had promised, he signed her out. She was making her way out through the sliding glass doors of Howard University Hospital draped in a fur jacket, and fur trimmed Prada boots. Tyra was exiting the hospital fresh to death thanks to her mom. With the clothes she wore the day of the crash and the gifts from well wishes inside of a shopping bag, she stepped over to a trashcan and threw them out. She didn't want anything that would remind her of her near death experience. Although that motto could've gone for her Benz as well, she wouldn't dare trash her baby.

She took a glance at the time on her watch. It was eight after eleven. Her mother was eight minutes late, and t she didn'thave her cell phone to call and see what was the hold up. She wouldn't dare risk the embarrassment of hopping on an outdated thing such as a pay phone. No one used those anymore, they were obsolete. So, she waited in front of the entrance of the hospital like a few others did.

Looking at the time again, she cursed. "Damn, it's twelve after eleven." Tyra wished she'd told her mom to get her cell from her house. However, if she had, her mom would've discovered her gun and she didn't want that.

Tyra huffed, wondering why her ride was not there yet. She remembered her mom telling her not to be mad if she was a little late, but she thought she was kidding. It was now obvious that she wasn't.

A black 745 LI BMW rolled up in front of Tyra. She peered through the window at the driver and recognized who it was behind the weel. Though she didn't know why he was there, she knew more than likely it had something to do with her. She watched the window lower.

"What's up, Tyra? I see you made it out okay," Roc said. His black, bearded face looked scuffed and beads of perspiration covered his forehead.

Tyra nodded her head. "I'm okay. What'cha doin' here?"

"Oh," Roc said, with a visibly forced smile, "I came to pick you up. G was busy so he asked me to come and scoop you up. He called me and said somethin' 'bout your Moms catchin' a flat so she couldn't make it on time."

*That's why she haven't showed up*, Tyra thought. She walked around the front of the car and got into the passenger seat.

Pulling off, Roc uttered, "I hope you don't mind, but I gotta stop and pick up some money for G."

Tyra nodded. "I don't mind. Do you have your cell on you?"

Roc shook his head. "I was in a rush and left it at the crib."

She stared at him suspiciously. How many people in this day and age leave home without their cell phones?

"I see you're still beautiful as ever despite the accident."

"Thanks," Tyra replied, then a thought came to her. *Why not come straight out right now and ask Roc about Dre. Def did say that it was Roc's hit on Dreand if I ask now, I can alleviate havin' to continue my investigationbut I wanna know more than I know he'll admit to. Ain't no way he gon' keep it real all the way around the board. I'm better off findin' out the rest of what happened from the streets. If he tells me that he gave the hit on Dre because he owed him money, that means either he, Def, or G was involved with sellin' drugs, because Dre was a drug dealer and whichever one of them is the drug dealer on the low, is more than likely the one who killed Cash.*

"Tyra!" Roc piped, breaking her thoughts. "I never thanked you for handlin' your business wit' that nigga, Def." Roc made a hog's grunt with his throat. He saw the look Tyra gave him but he continued. "You and that nigga together, y'all kill a whole block of niggas. Thanks for puttin' in that work."

Ten minutes later, Roc turned into a back alley of a neighborhood of row houses in Northwest. He came to a stop in front of a shabby fence that surrounded the house. He told Tyra he'd be right back then he exited the car.

She observed him walk into the fence then travel down about

four steps to the basement door of the house. When she saw Roc emerge from the basement, he had a blue backpack flung over his left shoulder, and what appeared to be a white washcloth in his right. She noticed he had a great amount of pep in his step and before she knew it, he was tapping on the passenger window, signaling her to roll it down. She did.

Roc let the backpack strap slide off his shoulder, down along his arm, then into his hand, where he flung it into Tyra's lap and when she lowered her head to look at the backpack, he swiftly took hold of her ponytail with his left hand, and with his right, smashed the washcloth that was laced with chlorofoam up against her face.

"Mmmm!" she wailed.

"Nightie night, bitch!" he bawled.

He was wide eyed as he looked on as Tyra struggled with what was happening to her. She kicked and clawed frantically. Her eyes were the size of two quarters staring at her attacker. Then, slowly but surely, her resistance subsided and she was out cold.

"Ahhh, that's right, bitch, go to sleep for daddy, I see now you're very real. You ain't no ghost after all. I fucked up that night, but it won't happen this time."

When Tyra awoke hours later, she found herself laid out on her back her wrists and ankles were tied to the four brass bed posts and her mouth was gagged.

"Baa...Baa!" Tyra spoke in a gibberish manner. She turned her head from side to side, squirming a little. She was trying to regain her vision, which was seeing double.

After a few seconds, her sight became better andshe was now able to focus more clearly and what she saw was a bedroom that looked to have gray, rocky, concrete walls and an old fashioned ceiling light fixture. The only sound that could be heard was the thumping of Tyra's heart and it wasn't until that moment, while listening to her heartbeat, that she looked down at herself and realized she was totally naked. Her heart sped up. Had she been raped?

"I timed it good," Roc said, as he made his way through the

room door. Tyra hadn't even heard him approaching. "You was knocked out for four hours just like the dude I got that sleepin' shit from, said you would." He made his way to the side of the bed, pinching his nose along the way. "I know you have a whole lot of questions, so I'm gon' stand right here and lay everythin' out to you without you askin' shit." Roc whipped out a tiny, brownish, Muslim oil type bottle and tapped some of the coke that was in it onto his hand. Sniff! The coke disappeared up his nose. He held his head back and pinched at his nostrils furiously.

Tears rolled down along the sides of Tyra's face, but she didn't speak. She didn't beg for her life, which she knew was at stake. At that moment she was more interested in hearing what Roc had to say. She had a feeling all of her questions about Cash's murder would be answered.

Roc dropped his head down, and he and Tyra locked eyes. He began, "First of all, I made your Moms late by flattin' the Benz tires. When G told me your Moms was gon' pick you up today, I stopped by her crib and stabbed a hole in the tires. I knew where she lived because I followed her after she left from seein' you at the hospital the same day I came to see you, and yeah, I'm the one that shot at'cha car, killin' that nigga, TimTim. I couldn't drive up to your side of the window because Florida Avenue is a two-way road. I was tryna get at you. I had my lil' cousin's Honda. You've been a ghost to me ever since I saw you at G's club. You were supposed to be dead years ago. I thought I killed you in that house. Yeah, that was me who killed your man, Cash, and the one who punched you in the face and left you to burn up in that fire.

"Your man brought that shit on himself. All he had to do was pay the 60 g's. That's right, I was sellin' coke behind G's back. I got Def to kill Dre under the pretense that Dre owed money. I told G the same, so he gave me the order to smash that nigga. But'cha man, Cash, I had to get him myself. TimTim told him what I said about my money and he said fuck me. So, after TimTim described Cash to me, I started layin' on him hard. I found out where his crib was and that was it. I knew how I was gon' get him.

"So, on the day I killed him, I followed him all day. When you and him stopped at a liquor store, I kept goin', headin' to your house.

I parked my car about three blocks from y'all crib. I climbed through the window y'all was stupid enough to leave unlocked. I waited behind the door until Cash came in. He had his gun out, but I had the up's on him. I took his gun and put it in my pocket and walked that nigga to y'all bedroom, where he said the money was. He cracked the safe, I bagged all the money that was in it, stepped him over to the bed, asked for his car keys, and told him to pull the sheets back. I told him to lie down on his stomach…again he listened. Then I shot him in the back of his neck and rolled him over, and placed the sheets over him. Oh, and I had a silencer on my burner, so that's why you didn't hear a gun shot. I was steppin' out y'alls bedroom when I heard you come in the house, yellin' his name. I quickly made my way to y'all bathroom and stayed there with the door cracked slightly. Then a couple minutes later, you climbed the steps and went into the bedroom, and that's when I made my move to y'all door and waited. I heard you scream loud as hell then the door popped open. I punched you in your face wit' a jab, knockin' your ass out. After that, I found two bottles of rubbing alcohol in y'all bathroom and poured both bottles all over y'all bed and lit that shit and jetted. I hopped in his Benz and peeled off. It wasn't until the next day that I came back for my car. Oh, and I sold his Benz to these car thievin' niggas I know. Oh, and his gun, well, I passed that off to Def. I think it was a chrome .38. A snob…"

Roc's words trailed off to Tyra. The mentioning of the .38 blew her mind. She knew at once that the gun she owned was Cash's gun. A faint smile slid across her face. Even in death her man was protecting her, just he had done when they were younger.

Now that everything was coming to her, she knew what the letters C&T stood for that were carved under the bottom of the handle of the .38, *Cash and Tyra.*

Roc tapped more coke into his hand and sniffed. Tyra gathered her emotions and tried to think of a way out of Roc's grasp.

"The only reason you gon' die tonite is cause of everything you know now. I was tryna get'cha at first cause I thought you was some type of ghost or somethin' tryna get at me for what I did to you and your man. I was buggin' out."

Tyra said something, but her words were muffled by the gag on her mouth.

Roc snatched the gag from her mouth. “Don’t scream bitch or I’ll kill you right now. Now, what’cha gotta say?”

“You don’t have to kill me, I’m not gon’ say nothin’ to nobody. What’s in the past is in the past.”

Roc stoopped down on the side of the bed and came back up with a black body bag. “You goin’ in this…” He slipped the gag back over Tyra’s mouth, just before she was about the scream. “Yeah, I beat you to it.” He smiled wickedly. “You expendable, we can always get another bitch to do what’cha was doin’ for us. Yeah, I know that nigga Def gon’ miss you cause he was fuckin’ you, but he’ll get over it.”

Tyra twisted and turned, trying to break free, coming to the realization that she was going to die. She yelled as loud as she could, although the gag softened her scream .

“Shhh! My grandmother upstairs, girl. We in her basement. She so senile, she doesn’t even know I’m down here, but that don’t mean her old ass can’t hear.”

Roc stepped over to the only dresser in the room, and withdrew a silenced .22 from his waist and placed it on top. Then he moved to the foot of the bed and stared down at Tyra’s nearly bald pussy. He recalculated the moment when G told him in so many words that Tyra wouldn’t fuck with him because he was a lil’ ugly nigga. That may have been the truth, but as it stood at the moment, he was going to get at the beautiful Tyra, whether she liked it or not.

He crawled up on the bed and positioned himself between Tyra’s widely parted, restricted legs. She raised her head and looked at him. Shaking her head no, as well as humming it, she fidgeted wondering what Roc was going to do to her.

“Relax,” he said, then flicked his tongue out like that of a snake. “I’m just gon’ eat’cha sweet pussy for now. I got much more planned for later though.” With his head an inch from Tyra’s protruding clitoris, he pulled her pussy lips apart to showcase her goodies. He flicked his tongue at it a few times. Then he placed his entire mouth on it and sucked. “Ah, your pussy is sweet. You had a chance to shower before leavin’ the hospital, huh?” Roc said, after releasing his mouth from Tyra’s pussy. “Look at it like this, at least you gon’ die tonite feelin’ good.” He laughed repulsively then stuffed his mouth with more pussy.

# THIRTY-ONE

G sat behind the cherry wooden desk in the office of his porno store. It wasn't often that he was even present at the adult establishment. He'd appointed, Nelly, a young, preppy, freckled faced, man he'd met through Jill as store manager years ago. However, today he had stopped by for a good reason. Nelly had phoned and informed him of the new black porn that had arrived and G always liked to view the DVD's in his office before taking them home. So for an hour now, he'd been watching male adult stars, such as Lexington Steele, and Mandingo plow the holes of female adult stars, such as Janet Jacme and Ayana Angel. His porno session came to a halt when the sound of his cell phone rang. He quickly lowered the volume on the television and grabbed his phone from atop the desk.

"Hello."

"Yes, hello…can I speak to G, please?" A feminine voice inquired.

"This me," G retorted, recognizing the Jada's voice. The hard on being suffocated within his jeans deflated slowly.

"Hi you doin' today?" Jada asked.

"I'm doin' fine," G answered, with a frown. He wondered why Tyra's mother was calling him. He'd only given her his cell number a week ago, during one of the days when he and Tammy visited Tyra in the hospital. He'd given her the number in the event that Tyra had awakened from her coma, so she could inform him.

"What may I do for you, Ms. Young?"

"I wanted to know if you've seen Tyra? I caught a flat tire this mornin', so I wasn't able to pick her up on time. I got there at twelve, but she was nowhere to be found. The doc that looked after her said he released her at ten-thirty this morning. That was the last he saw of her. But he also said that patients usually shower after taking a physical therapy test before leaving. He's guessing that's what Tyra did, so that means she didn't depart the hospital until eleven or a little after."

G flicked off the DVD player and sat up straight in his leather, highback chair. With a confused look on his face, he answered, "Nah, Ms. Young, I haven't seen her." G glanced at his watch, which read four o'clock. "So, she hasn't been heard from for about five hours now," G was saying more to himself than to Jada.

"Yep. No one's heard from her."

"Okay, Ms. Young. Let me make a few calls then I'll get back wit'cha if I hear anything and your number is?"

Jada gave him her number then said, "Okay, but as soon as you hear somethin' let me know."

"A'ight, I'll do that." G closed his phone and sat it back on his desk He slouched in his chair, his mind racing. He wondered where in the hell could Tyra be. *Maybe Def picked her up*, he thought. *Or maybe she could've made it home and didn't want to be bothered.* G snatched his phone up and dialed her cell number. It rung six times before her voice mail picked up. He left a concise message for her to call him when she could. He knew who he'd call to see if they'd heard from Tyra, but he decided he'd do that after watching the last few minutes of porn.

Def sat laid back with his feet propped up in the brown, leather Lay-Z-Boy recliner. Def and Old Man Bootney had been kicking it for nearly an hour now in the comfort of his bedroom. While the old man lay under the blanket on his bed, suffering from a bad cold, Def sat lounging next to him. They talked while Def flipped the T.V. from channel to channel. Though the old man had been demanding the remote, Def refused him. He continued to point it at the 32-inch television that sat on a twelve drawer dresser, laughing at the old man.

"Young soldier, whatever you do, don't stop on BET," the old man said.

"And why not?" Def asked. .

"Because I'm tired of seein' and hearin' all that ignorance, that's why. Now turn it to CNN or somethin'."

Grinning, Def uttered, "You know your old ass like to see those young girls shakin' their ass."

The old man let out a few coughs first then smiled, display-inghis off white teeth. He turned his head, which was the only part of his body that wasn't covered by the blanket, toward Def and stared at him. "You know I like that. What man doesn't? If he don't, he tellin' a bold face lie. Or it may be that he has a lil' sugar in his tank." They both giggled.

The sound of Def's cell phone ringing stopped his laughing. He tossed the remote to the old man and dug into his pocket for it. "Yeah," he answered.

"What's up, nigga?" G retorted.

"Hey, what's up, G? What's good, slim?"

"Ain't shit. Chillin' at the porn store?"

"That only means you checkin' out some new releases."

"And you know it."

"It's some black shit, right?"

"Yeah, that nigga Mandingo and Ayana Angel and all them."

"Make sure you hit me off wit' a copy."

"I got'cha. Aye, I called to ask have you seen Tyra."

Def frowned. "Nah, I haven't heard from her today. You said her mom was goin' to pick her up this mornin', right?"

"Yeah, but I just got a call from her Mom and she said she haven't seen or heard from her."

Def glanced at his watch. "It's four sixteen. You told me yes-terday that her Mom was gon' scoop her from the hospital at eleven, right?"

"Yeah, but somehow Ms. Young caught a flat tire and showed up at the hospital at twelve instead of eleven and when she got there, Tyra was nowhere to be found."

Def sat up in the recliner, causing the footrest to fold back within the chair. "You call her cell?" he questioned G.

"Yeah. Got no answer though. I left a message for her to call me."

Def sighed. "Somethin' ain't right. You don't just get released from the hospital and disappear. Shit, she just got out a coma."

"You right," G agreed. "So, what'cha think goin' on?"

"I don't know, but I'ma go stop by the shop and see if the girls have seen her. But first I'm gon' stop by her crib."

"A'ight. Hit me when you find out somethin'."

"Okay. I'll holla, slim." Def closed his phone and slipped it back into his pocket. He stood up from the recliner.

"You leavin'?" Bootney inquired.

Def grabbed his gray leather, jacket from the recliner and slid it on. "I gotta bounce. I'll holla at'cha maybe tomorrow, old man." Def looked down on Bootney.

"Everythin' good?" the old man asked.

Def shrugged his shoulders. "I don't know. I hope to find out." He made his way out the bedroom and out the front door of the apartment. He locked the door behind him with the set of keys the old man had given him. Since the old timer was under the weather, he'd given Def  keys to his crib so he wouldn't have to get up when Def came knocking.

In record time, Def was pulling into Tyra's reserved parking space in front of her townhouse. He hopped out of his Porsche and walked up to the front door. He banged on the door, as if he were a police officer. And when he received no response, he banged even harder. Although sturdy, the heavy wooden door rattled upon impact. It wasn't until his hand strated to ache that he relinquished his pounding, whipped out his cell and dialed Tyra's cell number and six rings later, her voice mail answered, and he said, "Tyra, this Def. Hit me when you get this message."

Def hopped back into his car and sped away. The entire ride to his next destination, he tried to figure out what was going on. Where could Tyra be? Though he was en route to her salon, something told him that she wouldn't be there either. He started to just call the salon to see if she was there, but thought better of it. He told himself that going there personally would be better.

As soon as he parked his car in the salon's small parking lot, he jumped out and headed to the door, where he was buzzed in by Ms. Carolyn. He moved up to the counter and hovered over it, peering down at the heavy-set woman.

"Hi you doin' Def? I know why you're here. Nope, she isn't here. I received a call about two hours ago from Tyra's Mom. She told me what was goin' on. I already asked all the girls have they seen or heard from her in the last six hours. They all said they haven't," Ms. Carolyn said. She had a perplexed look in her eyes. "I hope everythin' is okay. Tyra is a good young woman."

"If she shows up here, tell her I said to get in touch wit' me asap," Def said, while backing up.

"I will," Ms. Carolyn assured, with glassy eyes.

Def started his car but didn't drive away. He sat pondering. He couldn't, for the life of him, figure out what was going on. Tyra was missing. He knew for a fact that she wasn't with another man getting sexed. She just wasn't the promiscuous type. But what the fuck was going on? Where was she? Who was she with? Def asked himself all of those questions, but received no answers.

He thought of all the people he had met that knew Tyra, and out of all of them, it was only one person Tyra could be with, Cherry. But he didn't have Cherry's number nor did he know where she livedso he had no choice but to sit back and wait it out although he had already made up his mind that he wouldn't be waiting long. If it came to it, he'd plow the streets for answers. Somebody had to know Tyra's whereabouts andnd he would start with their circle of associates. As he sat, he told himself that if necessary, he would use his gun to get answers because Tyra meant that much to him.

# THIRTY-TWO

She knew she was awake so why was the room so dark? Then it hit her, she was blindfolded. Plus, there was a gag over her mouth.It all came back to her. She'd been put to sleep again by that washcloth that laced with something on it.

After Roc had somehow managed to make her orgasm twice by licking her pussy ferociously, he left the bedroom and returned with a plate of food and drink. He fed her chicken strips and french fries. Then he allowed her to kill her thirst with a punch soft drink. He left the room again, with the empty plate and bottle in hand, and when he returned, he held a soapy washcloth and a dry one in each hand.

With the soapy cloth, he scrubbed her pussy, and with the dry he wiped her clean. She had asked if she could use the bathroom to pee. He walked her to the basement's bathroom at gunpoint and watched with an ugly grin, while she hovered above the toilet to release herself. Before long, she was tied back to the bed.

Then he retrieved the small bottle of chloroform and the cloth from the dresser drawer, stood above Tyra while placing a dab of the liquid onto the cloth, then placed it over her face. She had wiggled her head in disobedience, but was still put to sleep. She wondered how long had she'd been knocked out? Maybe for four hours just like before.

She also wondered how long would she be used as Roc's sex toy. But, most importantly, she wonderd would she live or die. Though she was told she would die, she didn't want to believe it. It had to be a way out of it, and more than ever, she was determined to get from under Roc's grasp alive. But where was he? Where was the coked-out madman?

Roc slowly cruised to a stop in his BMW in the back alley of his grandmother's house. He sat with his car idling in front of the shabby fence that surrounded it. He gazed over at the woman who sat next to him. They exchanged smiles. He reached into his pocket and produced a bankroll. He peeled off bill after bill and passed it to her.

"That's five hundreds, girl. Nah…" He peeled more from his bankroll and passed it to her. "That's three more hundred. Everythin' I say goes tonite."

The woman smiled briskly, displaying the silver ball on her tongue. "Roc, you know I got'cha. Don't trip. Me and you been fuckin' wit' each other for a minute now. I'm a Tea Bag freak fo'real."

Roc whipped out the tiny bottle his coke was in and patted some out onto his hand. And sniff! The powder raced up his nose. He tilted his head back.

"Uh-uh! You ain't gon' give me none," the woman argued, staring over at Roc with a pout.

Roc dropped his head and grinned her way. He motion for her to stick her hand out. He placed a nice amount between her thumb and forefinger, and observed her sniff it. And when she tilted her head back, he took a handful of her hair into his right hand and leaned in roughly, sticking his tongue into her mouth. She responded by kissing him back.

"Now that's what the fuck I'm talkin' 'bout, bitch!" Roc piped, after freeing her hair and withdrawing his lips from hers. "Your strippa name fit'cha perfect, Nasty."

Nasty flicked her tongue out like that of a cobra. "That's right, I'm that bitch fo'real."

"You got everythin' I told'cha to bring, right?" Roc inquired, looking at the bag that sat in her lap.

"Yep." Nasty reached into her designer bag and brandished a big black, 10-inch dildo, anal beads, a bottle of lubricant and a large black bandana.

Roc grabbed the bandana from her and tied it around her eyes.

She didn't protest, she was down for whatever.

"Let's make this happen," Roc said, making his way out of his car after killing the engine.

No words could explain her current state of mind. She had been stripped of her clothing, confined to a bed and told she was going to die. The fact that no one knew her whereabouts sent fearful feelings throughout her body and to top everything off, she was now blindfolded, unable to see. Tyra's thoughts ended when she heard the sound of someone entering the bedroom.

"I have a surprise for you," Roc said, as he walked up to the bed and sat on the side of it. He removed Tyra's blindfold from her eyes. "I hope you into freaky shit."

Tyra squinted her eyes, trying to adjust to the light. When her sight cleared, she was staring at Roc's sweaty, black face.

"I changed my mind, I ain't gon' kill you," Roc lied, with a straight face.

His plan was to get his freak on with Nasty and Tyra, drop Nasty back off at the strip club and head back to take Tyra out. Since he was lying to Tyra, he had to make sure that Nasty stayed blindfolded throughout the whole episode. He didn't want Nasty to see who they were freaking off with just in case his plan didn't go off like he intended it to.

Tyra didn't believe a word he was saying, but she listened.

"All you gotta do is let me do what I wanna do to you, and I'ma let'cha go. Oh, and you gotta keep all that's happened to yourself. If you tell G or Def, I'll get'cha again. But next time, I'll kill you outright."

Tyra shook her head yeah in agreement.

"Now, I'm gon' untie your ankles, but not your wrist. Go along wit' this and you good." He freed her ankles, but slid her blindfold back over her eyes. Then he departed the room.

A few minutes passed then Tyra felt the soft touch of a woman. Then she heard Roc say, "It's on and poppin'. Most niggas that sniff wouldn't be able to perform coked-out, but not me."

Seconds later, Tyra felt someone station themselves between her legs. She could tell it was the touch of a woman. Then she felt a hot succulent tongue pressing up against her clitoris. Slowly up and down, then like a kitten licking milk out of a bowl. Then the licking stopped, but was followed by a grunting sound of pleasure only a woman could make. But although she couldn't see what was transpiring around her physically, she could sense it as well as feel the motion of it. Tyra knew what was going on. Roc had entered the woman that was eating her out from behind and the sway of the bed revealed that he was penetrating her with slow strokes. Slow enough for the woman to continue her assault on her pussy. This time Tyra felt not only a hot tongue working on her clitoris, but she felt her walls being perforated. The woman was stroking a dildo in and out of her, while licking her clit. Trying to resist what was going down, Tyra moved her legs back and forth trying to break the rhythm of the woman working her over. As hard as she tried, her body was screaming with joy so much so that her back arched and stomach contracted in a wave. Then it came, the big one. She released her juices all over the dildo.

"I see you like this shit, huh?" Tyra heard Roc say then she felt movement all around her that lasted for about thirty seconds. Tyra felt her legs go up by a pair of rough hands and before she could protest, since she knew it was Roc preparing to enter her, he plunged hard into her.

Within seconds, Tyra's body was in extreme pain. Roc was penetrating her anus as though it was her vagina. Ignoring her muffled cries, he was pushing himself into her like there was no tomorrow and assisting him was Nasty, who was sucking all over her breasts.

"I'm 'boutta cum" Roc shouted. "Nasty, reach your hands up to her face and slide her blindfold up. I want her to see this nut I'm 'boutta bust. Matter of fact, untie her hands."

Roc slowed his stride to decrease his buildup. But when Nasty got one of Tyra's wrist free, then the other, he sped back up rapidly and pulled out, sliding the condom off his dick and began stroking himself to an orgasm.

With both wrists freed, Tyra sat up and removed the blindfold from her eyes that Nasty didn't get the chance to remove and she took the gag from her mouth. That's when she saw Roc, masturbating with his dick aimed toward her chest and before she could even think of moving, his semen blasted from out him and landed all over her chest and stomach. As Roc held his eyes shut, still savoring in his ecstasy, Tyra's eyes shifted over to the dresser where the silenced .22 rested. Seizing the opportunity, she flung her body off the bed, knocking Roc sideways and jetted to the dresser, swiping up the gun. Roc leaped to his feet in pursuit, but was too slow. His naked body crumbled to the floor with a thud.

"What the fuck is goin' on!" Nasty piped, removing her blindfold.and for the first time since she'd taken off her blindfold, Tyra got a good look at the woman who had brought her to an orgasm with her tongue and a rubber dildo. It was Sam. It was her fault for not recognizing who it was when Roc shouted out Nasty, Sam's stripper name, which she knew. But how could she have really known? There were probably a dozen strippers in the city with the same name. Plus, Sam hadn't spoken a word since she had entered the bedroom. .

"Tyra!" Sam snapped. Her face showed complete bewilderment.

"Sam!" Tyra spat, anger shooting through her being.

Tyra took her eyes off Sam and onto Roc, who was making it to his feet. She stepped up to him and fired a silent shot to his exposed groin. He fell back to the floor, screaming and holding where he'd been shot. While wallowing around on the floor, Tyra placed the tip of the silencer to his head, and before firing said, "This is for Cash!"

Pfff! Pfff!

She dumped two into his skull. His body stopped moving, and blood oozed out from his head and out of her peripheral vision, Tyra saw Sam, who surprisingly hadn't screamed, creeping to the bedroom door with her clothes in hand. Tyra spun and aimed the .22 and before Sam could yell, Pfff! Pfff! Two bullets tore into her chest dropping her. Tyra moved up to her and put one in her head, just for the fact that Sam was a trifling bitch for even being there and for dissing her at the funeral home.

After cleaning herself off, Tyra gathered up all her clothes and got dressed unscrewed the silencer from the .22 and stuck it and the gun in her jacket pocket. She then made her way out of the bedroom and basement door without looking back.

Reaching Roc's BMW, she looked at it but walked away. Although she had retrieved the keys from the dresser, she thought it would be best if she hit a main road and flagged a cab.

An hour later, Tyra was climbing the spiral staircase in her townhouse to reach her bedroom. She emptied her pockets of everything and tossed it onto her bed. She slid out of her clothes and into her shower where sat Indian style on the shower floor as the water beat down on her.

Then, out of nowhere, she started crying uncontrollably, mumbling to herself, "I got 'em Cash. I…I got 'em baby. I got that nigga who killed you. I love and miss you so much. I got'cha gun. It's in safe hands now. Oh, and I…I took care of some drug dealers for you wit' it. But…but, the nigga that killed you raped me.  I feel so violated, Cash. I feel so dirty. And I got that bitch that helped him, too. I'm sorry, Cash. I swear, you were the only man I ever loved."

She paused from mumbling and lifted her head, as though she was listening to or for someone. She shook her head adamantly. "No…no, I don't love him. I only loved one man and that was you. I don't love him. I don't love, Def. I'll prove it. Anyway, he and G should've been more watchful of that nigga. Roc tricked both of them into believin' Dre owed money from borrowing it. What he really owed money for was from coppin' drugs. They both should've asked Roc more questions. If they had, maybe they would've found out he was lying and he was a drug dealer behind their backs and, most importantly, you would more than likely still be alive. So, it's no more than right that they get what Roc got, revenge for you, baby. Revenge."

# THIRTY-THREE

They stepped out of Stewart funeral home, in Northeast, dressed dapper-like but were in somber moods. They made their way through the parking lot of the funeral home, to G's Bentley.

"Damn, man," G grumbled, as he slid behind the wheel of his car.

"I can't believe this shit. Roc is dead."

"You think we should've stayed for the rest of the service, though?" Def asked, nonchalantly.

"I've already seen his body, that's all a nigga needed to see. I ain't goin' to the funeral. Damn, that bamma gone." G shook his head sadly.

Def nodded. "I don't know what that nigga was doin' on the side, but I know what we involved in didn't get him killed. We've been doin' this for years and ain't nobody came after us."

G shook his head in agreement. "That's what I'm sayin'. You know what though? You and I both knew somethin' was up wit' him, being that for a while he's been buggin out wit' that paranoia shit. And, like I told'cha on the low…I was 100% sure that he was on coke."

"You know what though? We should've said somethin' to him about that shit. You know we don't deal wit' no drugs in our circle. Maybe if we would've stepped up he would still be here. That coke probably had somethin' to do wit' him getting' slumped."

"Like I told'cha when I first said somethin' to you about it, I ain't into tellin' no grown ass man what to do."

"Check this out," Def began as G brought the Bentley's engine to life. "I've wondered for the past week now how in the fuck did that nigga get killed in his grandmother's basement wit' a strippa? He had a crib, he could've taken the bitch there or to a telly."

"I can't understand that shit either," G consented. "And another thing, I can't understand how he kept all his money in shoe boxes in his apartment. The police found all that shit when they went to his spot. My police connect said they confiscated around six hundred thousand."

"I guess the police station he lived by had him feelin' comfortable," Def said, watching as G drove slowly through the lot, heading for the exit.

"You know what's trippin' me out also?" G asked more to himself then to Def. "My precinct connect told me that they found some shit called Chloroform in the basement when they were investigatin' the scene. That's some shit that'll put you to sleep."

"That nigga, Roc, was into some crazy shit behind our backs, huh?" Def said.

"I guess so," G replied.

Both men were silent for a few then G broke their silence by laughing.

Def looked over at G. "What's funny? Let me in on the joke."

"Remember as a juvenile, when all three of us were locked up in Oak Hill and that lil' nigga swore he was the strongest on the pound?"

Def nodded and grinned. "Shit, he was. That nigga was cocked strong. Nobody was liftin' what he put up. Yeah, he was a lil' strong ma'fucka."

"Yeah, he was. That nigga was ripped up back then. Then he hit the bricks and let all his muscle turn into fat."

"Yeah, you right."

They fell silent again, then G broke it. "What's up wit' Tyra? You and her still tight after that day long disappearin' act she pulled?"

"I wouldn't call what she did a disappearin' act? Like she said, she was home that entire day. She just didn't wanna be bothered by nobody. She ws drained from her hospital stay, but as far as are we still tight…" Def shrugged his shoulders, "I can't say. I've only talked to her on the phone like you have since she returned our messages."

"Yeah, but I'm sure you've talked to her more than twice like I have."

"I've only talked to her three times actually. When I asked was she comin' wit' us to Roc's wake, she told me she wasn't."

"Okay, so what'cha feelin' 'bout how tight y'all are?"

Def lookzed out the passenger window, watching as the Bentley made its way onto the highway. "To be real wit'cha dawg, to me she sounded a lil' distant on the phone, like she wouldn't talk unless I asked a question."

G looked at Def and said, "I got the same treatment from her."

"It was like she wasn't really tryin' to talk. If you let me tell it, she sounded a lil' angry. So, as far as us bein' still tight, I can't say."

"It's funny how she was missin' the same day my police connect told me the homicide detectives believe Roc and that strippa was killed."

"Yeah, but..." Def stared at G strangely. "That's just a coincidence."

"Yeah, I know. I was just sayin'."

After being dropped off at home, Def stepped up on his porch to find the front door to his house ajar. He swiftly reached into his suit jacket and snatched his Taurus from its holster.

As he pushed the door open slowly, he thought, *who in the fuck breaks into a nigga's house at eleven in the morning*? With his gun in his right hand, he slowly closed the door shut with his left. He stood in front of it and scanned the floorallowing his eyes to land on the staircase that led up to the upstairs level. That's when he heardthe sound of his stereo system that he didn't remember leaving on, playing softly. He wondered who had or was in his bedroom fucking with his shit because as far as he knew nobody had keys to his crib but him.

Def crept toward the staircase at a turtle's pace, with his gun out in front of him. He methodically took one step at a time. It wasn't until he was halfway up that he heard the sound of the shower running. *What the fuck is goin' on? I hope ain't no crackhead or homeless person up in my shit takin' a shower.*

He moved a little faster up the steps. He passed the bathroom's closed door and entered his bedroom. He made his way up to a large picture frame, where a portrait of his mom hung on the wall and swerved it clockwise, revealing his safe that looked to have not been tampered with. He quickly looked under his bed and in his walk-in closet, then he walked out of his bedroom and into his spare bedroom. He checked it out then moved up to his bathroom door, where he heard the shower abruptly stop.

"Somebody in my ma'fuckin' house," he mumbled. He placed his ear up to the door, where he heard someone fumbling around. He had had enough. He wanted to see who was in his damn domain. He put his hand on the doorknob and turned it slowly. When the knob could turn no more, he paused and took a breather.

She'd been preparing all week for what she had to do. Although most of her preparation was mental, she felt it was necessary to put her anger and hurt aside and calm herself down enough to play a role that would sure enough bring about death, deceptively.

Tyra was taken aback by the sound of the bathroom door that slammed up against the wall with a loud crash. She had just grabbed a towel from the towel rack and wrapped it around herself. Standing with a shocked look on his face was Def, with his gun pointing at her. Though she had anticipated his entry into the bathroom, she was still shaken up by his intrusion.

"Boy! You scared the shit outta me!" Tyra barked, with a fake smile. She had both of her hands placed on her chest. She watched as Def's eyes bounced from her to her clothes and tote bag that sat atop the toilet. She saw his eyes ask a question that his mouth didn't, so she answered him.

"Sorry I never told'cha that I had a set of keys made when we switched cars a while back. You mad?" Tyra was speaking the truth, but what she didn't divulge to him was that she had only asked to switch cars with him after he had confessed to killing Dre. She wanted a set of keys to his house for leverage just in case she had to get at himand now she was glad she had because the time had come for her to do just that.

Def surveyed Tyra's entire body, his gun still semi pointed in her direction.

"What?" Tyra began. "This is your first time seein' me wit' a towel wrapped around my body? I don't think so."

Def slid his gun back into his holster. "Why did you leave the door open downstairs?"

"Oops, I thought I closed it. I guess I was in a rush to get in the shower."

Def looked at her strangely. He not only wondered what she was doing in his house, but he wondered what happened to the distant and angry sounding Tyra he'd just spoken to yesterday.

"I know what'cha thinkin'. I know I've been actin' funny lately, but I'm here now, not only to show you that I'm okay. But I'm here to cheer you up in case you're in a gloomy mood about Roc." Tyra unfastened the towel from her and let it crumble to the floor. She spun around slowly, giving Def a complete view of her nakedness.

He smiled wider than he had all day He watched as she moved up to him and cupped his crotch with her left hand, and with her right, she palmed the back of his curly head and threw her tongue in his mouth.

A few minutes had gone by and Tyra was riding Def's dick, as if it was the last piece of dick she would be getting. She had his bed rocking to her movement. Her hands were glued to his chest, while she thrust her ass up and down heavily on him. Loud slurping sounds escaped from their friction. They stared at each other without exchanging words, but they both had their fuck faces on.

"Oh shit, Tyra! Slow down or you gon' make me cum!" Def barked.

Tyra didn't slow her stride. Instead, she stopped her up and down movement in exchange for having his balls deep inside of her. She slid back and forward in a jerky manner.

"Oh shit! Now, you really gon' make me cum!" Def said, by closing his eyes. "Aw…Aw. It's comin'. Here it comes!"

Tyra quickly jumped off of him, but not before sliding her hand under the pillow, retrieving her .38, which she had placed there earlier. She stood on the right side of the bed and watched Def's semen blast from out of him and land all over his torsoand when he was done with releasing himself, he looked over at her and saw that she was aiming the chrome .38 he'd given her down at him.

"Don't say a ma'fuckin' word. Let me talk," Tyra ordered.

"Aye, Tyra, don't point…"

Pfff! Tyra let a silent bullet loose that grazed Def's left arm. He immediately grabbed at where he'd been hit and sat up. Blood trickled down his arm.

"I told'cha don't say a word!" Tyra snapped.

Def stared at Tyra with malice and confusion in his eyes.

"No, I'm here for one reason and one reason only. Revenge for my baby, Cash, that your man Roc killed. He wouldn't be dead right now if you and G would've only asked Roc more questions when he came to y'all wit' hits. Remember, I told'cha the dude, Dre, that you killed was just a childhood friend of mine. Well, he wasn't, he was a friend of my boyfriend, Cash. Since I know you didn't know, let me tell you everythin'." Tyra laid it all out for Def starting with why she got down with them in the beginning, her hatred for drug dealers since her childhood love was murdered, to being tied up in that basement bedroom by Roc, and killing him and the stripper. She had even told him that she knew Sam personally, and informed him that the gun he had given her was in actuality the gun Roc took from Cash the day he killed him.

"So, you gon' kill me and G, even knowin' we didn't have a clue what Roc was into on the side?"

"I have to," Tyra replied.

"If anythin', leave G out of this. That's a good dude. I'm the one who killed Dre, triggerin' Cash gettin' killed, too." Def looked Tyra straight in the eyes. "Let me ask you this. Did you ever feel anythin' towards me? Like…were you ever feelin' me?"

"Yes."

"Did you ever love me?"

Tyra took her eyes off of Def and stared blankly in no particular direction in the bedroom. It was as though she was listening for something.

Seizing that moment, Def rolled quickly off the bed and sprinted in giant leaps, heading out his bedroom en route to the bathroom where he'd left his gun. Pfff! He was struck in his left shoulder blade before he could even exit the threshold of the bedroom. His naked body fell out into the hall. When Tyra ran up on him, he was crawling, trying to reach the bathroom.

"Def, stop crawlin' and turn around!" Tyra demanded. She stood above him. Her legs gapped open with his body in between them.

Def relinquished his movement and flipped over on his back. His mouth was packed with blood. It looked as if he'd been punched in his mouth. He coughed and more blood sprung forth, running down along the sides of his face. He gawked at Tyra's naked body. She held the gun, aiming down in the direction of his face. He noticed that both of her hands, which were wrapped firmly around the silenced .38, were steady. She wasn't nervous.

"Take your death like a man. Don't run from it. It's your turn now. It was all your victims turn to die when you got at them. So, now it's your turn." Tyra smiled wickedly.

Remembering seeing that wicked smile once before, Def knew he was going to diebut what he couldn't believe was that he was going to die by the hands of a woman he had feelings for, so in coming to grips with the reality that was staring at him, he gave in.

"Bi…Bitch, don't talk to me…to Def. Put that shit in me." His lips curled into a smile that he could tell instantly infuriated Tyra.

"Oh, this a joke, huh? And to answer your question whether I ever loved you or not. No, I never loved you, nigga!"

More blood oozed out of Def's mouth when he coughed.

"G will be an hour or so behind you, so hold the gate open for him," Tyra said.

"Fuck you! Tha…that's why your man, Cash, already there." Def drew in a deep breath and let loose a glob of blood, which replaced his saliva and hurled into the air en route to land on Tyra, but two silent bullets ripped into his face in succession beating his disrespect to the punch. His glob of blood, which his lungs weren't strong enough to push out properly, missed its target and landed on him.

Tyra stepped away from his body and swifly gathered all her things to exit the house. She had another mission to accomplish, and it was sure to be as deadly as her last.

# THIRTY-FOUR

G sat on the side of his bed, wearing nothing but a pair of black boxers and a white wifebeater. He held his cell phone up to his ear with an irritated expression on his face. *I just dropped this nigga off an hour ago. Why the fuck he ain't answerin' his cell*, G thought. His gaze shot over on Tammy, who had entered the spacious bedroom.

"Baby, you still tryna get in touch wit' Def?" Tammy asked. She sashayed over to where he sat and stood before him. A pink Versace, silk robe with matching slippers adorned her petite body. She licked her fairly thick lips as she stared at her man. Just looking at G seemed to always stir something in her.

"Yeah, and I don't know why that nigga ain't answerin' his cell," G responded, in a harsh tone.

Tammy gently took the phone away from his ear, pried it out of his hand and tossed it on the far side of the bed. "Baby, you a lil' upset now. You've had a hard mornin'. You know...goin' to Roc's wake and all." She stood in between his legs with her hands massaging his shoulders. She bent forward and planted a soft kiss on his forehead. "Daddy, let mommy make you feel better."

G looked Tammy in the eyes. He tried to hold in his smile but he couldn't. He beamed brighter than the sun. That was one of the many things he loved about her. She knew just what to say and do at the right times.

"Make daddy feel good, mommy." G settled his hands around Tammy's small waist.

Tammy moved his hand and dropped to her knees. She reached her right hand into the slit of his boxers and brought out his ¾ erect dick. She didn't waste any time sliding it into her warm mouth.

G tilted his his back and stared up at the ceiling for a second, before dropping his head back down to observe Tammy put in work.

"You like that, daddy?" Tammy inquired, before she started licking G's now fully erect dick like a lollipop. She ran her tongue from the base of the thick vein under his shaft to the head. Then she rose to her feet, cupped his balls in her hands, placed the head into her mouthand swoosh! She took in six inches of dick.

G smiled briskly, while looking at Tammy. He knew what she was about to do, so he waited in anticipation. He observed as she arched her neckand relaxed the back of her throat. Then swoosh! She took in his last three inches, and now she had him ball deep in her mouth, all nine inches.

"Oh God!" he howled.

The sound of the downstairs doorbell ringing caused Tammy to slide her mouth off G's dick, leaving trails of saliva on it.

"Damn, who the fuck is that?" G piped, visibly upset.

"I don't know..." Tammy was wiping her mouth with the back of her hand. "You expectin' someone?" She smiled, while looking at G's shiny dick.

"Nah."

"I tell you what, I'll go downstairs and see who it is, while you keep my thang hard." Tammy grabbed G's hand and settled it on his dick. "Play wit' it until I get back." She dashed out of the bedroom.

When Tammy made it to the door, she raised on her tiptoes to look out the peephole. When she saw who it was, she frowned. *I know I can't go back upstairs and finish puttin' my head game down now. Damn! I hope his company don't stay long*, Tammy thought, while she unlocked the door to open it.

For some strange reason, while she had driven to her destination, she second guessed what she intended to do. It wasn't the fact that she was afraid, because she wasn't. It was the fact that she knew she didn't really have to carry out the rest of her mission. But on the other hand, she had made a promise to take out all parties that were involvedso she had to adhere to that. When she heard the clacking sound of locks being detached, she stood up straight, placed her gloved right hand into her tote bag and gripped her gun. When the door opened, she went straight to work.

"Hey, Ty…" Tammy's words were abruptly cut short by the blow she caught to her forehead by the butt of the .38. She stumbled backwards in her slippers and fell to the travertine floor on her ass. She sat upright, holding her forehead with a dazed look on her face.

Tyra slipped into the house and shut the door behind her. She moved up to Tammy and hovered above her, wishing the woman hadn't been present. She only wanted one person, G. With her tote bag straps over her left shoulder, she reached down and palmed a handful of Tammy's hair. She yanked upward, causing Tammy to make her way to her feet. With Tammy's back to her, Tyra pressed the gun into her backand it wasn't until that moment that Tammy spoke.

"Tyra, what's goin' on? I don't understand." Although Tammy knew what kind of relationship Tyra had with G, since he had told her about Tyra's job working as a set-up girl for him, she was oblivious, just like G, to the damage Roc had caused to his establishment.

"Tammy, just shut the fuck up and talk only if I ask a question. Now, is G upstairs?"

"Yeah, but…"

Tyra nudged Tammy in the back with the gun. "Bitch, shut the fuck up and let's go upstairs."

They marched up the staircase then into G's bedroom, who sat doing what Tammy had asked him to do. It wasn't until he looked up and saw Tyra standing behind Tammy that he stopped playing with his dick and bounced to his feet. He stood at a loss for words and maybe that was because of the tears he saw pouring down Tammy's eyes and the grip he saw Tyra had on his girl's hair, not to mention the scowl Tyra wore plastered on her face.

Tyra couldn't help but to look at G's dick that was deflating by the secondand when he noticed her eyes was on it, he swiftly pushed it back into the slit of his boxers.

"Tyra, what the fuck"

G's words were cut short by what he witnessed, Tyra slamming the butt of the .38 down on Tammy's head forcefully, knocking her out. Her body collapsed to the floor with a thud.

"Aye, what th..." G motioned to move, but Tyra smoothly stepped over Tammy's body and backed him up with her gun extended. He sat back down on the side of his bed. His face depicted bewilderment, anger and disbelief all rolled into one.

"I know this is a big surprise for you," Tyra uttered, with the scowl she had entered the bedroom with still on her face. She stood a couple of feet in front of G with her .38 directed at him. "Because it's a big surprise to me that I'm doin' this. You'll be the last to go. Roc was first, then came Def, and now you."

G stared at Tyra. He didn't blink an eye.

"I know you're askin' yourself what the fuck am I doin'." Tyra's face softened. The scowl she wore evaporated. It looked as if her eyes were becoming glassy. "I'll tell you. I'm...I'm gettin' revenge for Cash. The only man I ever loved. I loved him so much and Roc took him away from me. And it's partially your fault."

G shook his head and hunched his shoulders. "Tyra, what the fuck are..."

Pfff! Tyra fired a shot that whisked past G's head and lodged into the wall, causing plaster to fall from it. "Shut the fuck up! Just shut up! I don't wanna hear it!" A tear fell from her eye.

Her face turned into an ugly cry; a sure warning that more tears were on their way. Sure enough, seconds later, tears began to roll down from her eyes and down her face.

G placed his palms up, as if to say he surrender and that he'd do as she wanted, shut the fuck up.

"I loved him so much, G. Why did'cha let...let Roc kill him? Why?" Tears continued to fall from her eyes, which had turned blood red. "You...you should've checked some of the hits he came to you wit' out. You should've known he was sellin' drugs on the side."

G frowned. He was really confused now. What Tyra had just said to him didn't make sense. He wanted to speak, but she had told him not toand he didn't want her to become more crazed than she was if he spoke.

Shaking the gun at G, Tyra spat, "Say somethin', dammit! Why? Why didn't you know he was sellin' drugs on the side? Talk G or I'll blow your fuckin' head off!"

Now given the opportunity to talk, G was at a loss for words-but seeing how erratic Tyra was becoming by the second, he knew it would be best if he spat something out. So he unconsciously said, "Tell me what happened. How did you come to this point?"

With tears still tumbling from her face, Tyra told G everything that led up to her standing before him with her gun pointing at him.

Now, seeing a clear view of everything, G knew he had to try to say or do something, or his life would surely end. If she had killed Roc and Def, a man in which she was intimate with sexually, he knew his life meant nothing to heralthough he had done so much for her since they'd met. So, he thought he'd try the guilt approach first, hoping it would work.

"Tyra, you gon' kill me after all that I did for you?" G put on his disappointed look. "I looked out for you like crazy and this is the thanks I get. You comin' in my house knockin' my girl out and threatening to kill me." He stood up, his palms still in the air though. "Since when did a nigga doin' somethin' good for a person start gettin' paid back by gettin' killed? Huh?" He took one small step forward.

Hysterically Tyra shouted, "You take one more step and I'll shoot you in your fuckin' face! Now sit back down! I'm not finished talkin'!"

"No, you won't. You ain't gon' shoot me, cause if you was you would've already done it. You know I've been nothin' but good to you since you came on my team. Now, put the gun down, Tyra, and let's work this shit out." G took another small step forward.

Tyra took one step back. Her face was a wet mass from her tears. Mucus started to escape from her nostrils with each heaving breath she took. Her face depicted perplexity rather than anger. Her right hand that held the gun waseven shook as though she was nervous.

"Tyra, things are not over. I understand why you killed Roc and Def."

Tyra shook her head no. "You under…stand, but can you feel my pain? Can you feel the pain of losin' someone you love deeply, huh? I loved Cash wit' every bone in my body. I thought me and him was gon' get married some day. You know, people used to tell me and him that we were too young to be so serious. That shit irritated us both. He used to tell me to pay that shit no attention because nobody knew what we were feelin' but usand that was the only thing that mattered. What we felt."

As soon as Tyra sounded like she was finished talking, G said with his palms now down and arms to his sides, "Tyra, let me get the gun and we can sit down and talk. I'll listen to you."

"I'm not here for you to listen to me!" Her face transformed from a picture of perplexity to pure anger. "I'm here for revenge for Cash." She cocked the hammer back on the .38, causing G to take a step back.

"Hold on, Tyra, he uttered.

"Hold on for what? I came here to kill you."

G stationed his hands out in front of him. "Just hold on, Tyra. Think about what'cha doin'. It's me, G."

"I don't have to think about shit. I came to get revenge for Cash and I'm getting' it!" Tyra aimed directly at G's face, but when she did, she didn't expect to see what she saw. What should've been a frightened look on his face was actually a grinand his eyes seemed to look beyond her instead of at hers though he was looking over her shoulder. Now curious, she followed his gaze and turned to look behind her and a crackling sound was the last thing she heard proceeded by darkness that welcomed her.

# THIRTY-FIVE

Two months and eleven days later, on Tyra's 21st birthday, she sat in front of her vanity dresser staring into the mirror while applying lip gloss on her lips. Though she was paying attention to what she was doing, her mind was on something else. She couldn't stop thinking about what had happened. It was a miracle that she was still alive and breathingand that was only so because of the good heart of G. He had allowed her to live in spite of what she'd done, murdering Roc and Def, then attempting to murder him.

She had to admit, if it had been the other way around, she would've murdered him three times over. It would've been no rationalization that would've kept him alivebut deep down G was a kind soul.

That's why that day when Tyra held her gun on him, presumingly about to fire, Tammy woke up from being knocked out by Tyra and hit her across the head with a vase, knocking her out cold.G hadn't took revenge and did to her what she was going to do to him. Instead, he and Tammy got dressed, gathered all of Tyra's things except her gun, carried her body out to his Escalade, drove her to her townhouse and left her there. Before leaving, Ghad placed a note on her coffee table.

*Tyra,*

*I can't believe what you tried to do. I looked out for you like I never have for another woman besides my sister, and we wasn't even fuckin'. I'm not gonna make this long so I'll say what I have to say. I'm dead to you and you're dead to me. There's no more me and you. I never wanna see or hear from you again. I'm takin your Benz cause it's still in my name. I'm givin' it to Tammy. Since everythin' pertainin' to your shop is in your name, you good on that. I'ma do you one last favor though cause I'm just that type of nigga. I'ma get rid of your .38 for you, that you popped Def wit' it. Keep your mouth shut and I'll keep mine shut, too.*

*P.S. I still wish you well,*

*Have a nice life.*

Tyra broke out of her thoughts and slid her chair out from her vanity dresser as she moved over to her bed. She snatched up her black Prada purse and made her way before the full length body mirror. She admired her clothing. She wore black stiletto three-inch heel boots, satin pants, a long sleeve turtleneck sweater, and a fur jacket. . She smiled at her reflection because there was no doubt she looked good enough to attend the club she was going to, along with Cherry, to celebrate her 21st birthday.

She just hoped Cherry, who surprisingly to her had come back into her life just a week ago after phoning her, was dressed as fly as she was. Over the past three days, she and Cherry had been chatting on the phone. Cherry had called to say that she really missed her and wanted to reconcile their relationship. She stated that she was trying to do what she had told Tyra she needed to do so many times before, move on with her life, after the loss of her true love.In fact, it was Cherry who had suggested they go out to a club to celebrate her birthday. Tyra had agreed, and now she was just waiting for Cherry to arrive

The ringing of her house doorbell caused Tyra to glance at the time on her watch, which read nine-thirty. She shut off her bedroom light and headed downstairs. When Tyra reached the front door, she didn't bother to look out of the peephole because she knew it was Cherry and after opening the door, she was correct. It was Cherry, but not the physical looking Cherry she once knew. The big boned Cherry was gone and had been replaced with a petite frame. If Tyra had to guess, she would say that Cherry had lost at least thirty to thirty-five pounds and she displayed a radiant smile on her face It looked as if Cherry had been a recipient of an extreme makeover show,even her once short, cherry colored, spiky hairdo had changed. She now wore it in long flowing black braids. She was sporting black suede from head to toe. In her right hand she held a black purse, and in her left, a brown paper bag with a bottle of Hennessy in it.

"Hey, Cherry, you lookin' good, girl," Tyra said, with a smile. C'mon in here."

Cherry stepped into the house and Tyra shut the door. Afterwards, Tyra paced a circle around Cherry checking her out.

"Dammmn! You lookin' real good, Cherry. You lost a lot of weight, girl."

Smiling, Cherry replied, "Yeah, I took it down a lil'."

"Pss…a lil'. Shit, you almost look like a totally different person."

Cherry slid the bottle of Hennessy from the bag. It was a quarter of the drink missing. "I drank some already. I remember how much you used to like Hen Dog when we were livin' together, so I brought you some over. I thought'cha could start gettin' bent before you reach the club. It's your day. You get twisted and I'll drive."

Smiling, Tyra responded, "I'll be right back. Let me get a glass and get some of that before we hit the road." She disappeared through her living room, into her kitchen where she rambled through her cabinet and found a small drinking glass. She made her way back into the living, where she spotted Cherry seated on her sofa. She joined her.

Cherry held the bottle out to Tyra and filled her glass half way. Afterwards, she sat the bottle on the coffee table.

"What time the club close tonite?" Tyra questioned, with her glass up to her lips.

"I think around two or three."

Tyra took a swig of her drink and her face took on an unpleasant frown. "Damn, this stuff strong, maybe because I haven't drunk it in a while."

"Tyra," Cherry said, followed by silence. Se was staring into Tyra's face. She watched her take another swig of her drink.

"Yeah," Tyra said.

"Tyra," Cherry said again, followed by silence.

Tyra sat her drink down on the coffee table. She rubbed her eyes as if they were itching. She fanned herself with her hands. "It got hot in here all of a sudden. Girl, you feel that heat?" Her eyes were blinking rapidly.

"Tyra, why?" Cherry's eyes were glued on Tyra.

Tyra slid her arms from out of her fur jacket and tossed it on the sofa next to her purse. "Damn, it's hot in here."

Cherry observed Tyra's blinking eyelids. Her eyeballs had suddenly turned red. "Tyra, why?" Cherry asked again.

"Why…" Tyra scratched at her neck. "Why what?" Her body was twitching a little.

"Why did you kill Smoke?"

The look on Tyra's face read guilty and Cherry saw it. "I…I don't know what'cha talkin' 'bout." Tyra's eyelids stopped blinking andher body stopped twitching. She suddenly and calmly set back on the sofa. Her body wasn't moving.

Cherry stood up and posted up in front of Tyra, looking down on her with a wicked smile. She opened her purse and produced a box cutter. "Sam saw you, bitch. She saw you leave out that motel room Smoke was killed in. It was her who yelled out your name just before you hopped into your car and drove off. She was at that motel wit' one of her tricks that day and after you sped out of the lot, she went to the room Smoke was in and saw his body. You killed him, bitch. Plus, the description the detectives gave me of the bitch he was last seen wit' fit you. It didn't register with me until after Sam told me what she knew and I thought on it. Plus you fucked up that day you was consolin' me and said Smoke was in a better place and God will take care of him, when I hadn't even told you he was dead."

Tyra stared up at Cherry who looked to be possessed, as if the devil had overtaken control of her body. By now, Tyra's body had zero movement and her eyes were barely blinking.

"I poisoned you, bitch!" Cherry hiked up her skirt and straddled Tyra. "That's why you can't move your limbs or talk. You gon' die from the poison in about five more minutesbut before you go, I want'cha to see what I'm goin' to do to you." She pushed the razor up and out the box cutter. She placed the sharp tip of it up against Tyra's left cheek. She pierced into Tyra's cheek and drew blood that trickled down along Tyra's face and neck.

"Did my baby die slow like you are, or did you kill him instantly? Huh? Bitch, did you fuck him in that room? Huh?"

Cherry took a hand full of Tyra's hair into her left hand after tossing her purse to the side. She then ran the razor from Tyra's left cheek and down under her lip and up to the right side of her cheek. Tyra's white meat was showing and blood spilled out from her face rapidly.

"It's a good thing that poison numbed your body before you die or you'd be in great pain right about now." After those words, Cherry went back to work, slicing and dicing into Tyra's face. Blood was everywhere.

Cherry unstraddled Tyra and stood up. She stared down at the ripped piece of flash that once was Tyra's face, but now looked like raw, sliced, bloody meat. As soon as she saw Tyra's chest rise up then down then cease to rise again, she knew the woman who was once her friend had taken her last breath. So, she grabbed her purse, the half empty bottle of Hennessy that she placed back into the bag, and headed for the front door.

When she reached the door, she slid her hand back into the sleeve of her coat to touch the knob. But when she opened the door she was taken aback by the four pair of blue eyes that were peering at her.

"No! No!" Cherry barked, while backing up. Tears instantly started pouring down her face. She dropped the bottle of Hennessy and dug into her purse, recovering the bloody box cutter. She held it out in front of her, wavng it recklessly. "No! Get back! I was supposed to get away wit' this! Nooo!"

Both young white detectives drew their service weapons from their belt holsters. They wore expressions that said, '*we only came here to ask Ms. Young more questions about the accident she was in that resulted in the death of the fellow named TimTim and we bump into this'*. Both men inched inside the house.

"Put your weapon down Miss!" Detective Stone said.

"Yes, please put it down!" Detective White echoed.

Cherry glanced into the living room at Tyra's bloody corpse, causing the detectives to follow her eyes. They both saw what she saw.

"Drop the weapon, now!" they both yelled in unison.

In a fit of rage, Cherry screamed and charged at the detectives with the box cutter held above her head in a knife stabbing position. And before she could reach them, Pop! Pop! She was shot. She hit the floor and two pairs of expensive shoes was the last thing she saw before her eyelids fluttered twice and closed.

# EPILOGUE

One month later, Cherry, who hadn't died form being shot, sat in an aluminum fold-out chair behind a large wooden table in one of the many confidential rooms of Saint Elizabeth's Mental Hospital. She had been sitting there for twenty minutes, waiting for the visitor she was taken from her ward to see.

Cherry watched as the only door into the white wall painted room opened, and a short, brown suit wearing, fat white man came in, shutting the door behind him. He walked up to the table and sat his black briefcase down. He sat in a fold-out chair and stared across the table at Cherry. He shook his baldhead sadly.

"Young lady, you would've been better off not pleading crazy to that murder. If you wasn't crazy before you will be after staying in here for the ten years that you were sentenced to," the white man was saying more to himself then to the zombie like woman he sat before. He snapped the briefcase open and pulled two pieces of paper and an ink pen from it.

Cherry's attention moved towards the paper.

"One is a written Will and the other is an…" he paused. "Oh, and by the way, I'm Jonathan P. Pheingold. I'm an attorney for Ms. Young, Tyra Young's mother. But like I was saying, one of these pieces of paper is a written Will and the other is an ownership contract that gives you full ownership of Tyra Young's hair salon. In her Will you're entitled to her house, car, clothes and half of her money that's in the bank. However, since you murdered her and her mother resents you for doing so, she wants you to forfeit your rights over to her since in both, the Will and the ownership contract, she is second and last named to own it all." He produced another piece of paper from his briefcase and sat it in front of Cherry. He sat the pen on top of it. "Just sign your name and the date on that line and I'll be out of your hair." He smiled.

Cherry picked the pen up and slowly scribbed her name on the line and the date. She dropped the pen back on top of the paper and grinned.

Seeing Cherry's grin, the attorney said, "What's funny?" He gathered the papers and pen up and stuffed them into his briefcase, locking it as he rose to his feet.

"How bein' *dangerously in love*, can impair one's judgment and cause a normally good person to do awful things…murder." Cherry laughed crazily, while rocking back and forth in her chair. She paid no attention to the attorney who had slipped out of the room, leaving her to dwindle in her world of madness.

The
DIRTY
Divorce
Part 4
A NOVEL BY
MISS KP

# COMING SOON

**MAIL TO:**
PO Box 423
Brandywine, MD 20613
301-362-6508

# ORDER FORM

| | |
|---|---|
| Date: | Phone: |
| Email: | |

| | |
|---|---|
| Ship to: | |
| Address: | |
| | |
| City & State: | Zip: |

*Make all money orders and cashiers checks payable to:* **Life Changing Books**

| Qty. | ISBN | Title | Release Date | Price |
|---|---|---|---|---|
| | 0-9741394-2-4 | Bruised by Azarel | Jul-05 | $ 15.00 |
| | 0-9741394-7-5 | Bruised 2: The Ultimate Revenge by Azarel | Oct-06 | $ 15.00 |
| | 0-9741394-3-2 | Secrets of a Housewife by J. Tremble | Feb-06 | $ 15.00 |
| | 0-9741394-6-7 | The Millionaire Mistress by Tiphani | Nov-06 | $ 15.00 |
| | 1-934230-99-5 | More Secrets More Lies by J. Tremble | Feb-07 | $ 15.00 |
| | 1-934230-95-2 | A Private Affair by Mike Warren | May-07 | $ 15.00 |
| | 1-934230-96-0 | Flexin & Sexin Volume 1 | Jun-07 | $ 15.00 |
| | 1-934230-89-8 | Still a Mistress by Tiphani | Nov-07 | $ 15.00 |
| | 1-934230-91-X | Daddy's House by Azarel | Nov-07 | $ 15.00 |
| | 1-934230-88-X | Naughty Little Angel by J. Tremble | Feb-08 | $ 15.00 |
| | 1-934230820 | Rich Girls by Kendall Banks | Oct-08 | $ 15.00 |
| | 1-934230839 | Expensive Taste by Tiphani | Nov-08 | $ 15.00 |
| | 1-934230782 | Brooklyn Brothel by C. Stecko | Jan-09 | $ 15.00 |
| | 1-934230669 | Good Girl Gone bad by Danette Majette | Mar-09 | $ 15.00 |
| | 1-934230804 | From Hood to Hollywood by Sasha Raye | Mar-09 | $ 15.00 |
| | 1-934230707 | Sweet Swagger by Mike Warren | Jun-09 | $ 15.00 |
| | 1-934230677 | Carbon Copy by Azarel | Jul-09 | $ 15.00 |
| | 1-934230723 | Millionaire Mistress 3 by Tiphani | Nov-09 | $ 15.00 |
| | 1-934230715 | A Woman Scorned by Ericka Williams | Nov-09 | $ 15.00 |
| | 1-934230685 | My Man Her Son by J. Tremble | Feb-10 | $ 15.00 |
| | 1-924230731 | Love Heist by Jackie D. | Mar-10 | $ 15.00 |
| | 1-934230812 | Flexin & Sexin Volume 2 | Apr-10 | $ 15.00 |
| | 1 934230748 | The Dirty Divorce by Miss KP | May-10 | $ 15.00 |
| | 1-934230758 | Chedda Boyz by CJ Hudson | Jul-10 | $ 15.00 |
| | 1-934230766 | Snitch by VegasClarke | Oct-10 | $ 15.00 |
| | 1-934230693 | Money Maker by Tonya Ridley | Oct-10 | $ 15.00 |
| | 1-934230774 | The Dirty Divorce Part 2 by Miss KP | Nov-10 | $ 15.00 |
| | 1-934230170 | The Available Wife by Carla Pennington | Jan-11 | $ 15.00 |
| | 1-934230774 | One Night Stand by Kendall Banks | Feb-11 | $ 15.00 |
| | 1-934230278 | Bitter by Danette Majette | Feb-11 | $ 15.00 |
| | 1-934230299 | Married to a Balla by Jackie D. | May-11 | $ 15.00 |
| | 1-934230308 | The Dirty Divorce Part 3 by Miss KP | Jun-11 | $ 15.00 |
| | 1-934230316 | Next Door Nympho By CJ Hudson | Jun-11 | $ 15.00 |
| | 1-934230286 | Bedroom Gangsta by J. Tremble | Sep-11 | $ 15.00 |
| | 1-934230340 | Another One Night Stand by Kendall Banks | Oct-11 | $ 15.00 |
| | 1-934230359 | The Available Wife Part 2 by Carla Pennington | Nov-11 | $ 15.00 |
| | 1-934230332 | Wealthy & Wicked by Chris Renee | Jan-12 | $ 15.00 |
| | 1-934230375 | Life After a Balla by Jackie D. | Mar-12 | $ 15.00 |
| | 1-934230251 | V.I.P. by Azarel | Apr-12 | $ 15.00 |
| | 1-934230383 | Welfare Grind by Kendall Banks | May-12 | $ 15.00 |
| | 1-934230413 | Still Grindin' by Kendall Banks | Sep-12 | $ 15.00 |
| | 1-934230391 | Paparazzi by Miss KP | Oct-13 | $ 15.00 |
| | 1-93423043X | Cashin' Out by Jai Nicole | Nov-12 | $ 15.00 |
| | 1-934230634 | Welfare Grind Part 3 by Kendall Banks | Mar-13 | $15.00 |
| | 1-934230642 | Game Over by Winter Ramos | Apr-13 | $15.99 |
| | 1-934230618 | My Counterfeit Husband by Carla Pennington | Aug-14 | $ 15.00 |
| | 1-93423080X | Mistress Loose | Oct-13 | $ 15.00 |
| | 1-934230626 | Dirty Divorce Part 4 | Jan-14 | $ 15.00 |
| | | | **Total for Books** | $ |
| | | | **Shipping Charges (add $4.95 for 1-4 books*)** | $ |
| | | | **Total Enclosed (add lines)** | $ |

* **Prison Orders- Please allow up to three (3) weeks for delivery.**

**Please Note: We are not held responsible for returned prison orders. Make sure the facility will receive books before ordering.**

***Shipping and Handling of 5-10 books is $6.95, please contact us if your order is more than 10 books. (301)362-6508**

Made in the USA
San Bernardino, CA
27 September 2015